Access

Going Places

Paul Ward

outskirts press

Access
Going Places

v3.0

Outskirts Press, Inc.
http://www.outskirtspress.com

ISBN: 978-1-9772-6266-0

PRINTED IN THE UNITED STATES OF AMERICA

1

"Friday afternoons just seem to drag on" Joe said as he passed Dave's cubicle. Dave chuckled and nodded, his day seemed to go by quickly since he just kept busy. Dave Smith had been working for Jonstone Services for nine years doing data entry. Dave looked to be in his mid-thirties, and in pretty good shape for someone who works at a desk.

"Hey Joe, you coming for poker tonight?" Dave asked.

"Don't think so" Joe responded, " I'll be keeping my money, thank you very much."

"Oh well, nothing ventured, nothing gained." Dave said with a shrug.

Joe looked at him and said "My mother taught me that if I can't afford to lose I can't afford to play." Joe turned and continued on to his cubicle.

From around the corner someone says "Good advice for a pussy!"

Dave asks "That you Rob?"

"Yeah," Rob said, "too bad, I could've used the money."

Joe just shook his head as he sat down at his desk. Joe is a tall good looking black man with a wife and three kids, a teenage son and a seven year old girl and a six year old boy. He married his high school sweetheart shortly after she got pregnant at their senior prom. He had no regrets and loved his wife and family dearly.

"So I take it you'll be there tonight, Rob?" Dave asked.

"Of course I will," Rob said, "but, eh, who else'll be there?"

Dave paused, "Not real sure yet, you, me, Mr. Jonstone,"

"Wait a minute." Rob interrupts, "you invited the boss?"

"Sure, why not? His money is good, and his poker is not." Dave explained, "You still coming?" he asked. "or are you a pussy?"

A laugh is heard from Joe's cube. When Joe had gotten back to his desk, he found a CD. He wasn't sure, but he had an idea who put it there. He also knew it would mean a production bonus.

"Ok, ok, "said Rob, "who else?" He asked as he came around to Dave's desk.

Dave looked suspiciously at Rob, wondering, why all the interest? "Well," Dave continued, "I asked Joe and Quinn, also my neighbor, Dan, and maybe his sister Chrissy. She's in for a couple of weeks vacation."

Dave paused, then looked up at Rob, "Who do you owe?" he asked. Rob looked down and said "I owe Quinn a hundred from last time I played."

"You mean you haven't paid him yet?" Dave asked incredulously, "that was two months ago, you sure you want to play tonight?"

"Yeah, I'm sure, and I'll bring Quinn his money. Like it matters to him, he's barely conscious." Rob said, with almost a sneer.

"What's that supposed to mean?" Dave asked, clearly agitated.

"Ok, ok, sorry, I know he's your friend. But he's, like, autistic or something, he never looks at me and it creeps me out." Rob replied.

Dave looked at Rob, he could tell Rob regretted saying that, out loud at least, but probably couldn't help it. That's just how Rob was.

"Well, he is an acquired taste." Dave offered.

"I guess I ain't acquired it yet." Rob said as he walked back to his space.

'Well,' Dave thought, 'might as well stretch my legs.' As he stood up a slight groan escaped from his lips.

"Old man noises." someone said in the background.

'Old man noises indeed' thought Dave. His back and knees weren't fans of sitting at a desk all day.

He liked taking the long way to the water cooler, he

got to see more people this way. He walked amongst the cubicles, nodding and saying "Hi", until he approached Amanda's cubicle. He knew in his heart this was why he came this way.

He found Amanda to be simply adorable. She was a cute little hardbody, with natural dish-water blonde hair, and definitely a lot smarter than she appeared. He believed she was in her late twenties.

He stopped and asked "How's things on your end? They look pretty good from here."

Amanda giggled and said "I can still get a rise out of people."

'I'll bet you can' thought Dave. He looked at her and asked "Everything good with the new beau?"

She lit up and said "Real good, three dates and he's still listening to me!"

"Sounds like a keeper, keep me informed." Dave said as he turned to continue on to the water cooler.

"Thanks for asking,...and for everything." she said as he left.

Amanda liked Dave. She found him easy to talk to, and he was always willing to help...no matter what. She did sometimes wonder why he had never hit on her when they first met, but was happy they had become good friends.

As Dave got his first cup of water the cooler made a gurgling noise, that's when a voice came out of the only corner cubicle in the office.

"I was just thinking," Quinn started.

"And what's holding your interest today?" Dave queried.

"Pistachios, are a good nut. They would make a good snack for poker." Quinn said.

"What about the shells?" Dave asked.

"A small price to pay for not having greasy fingers!" Quinn retorted.

"Good point," Dave said, "so I assume you'll be there tonight?"

"Of course I will." Quinn said as he turned to continue typing.

Dave nodded and headed back to his workspace. As he passed Amanda's cubicle he looked in to see, as she turned in her seat, a glimpse of her panties. 'Light purple, nice' he thought. Amanda looked up to see him looking up her skirt, with a quick glance at his crotch, looked at him and said "Good luck tonight."

He grinned and said "I feel I've been blessed." He walked back to his cubicle thinking ' if only I were a younger man.'

2

Dave got home from work and immediately started making sandwiches and putting chips and salsas into bowls, it was the third Friday of the month and that meant poker. He always made sure everyone had enough to eat, so they wouldn't get drunk. Everyone knew to bring their own beverages, and he had no restrictions on what or how much you drank. But he made sure everyone understood that being drunk is no excuse, you get drunk and somebody will take advantage of you. Forewarned is forearmed.

He had turned his dining room into a poker parlor, he had two round tables that would each seat seven people comfortably. Although it had been a while since he had used the second table. He also had several small fold-out tables for drinks, ashtrays, and such. He had, over time, acquired a variety of folding chairs, mostly padded (some better than others), but all solid. None of which were set up. He knew Quinn liked to help set up the room, so he waited for the help.

Dave looked at the clock, it was five thirty, everyone knew to be there around six. He knew Quinn would be there at a quarter to six, so he was surprised when the doorbell rang. He answered the door to find Quinn standing there with their boss, Jim Jonstone.

Quinn smiled and said "A good night for poker, let's get this set up."

"You're early." Dave said.

Jim spoke up, "I saw him waiting for a bus, so I stopped."

"I think you should get in." Quinn interrupted, using his 'boss' voice, "that's what he said."

They all laughed and got to work setting up the room for the evening's game.

"How many places do we need?" Jim asked.

"I think seven." Dave responded.

At that there was a knock on the door. "Come on in." Dave called out. The door opened and in came Rob with Joe right behind.

"You two ride together?" Jim asked.

"Nope" Joe said, "different sides of town."

'Different sides of town, indeed' thought Dave. Joe lived a block over from Dave, in an upper-middle class neighborhood, Rob, however, lived in the lower income part of town. 'Cheaper rent.' Dave supposed.

Through the window Dave saw his neighbors headed over, so he went to the door to greet them.

"Howdy folks!" Dave said as they reached the porch.

Dave's neighbor, Dan, was about forty, an average looking man, who's only problem seemed to be a mild case of cerebral palsy. It wasn't real bad, but he was often taken for being drunk.

His older sister, however, was almost perfect. A natural redhead with a killer body and an even deadlier wit.

"Ok," Dave said, "I guess the only people who haven't met are...Dan's sister, Chrissy, this is Jim, my boss, and over there, staring at Chrissy's tits, is Rob. Rob visibly reddened as he waved to her.

Jim shook Dan's hand, "Good to see you again, and good to meet you." he said as he nodded to Chrissy. Jim continued, "I just want everyone to know I have to leave at nine o'clock, up or down I have got to go." Everyone agreed.

"Well then, let's get our chairs and chips and get started." Dave said with a smile. Everyone found a seat at the table except Dan.

"You playing tonight?" Dave asked Dan.

"Nah, I'm just here to administer first-aid to whoever pisses off my sister." Dan replied. Everyone looked at Rob.

"Screw all of you." Rob said, looking visibly annoyed. Everyone, except Rob, got a good laugh. Dave liked needling Rob before the game, it made him easier to read.

With the players seated, everyone put in one hundred dollars for the buy in, except Quinn, Rob put in two hundred and said "That's for me and Quinn." He looked over at Quinn, and Quinn gave him a nod.

"All good?" Rob asks.

"Yes sir." Quinn replied.

"Ok then, first ace deals." Dave announced, then starts dealing face up, "Jim: king, Quinn: eight, Chrissy: deuce, Rob: six, Joe: a jack, me: deuce. Around again, Jim: king, Quinn: five, Chrissy:ace, finally, your deal, lady.

"Can I keep these?" Jim asked, with a pleading look.

"You're probably going to need them." Joe said, with a laugh.

"You got that right." Chrissy said as she gathered up the cards.

Dave watched as she shuffled the cards, her hands seemed to move with much more ease than his. He had to admit to some arthritis in his hands, and knees for that matter.

"Five card draw." Chrissy announced, then started dealing the cards.

As the cards were being dealt Jim asked Dave "So where are you going for your vacation?"

Dave smiled, "Belize" he answered.

"Belize? Why Belize?" Joe asked.

"Why not? I don't know anything about it, except that it is very different from here." Dave said, then looked at Quinn, "and I don't want to know 'til I get there, Quinn Tucker!"

Everyone, including Quinn, laughed at that. They all knew that if you needed information about somewhere on earth, chances were Quinn had read about it.

"You open, Rob." said Chrissy, and everyone started paying attention to the game.

The game was going well for Dave after an hour and a half when he said "I sent in one of those DNA test kits a few days ago."

"Oh no" Quinn said, "now the government has your DNA."

"I don't think that's how it works." said Jim.

"I would never discount any opinion Quinn has." Joe interjected.

"Thank you, Joey." Quinn said.

"Well, I thought it might be fun. What with me being an orphan and all." Dave said, "besides, Quinn, I thought you could appreciate one getting some info on ones self."

Quinn was already working at Jonstone Services when Dave started there. Quinn took a liking to Dave right away, and soon discovered they had both been orphaned as babies.

"You were an orphan?" Rob, looking surprised, asked Dave.

"That's right, but as Quinn informed me I was not an abortion, so all is well." Dave responded, with a smile directed at Quinn.

"Wow that must've been hard" Rob contemplated.

Joe lit up, "Hey, can we make bets on the results of the test?" he asked.

"I don't see why not." Jim said, "We could have an office pool." he suggested.

"Hell, I'd be willing to throw some money at that." Dan said, from the kitchen. He had been setting out plates and the sandwiches for the upcoming break.

It was Rob's deal, "Seven card stud." he said, after the cards were cut. He dealt the first two cards down, paused to look at everyone, then started the up cards, first to Joe.

Rob called out the cards as he dealt, "Eight of diamonds to Joe, two of spades to Dave, Mr. Jonstone, a queen of spades, Q-ball gets an ace of hearts, the lady gets the ten of hearts, and I get the king of clubs, ace bets." Rob looked at Quinn, he was trying to annoy Quinn with the names, but he couldn't tell if it had an effect.

"Ace is good for a buck." Quinn said, he knew he had a three and four, off suit, so three to a straight. Worth seeing another card and, maybe, get a couple of them to drop out.

"I call." Chrissy said as she looked again at her hole cards, a pair of tens, and threw in a chip.

Rob had king-five off suit in the hole and felt pretty good about calling. He had the short stack at the table, with about sixteen bucks in chips left, but threw in a chip.

"I fold." Joe said and set his cards down in front of himself.

"Me too." Dave chimed, and dropped his cards on top of Joe's.

Jim looked at Rob, he looked excited and trying to hide it. Looking at Chrissy revealed she looked a little apprehensive, and Quinn looked the same no matter what. He could have four aces or a nail in his foot and his facial expression wouldn't change, he thought. He had three to a straight, queen high, but decided, "I'm folding." Then tossed his cards on the others in front of Joe.

"Ok then," Rob said," here we go. Quinn, a five of spades. Chrissy gets six of clubs, and I get the five of diamonds." Rob looked around the table, "Ace still bets." he said.

"Ace bets two." Quinn said.

"I call." Chrissy said, after a pause.

"I raise it to five." Rob said quickly, throwing in his chips.

"I will call this time." Quinn responded.

"I should watch, but..." Chrissy said, putting in her chips.

"Ok then, "Rob said, as he started to deal, "Quinn, gets my king, Chrissy gets herself an eight, and I get the three of hearts." Rob paused, then said "Wow! the ace is still in charge, waddya say there, Q-bert?"

Quinn looked at Rob's cards, "The bert part of me is going to check." he said as he tapped the table.

"Me too, check." Chrissy said, also tapping the table.

Rob looked at both of them for a moment, then also checked. "Ok then, "he said, "last show card, Quinn, you get a seven. Chrissy, the six of diamonds for a pair, and I get the three of spades for a smaller pair.

Rob looked at Chrissy and said "pair of sixes bets."

Chrissy appeared worried, looked at Rob, then at Quinn and said "Sixes bet two."

Rob immediately said "raise to five."

Quinn tossed his cards to Joe and said "Q-B folds."

Chrissy looked at Rob and said "His last chips, that's what I want, I call."

Rob glanced down at his last five chips and gave a little smile, then said "Last card, down and dirty." as he dealt the last two cards.

Chrissy looked at the card she had been dealt to find the queen of hearts, no help. Rob picked up the card he dealt himself and felt both dread and excitement, it was the three of clubs, he had a full house.

"Sixes still lead." Rob said, trying to look unaffected.

"I bet five." Chrissy said.

"I gotta call." Rob said, and with that he showed his cards, "I gotta boat, threes full of kings. Beat that, little lady!" he finished, with a smirk.

"If you say so," Chrissy said, "Tens full of sixes." She

watched as the color drained from Rob's face.

"Now that's a burn." Joe said.

Dave spoke up "I'm ready for a break." Everyone agreed and started for the kitchen, except Rob, who sat bemoaning his losses. As Joe walked by he put a hand on Rob's shoulder and gave him a little shake and said "C'mon man, get a sandwich, free food always helps."

Rob got up, and as they walked to the kitchen, he asked Joe "I thought you weren't going to be here tonight."

Joe smiled and said "My wife gave me the ok when I told her my production bonus would be doubled this week. So here I am, taking your money."

"Ha, ha, "Rob said with a sneer, "I have never missed the quota, but I never get a bonus."

"Hey, you know the difference between a bonus and a boner?" Joe asked.

Before anyone could respond Jim spoke up "You gotta make me money to get a bonus, the quota merely covers the cost of having you as an employee. You make the quota, you don't cost me to have you there. You get over the quota and I start getting paid, do well enough, and I give back."

Rob looked confused, he shook his head and said "I've been there almost two years and I had no idea. I never heard of a company doing that."

"Most people start getting perks by just naturally getting faster at what they do." Jim said.

"I was just thinking, it helps to have a little drive." Quinn interjected. This got a few chuckles around the room.

"Yeah, what do you know about it?" Rob asked.

"Two of my cubicle walls are windows." Quinn said with a smile. Rob still looked confused.

Jim spoke up "I've got fifty employees, forty -five of which do data entry. Of those, there are six that only do the quota, and of those, four are handicapped."

"Is Quinn one of them?" Rob asked sarcastically.

Jim got serious, "I never considered Quinn to be handicapped." he said sternly.

Quinn was beaming, he had been with Jonstone services for sixteen years plus and, unknown to most, was the company's best producer.

"Hell, you're more handicapped than anyone in this room." Jim said.

"At least his poker is." Dave said to ease the tension, and got a few courtesy laughs around the room.

Dave looked over at Quinn as he was laughing and joking with Joe and Chrissy. He found Quinn to be amazing. As far as he knew, he and Jim were the only people Quinn had let in on his history.

Quinn had been dropped off at an orphanage with a note pinned to him that said 'my name is Quinn'. He was four or five months old, didn't like being held or touched, and would not make eye contact. His first word wasn't uttered until he was six years old, and always started with 'I was just thinking'. Startled the hell out of the nurse the first time he spoke, he had fallen out of a tree and broke his arm, "I was just thinking, my arm is broken." he said when they set him on the table.

The other kids picked on him relentlessly from the age of three until he reached ten, one of the staff, "A foreigner" Quinn had said, took to calling him tucker, because where he was from 'tucker' was their word for food. He thought Quinn was food for the wolves.

He had never been officially diagnosed by anyone, the orphanage didn't have funds for things like that. Around the age of four he started reading everything he could get his hands on, a few years later it became non-fiction only. He would ignore all the teasing and verbal abuse the kids would throw at him, but he did not like when they touched him, mostly punches and pushing, that ended when he was ten. At that point he was strong enough to defend himself. He had bought a copy of 'Greys anatomy', and figured out how to use range of motion against his opponents. If someone touched him with ill intent, he would grab their fingers then duck under their arm and have them twisted like a pretzel and at his mercy.

When he had been there seventeen years they threw him a party then told him he had to leave.

Jim called out "Hey Dave, can you come over here and witness this?" Dave walked over to find Jim with Rob, and now everyone was looking at them.

Jim opened his wallet and pulled out a hundred dollar bill and as he handed it to Rob he said “You agree to pay this back by next Thursday or it will be deducted from your paycheck as an advance, right?”

“Right. “Rob said.

“I got witnesses.” Jim said as he pointed around the room.

Rob took the money, turned to Dave, and said “I want more chips.” Dave obliged by taking the money and counting out chips.

Rob had insisted on playing when, shortly after hiring on, he heard some people talking about the game. Rob believed he was a much better poker player than he actually was, that was probably because he believed he was much smarter than he actually was.

Robart Bott, his parents misspelled Robert, was twenty-six years old, just under six foot tall and weighed about two-fifty. He looked soft, not a lot of muscle tone, and after dealing with him for five minutes you got the impression he felt someone owed him something.

Joe looked over at Rob and said “You think you can make that last a little longer?”

Rob gave Joe the evil eye and didn’t say anything. Rob didn’t much like Joe, partly because he was black and partly because Joe had a quicker wit than he. Rob had a hard time accepting people different from himself, he tried to hide it, though not very well.

Rob stacked the chips at his spot, then went in for

more sandwiches and some chips with some of Dave's homemade salsa.

Dan caught Jim's eye and asked "What do you think of the President?"

"No politics!" Dave interrupted quickly.

"Sorry, I forgot." Dan said, "So what do you think about climate change?"

"Hey, no religion either." Quinn said with a smile. That got a few laughs around the table, but Rob clearly didn't get the joke.

Jim looked at Chrissy and asked "So, Chrissy, I know your brother is a C.P.A., I was wondering what line of work you were in." Jim, upon meeting Chrissy for the first time, found her fascinating.

"I'm an auditor," Chrissy responded, "mostly forensic auditing, to figure out what happened to missing money." She looked into Jim's eyes, she found him to be interesting. It wasn't often that she ran across a boss who actually cared for the people working for him.

"I could set you up with a program to monitor your employees computer use." She offered.

Rob looked over and said "Wait, what? You can do that?" He looked nervous.

Jim smiled, "Thanks, but that won't be necessary," he said, "I already have one that Quinn and I wrote ourselves." Jim looked at Rob and said "Don't worry, I just know how many e-mails are sent and received and periods of inactivity, like when someone is streaming a movie or something. And I got that whitelist anti-virus protection so I know nothing bad is getting in."

"Sounds like you got it covered." Chrissy said.

"Yeah, covered." Rob grumbled. Rob spent around two hours a day watching shows and now he felt he couldn't.

"Hey, Dave," Joe said, "I want to hear more about your vacation."

"Why?" Dave asked, "you'll just end up hating me."

Chrissy looked over and said "I want to hear about it too."

"In that case, ok," Dave said, "through an old friend I met the ambassador to Belize and he needs to have his new diplomatic vehicle delivered to the embassy in Belize, so they're going to pay me to drive it down."

"How much?" Rob asked.

"Enough." Dave replied. He didn't want to tell he was making five hundred plus expenses. Dave continued "I have seven days to get there, but I figure to get there in four. Then it's three weeks in a cottage in a western suburb of the capital."

"That would be Belmopan." Quinn interjected.

"Yes, it would," Dave said, "and I figure to do a little hiking, maybe take a couple of tours, check out the local cuisine, you know, touristy stuff."

"How you getting home?" Dan asked, "Bus or plane?"

Dave answered "Plane, then a taxi here, where my

plants will all still be alive, right Quinn?"

Quinn chuckled, "Yes David, they will all be alive." Quinn had offered his services when Dave first mentioned going on vacation. This was the kind of thing, when he was younger, he would do to prove he could handle the responsibility. Now he just liked the feeling of helping out a friend.

"It's been a while since I've had a vacation, so I thought it was about time I treated myself to an adventure." Dave said.

"Yeah, it'll be an adventure getting past the border town, it's all controlled by the cartels." Chrissy said, "The first fifty miles are like a giant toll road for them, no money, no pass."

"I was just thinking" Quinn started.

"Please let us know about what" Dave said with a smile.

"That we should be playing poker" Quinn finished.

"And that we should," Dave replied, " everybody ready to play?" he asked.

Jim spoke up "I know it's early but I think I'll call it a night. I'm down about twenty bucks and I don't see me getting it back in the next half-hour."

"Well, thanks for paying, I mean playing," Dave said, "let me get you cashed out."

"Cute, I got seventy-eight in chips. "Jim said.

"Well then, we know at least a hundred 'n twenty-two has been lost so far." Joe said.

"Question is, who has it now?" Joe posed.

"Don't count your chips until it's over." Quinn insisted. His stack was looking pretty good and he, obviously, didn't want anyone to notice.

Dave counted out the money and handed it to Jim, who accepted the loss with a smile. Jim really enjoyed the game and getting to know his employees as people. He had been in the game, on and off, for about five years now, since shortly after his divorce.

It was around six years ago when Jim had caught his wife in bed with his office manager, Al Pagninski. He only found out about it because his daughter, Trish, said he hit on her. When asked to explain she told him she had gotten off work early one day and Al was at the house when she got home. Her mom told her he was there to pick up something her dad had left behind. She said she felt uncomfortable the minute she walked in, and it got worse when her mom left the room. That's when Al asked if she would like to party sometime.

After talking to his daughter, the next time Al stuck his head in his office to ask him to watch the workers because he had to run to the office supply store, he followed him. Thinking back, Al seemed to run an errand three or four times a week. This time he was going to find out what Al was taking care of.

When Al turned to go down the street where Jim lived, Jim didn't turn. Instead, he drove past and parked on the next street and called his lawyer. After talking to his lawyer, he drove around the block and parked about three houses down from his own. He walked to his house, entered, and went to the bedroom to find his wife riding Al like a carnival pony. He stood and watched them panic for a moment when he said "Al, you're fired."

The next year would've been really hard except for Quinn and Dave, they turned out to be really good friends to him.

After that he decided he didn't need an office manager, instead he gave everybody a raise and an opportunity to earn bonuses. Suddenly everyone was happier, productivity went up and his stress level fell drastically.

Dave watched as Jim was leaving he stopped to talk with Chrissy. 'That would be a good match.' he thought.

They were taking their seats when Joe asked "So Dan, you gonna change the luck of the empty chair?"

Dan answered "Sure, who wants to sell me fifty in chips?" Quinn started counting out some chips and handed them to Dan.

"You sure that's enough?" Rob asked.

Dan just grinned, he figured if he didn't start winning with the first fifty bucks the cards were not with him that night.

Joe watched out the window until Jim pulled away then pulled out a joint and asked "Any body else?" He then lit up and inhaled deeply, then offered the joint to the others.

Dave took the joint and took a good hit, then passed it to Dan. Dan took a couple of small hits when his sister said “Hey, don’t bogart.” Dan looked at her and grinned, they had been saying that to each other since they were teens. Dan passed it to Quinn who passed it to Chrissy without taking a hit. Chrissy took the joint and took a good sized hit, then handed it to Rob who immediately handed it to Joe.

Rob knew that he couldn’t handle pot if he had been drinking, and he had already had five beers. He knew, from experience, that one hit would give him the spins and he would puke on his shoes.

Joe took another hit and around it went.

They were all settled in when Rob asked “So Joe, whaddya think about reparations?”

Joe gave Rob an ‘are you serious?’ look then said “I have never been a slave, and I am not a victim. I make my own money and my own way.”

Quinn spoke up “I was just thinking... if someone wanted reparations, they should go after the tribes in Africa that sold their ancestors to the whites in the first place.”

Joe cracked up laughing, “I don’t think I’ve ever heard anybody say that before, but, damn.” he said.

“That makes more sense than anything else I’ve heard.” Dan interjected, “I mean, who in America today should pay? Not everyone’s family owned slaves, immigrants since 1865 didn’t own slaves, and what about blacks who owned slaves?"

"And what about Native Americans?" Quinn asked.

"Ok, ok, that's enough. Sorry I brought it up," Rob said, "you're making my head hurt."

Joe looked at Rob and said "That thinking stuff is strange to you, huh?" This elicited a few laughs around the table.

"Don't pick on Rob, it's not his fault." Dave said, "He was taught 'Common Core' by people who were taught 'Common Core'."

"That's why my parents home schooled me, "Joe said, "they believed that 'Common Core' was the most racist program ever enacted by the government, lowering standards so blacks could keep up." he finished with a look of disgust.

"Sounds like the progressives don't consider blacks to be equal, do they, Joey? "Quinn interjected.

"Don't git me started" Joe said

"What's wrong with progressives?" Rob asked, "I mean what's wrong with progressing into the future?"

"I was just thinking," Quinn started, "that it wouldn't be bad if that was what they stood for, but it isn't. They have an agenda, and it supersedes everything else. Laws, people's rights, the Constitution, everything." he finished.

"And," Joe spoke up, "they have a serious case of 'cheating spouse syndrome', they're always accusing their opposition of doing what they're doing. You want to know what they're up to, just listen to what they accuse their opposition of doing."

"Ok boys, all this chatter is slowing down the game." Chrissy said.

"The slower the game, the longer my chips last." Rob replied. He looked down at his stack, it was depressing, just over thirty in chips left.

It was just after ten o'clock when Rob won a hand that brought his stack to just over fifty dollars. "I think I've had enough." he said counting his chips.

"Well, you look ok to drive." Dave noted aloud.

"Haven't had a beer in over an hour." Rob said. He cashed in his chips, said his good-byes and headed home. He did not look happy.

Chrissy looked at her brother and said "I don't think you were ever that young."

"Maybe, but never that dumb!" Dan replied. Everyone got a laugh at that.

Dave felt bad for Rob for a moment, but that passed as he remembered how Rob had insisted on playing. "Maybe someone could coach him?" he asked.

"I gave him a book on poker strategy," Joe said, "I think it made him worse."

"You sure he read it?" Chrissy asked.

"Pretty sure," Joe responded, "He tried some of the strategies, but always at the wrong time."

"He'll get better or he'll get broke." Quinn said. Everyone agreed and the game went on for another hour.

As Dave was cashing everyone out, he noted "Looks like everyone here got a piece of Rob's pie."

"Yeah, that was fun," Chrissy said, "Maybe I shouldn't go three years between games."

"I completely agree," Dave said, "You know you're always welcome here, with or without the calculator." He nodded at Dan as he said that.

"I'll keep that in mind." she said with a smile, She and Dave had dated when they first met but found they made better friends.

"Thanks for everything." Dan said as Dave walked them to the door. Dave stood and watched them as they went down the walkway.

"Damn fine view, if I may say so." Joe said as he walked up behind Dave.

Dave smiled and grunted "Uh huh." They turned and walked back to the dining room where Quinn was folding chairs.

"You need more help?" Joe asked.

"Nah, we got this, but thanks for asking." Dave replied.

"Ok then, I'm going out the back, you guys have a good weekend." Joe said.

"You too, Joey." Quinn said.

With that, Joe went out the back door, through the back gate then down the alley to his house on the other side of the block. The back porch light was on and his wife came to the door when she heard him coming through the back gate.

"I got fed and I won sixteen bucks, not too bad. Huh, baby." Joe said, beaming at his wife. She smiled and gave him a hug and a kiss, and they went into the house.

Back at Dave's they are finishing cleaning up the kitchen when Dave asked "You gonna need a ride home, or, you could stay here?"

Quinn looked Dave in the eyes, "I was just thinking... I would like to try staying here tonight, for a change." he said. 'For a change, indeed.' Quinn thought. It had been ten years since he slept anywhere but home, but somehow he felt he would be comfortable enough to sleep here.

Dave was caught off-guard, "That would be great, you can use the guest room or the couch, or anywhere you want, except my room. You're not my type." he offered with a smile. Dave felt honored that Quinn trusted him enough to sleep over. He had been offering him to stay the night for years, and now he was actually going to stay.

Quinn chuckled and said "Are you sure?" He paused for effect, then added " the guest room should suffice."

Dave felt relieved and honored, relieved because he didn't have to drive Quinn home. He did not like driving at night. Honored because he felt this was a trust breakthrough for Quinn.

"Ok man, you know where everything is, I'll be on

the porch winding down." Dave said. He turned and went outside, sat down and lit up a joint.

As Dave sat enjoying the cool night air, he could hear furniture being moved in the spare bedroom. He almost choked on his hit as a laugh escaped.

Quinn came out a few minutes later, put his hand out and said "I think that will help me sleep."

Dave handed him the joint, "You could've asked me to help move...whatever it was you moved. It sounded heavy." he said with a smile.

"Can't sleep with a window over my head, don't want glass over my face while I'm sleeping." Quinn said, almost compulsively.

"You know that actually makes sense." Dave agreed.

They finished the joint and sat talking, mostly about different women in the office, for the next half-hour. at which time Quinn got up and said goodnight. Dave followed him into the house, and they retired to their rooms for the night.

3

The next morning Dave got up and went to the kitchen to find Quinn finishing the dishes left over from the night before.

"Apparently you've been busy." Dave said as he looked around. The house had been tidied up and he hadn't heard a thing.

"Coffee is made." Quinn responded.

Dave looked to the coffee maker, and it was off, so he looked to the stove and saw Quinn had dug out his old percolator. He had stopped using it because the coffee maker saved time.

Dave grabbed his mug and filled it with coffee, as he took a sip he found that he had forgotten how smooth and mellow coffee could be. He could see Quinn smiling at him. "The coffee is real good." Dave said, "So, what, you couldn't sleep?" he asked.

"I slept fine," Quinn answered, "I just got up early."

"Would you like me to fix you some breakfast?" Dave asked.

"I normally don't eat breakfast." Quinn said.

"Oh good," Dave said, "I don't either, not sure what I would've made."

"Coffee is enough." Quinn stated. Dave nodded in agreement.

They sat sipping their coffee in comfortable silence until Quinn got up for more coffee.

"I was just thinking," Quinn started, "It's hard to find a good place to worship. I have been to several chapels in the last couple of months and I haven't been comfortable in any of them." he finished.

"What seems to be the problem?" Dave asked.

"Most just want my money," Quinn said, "You know, give a seed and reap riches and blessings."

"And the rest?" Dave wondered aloud.

"They tell you everything is ok and God wants us to be happy with however we are, and that Jesus loves us no matter what we do." Quinn paused, then went on, "First; some things are not 'ok', second; Yeshua is his name, not Jesus, Yeshua."

"I never said being a Christian would be easy." Dave said.

"They do," Quinn went on, "They tell you everything is good, and you will be blessed if you plant a seed, but I've got nothing but teasing and being looked down on."

"Yeshua told us it would be bad." Dave said.

"Well, He knew what He was talking about." Quinn said with a smile, "And I'm not sure I like 'Christian',

I think 'follower of the Nazarene' is more appropriate for me."

"I think the Jews and Moslems would find it so, also." Dave said, " I like to think I'm 'part of the Church', just your basic definition. Perhaps we could start a once-a-week Bible study, when I get back from vacation."

Quinn nodded, "I think that would be good," he said, "maybe others would be interested." he wondered aloud.

"If we praise Him, they will come." Dave semi-whispered. Quinn didn't get the reference and had a puzzled look on his face. "Never mind, you find people you're comfortable with, ok?"

"I can do that." Quinn responded as he turned to finish cleaning up.

Dave poured himself a second cup of coffee and scanned the paper for anything useful. When he had finished his coffee, Dave turned and asked "You want a ride home? I'm going to the bank and run some errands, so..."

Quinn paused what he was doing and said "I'm thinking I would like to take the bus."

"Ok, you know best." Dave said.

"It's a nice day and there are always interesting people on the bus." Quinn responded.

"And I'm sure you're one of them, aren't you." Dave teased.

"I would like to think so." Quinn answered, with a smile.

Dave got up and went to his room to shower and get dressed, Quinn got another cup of coffee and went to sit on the front porch.

As Quinn sat enjoying his coffee in the cool morning air, he heard a door close next door. He looked over to see Chrissy had come out. He smiled and waved to her as she walked to her car. Chrissy smiled back and gave a nod. She reached into her car and started it up, as it warmed up, she walked over to Quinn.

"Top o' the morning to you." Chrissy said.

"And the rest of the day to you, lassie." Quinn replied.

"I was just wondering," Chrissy started, "you've worked for Jim for a while now, right?"

Quinn made eye contact for a brief moment, then said, "I have worked for him for a long time." He could tell she liked the boss at the game last night. "James isn't dating anyone at the moment."

Chrissy blushed a bit and said "That obvious, huh." Quinn grinned and nodded enthusiastically.

"I gave him my number last night," she said, "that wasn't too much was it? I wouldn't want to scare him off." She looked at Quinn, who sat grinning.

"Not too forward, I think," Quinn said, "he hasn't dated in a while, so I think you should expect a call."

Chrissy felt a wave of relief pass through her,

it caught her off-guard. She normally didn't worry because she thought she knew what men wanted. Jim felt different, and it had been a long time since a guy had made her feel like a schoolgirl. "Thanks, Quinn." She said with a smile.

"Besides," Quinn replied, "look at you, who wouldn't be honored to go out with you."

"Yeah, what about you. Would you want to go out with me?" Chrissy teased.

"Redheads scare me." Quinn said, trying not to smile. With that Chrissy raised her hands like claws and growled at him. Quinn turned away and said "Thanks, now I got that in my brain." They both laughed, then she gave him a big hug and walked to her car, a yellow '72 fastback Mustang, that she called Elenore. As she got into her car she gave him a wink, then closed the door and drove away.

As Quinn sat watching her drive away, he thought 'If only she wasn't a redhead'. He wasn't kidding when he said redheads scared him. There was something unsettling about his perception of redheads, 'they have a different glow about them' was the way he put it.

For Quinn everybody glowed to some extent. Most people had a really soft glow, but some were relatively bright and a rare few shone nearly pure white. Dave was one of those. Quinn didn't know if he glowed, it didn't translate through mirrors and he needed a short distance in order to have a proper perspective.

It was that glow that initially got him talking to Dave. He couldn't explain it, but he felt he could trust Dave right away. He had seen that glow only once before, when he was only six years old, when an old man walked past the orphanage. The old man never even looked over his way as he passed by.

Then there was the darkness, Quinn supposed what kept people from brightness were the little flecks of dark light. The more miserable someone was, the more dark bits about them. Quinn had never seen darkness approaching the level of light that Dave had, but he figured that it had to be out there somewhere. The thought of that much darkness in one place always gave him a shudder.

The door opened behind Quinn and Dave stepped out onto the porch. "It's going to be a nice day." Dave observed.

"I'm thinking you are right." Quinn responded.

"Ok then," Dave said, "I'm off to run errands, lock it up when you leave and I'll see you on Monday."

Quinn sat and watched Dave drive away in his late nineties, silver mini-van and wondered why Dave didn't drive a newer car. He finished his coffee and went inside and checked all the plants before he locked up and headed to the bus stop.

The walk to the bus stop seemed shorter than usual, Quinn took this as a good sign. He had been waiting about five minutes when he spied the bus at a distance, 'pretty good timing' he thought.

As the bus neared he could see the driver, it was Donald. Quinn liked Donald because he always treated him the same as anyone else, no special treatment and especially no baby talk.

Quinn had gotten to know most of the bus drivers on his side of town because he rode the bus everywhere. It didn't take him long to figure out which ones were worth talking to. They were all respectful, the job required that, but some had a better sense of humor. He knew that made them easier to talk to.

Donald had a sparkle in his eyes that told Quinn that he had the rare quality of being able to accept the differences in people.

As the bus slowed Quinn could see Donald smile when he recognized him. The bus stopped with a loud puff and the door opened. Quinn looked up and smiled at the driver, "Good morning, Donald" he said.

"Good morning to you sir," Donny said, "I didn't expect to see you out this way this early."

"I try to not be predictable." Quinn responded. Donny laughed, he had been picking Quinn up at the same stop, at the same time in the morning, every Wednesday, Thursday and Friday, for the last eight years, ever since he started this job. Plus, Monday and Tuesday when he filled in for the other driver.

Quinn scanned his pass and sat down in the first open seat past the handicapped section. A quick scan told Quinn that there were several people riding today, an older couple, a small group of teens, two guys that looked like they worked construction, and a pretty, young Asian woman sitting across from him.

They had gone about four stops when Quinn heard Donald say “Oh shit” under his breath. Donny pulled the bus over at the next stop and two large skin-head types got on and walked past him without paying. Donny pressed a hidden panic button which alerted the police. They usually took three to four minutes to arrive.

The slightly smaller of the two walked past Quinn and stopped next to the construction guys, staring at the group of teens which consisted of two boys and three girls. They looked to Quinn to be fifteen at most.

The second ass-hole stopped in front of Quinn and turned to the young woman across from himself.

“You look like you could use a friend.” the skin-head said, as he forced his leg between her knees to open her legs.

“I was just thinking,” Quinn said, louder than usual.

“Oh yeah, rainman, you can think?” the large man turned around and pounded his fist into his other hand.

“I don’t think the lady is ready for a friend of your caliber.” Quinn stated.

“What the hell does that mean.” the angry man said, reaching for Quinn. As his hand touched Quinn’s jacket, Quinn grabbed two of the large man’s fingers, ducked under his armpit and folded the man down to the deck. Grabbing the other two fingers, Quinn pulled them apart, wishbone style, but stopped short of doing any real damage.

"If your friend touches me, you will take a long time to heal." Quinn said, matter-of factly. The man's eyes got big as he stopped his friend with a look. Quinn looked up as the police entered the bus.

"Let go of him." the first cop said authoritatively. Quinn immediately dropped the man and put his hands out to his sides and sat back down in his seat.

After twenty minutes of talking to the driver, downloading video, and getting statements from everyone, the police headed back to the station with their two new friends. One got a ticket for not paying, the other had to post bond for assault.

As the bus continued on its route the young lady got up and sat down next to Quinn. "My name is Emma," she said, "and I would like to thank you for what you did."

"It needed doing," Quinn said, "and my name is".

"Quinn" Emma interjected, "I've seen you on the bus before."

"Yes, Quinn." he said, glancing at her eyes. "Those dark men shouldn't be allowed on the bus." Quinn stated.

"You know that I have to stop for everyone, don't you?" Donny said, "and the union would ruin me if I got out of the driver's seat to try to stop them. So I hit the button as soon as possible."

"I know this, Donald." Quinn said, apologetically.

"And Donny, thank you for reacting so quickly." Emma offered.

"You are so nice." Donny replied, "I appreciate that."

Quinn could see Donald was upset at not being able to help. "You can not afford to lose your job, you have a family to take care of." Quinn said. Donald nodded and settled back into driving the bus.

Emma looked at Quinn, "I would like to learn how to do what you did to that man." she said shyly. Quinn sat up a little straighter. Emma continued, "You could come over to my house and give me lessons." She smiled hopefully at Quinn.

Quinn made momentary eye contact with Emma, he felt comfortable, even with her sitting so close, which also made him a bit nervous, but in a good way. "I was just thinking," he started, "you would be a good person to teach what I do." he finished with a nervous smile.

Emma let out a sigh of relief and said, "Oh, thank you so much. Let me give you my card." She opened her purse and pulled out a small leather business card holder. As she handed her card to Quinn she explained, "I'm getting new cards, I already ordered them. The old ones just have my first name and my number, but the new ones will have my full name, my number and what I do."

Quinn took the card from her and said, "I was just thinking, I like the one name effect, it gives you 'gravitas'."

Emma smiled, "You are too kind." she replied. She looked up and realized her stop was next. "I hope you will call soon." she said as she got up and moved to the door. The bus stopped and when the door opened she waved at Quinn as she stepped off. Quinn sat quietly trying to process all that had just happened. The bus stopped and Donny said "Hey Quinn, I think this is your stop." Quinn snapped back to reality and said, "I was distracted."

Donny smiled, "I would be too." he said.

"Thank you for keeping the wheels on the ground." Quinn said as he disembarked. Donny gave him a wave as he closed the door and then drove away. Quinn turned and walked down the side street to his apartment at a private assisted living facility.

It was a group home owned by a LPN named Heather. It had twelve apartments, each with one or two tenants. Heather lived on the first floor with her brother, who had severe Down's Syndrome. The rest of the first floor was filled with people who also had Down's. Quinn saw a soft green glow about them that meant they were mostly happy and content, he liked talking with them, they could always cheer him up. The second floor had a variety of medical reasons for not living alone, Quinn lived on this floor in his own apartment. The third floor was mostly occupied by Heather's friends.

Quinn spent the better part of twenty minutes saying hello and chatting with his neighbors as he made his way to the stairs. Once inside his place everything else melted away and he could let his guard down and relax.

Quinn's apartment was spartan. There were two rooms and a full bath, one room had a galley kitchen with a small table and three chairs. The other had a bed, some shelves and a desk with a computer and a stereo/CD player.

He liked to sit and watch the cottonwoods, in the courtyard, move with the breezes. When he wasn't doing that, he was reading.

He read non-fiction only since he was eight, before that it was whatever he could get his hands on. He had been reading since he was three, but everyone around him thought he was pretending since he didn't speak. He liked going to the library because he liked the feel of real books, also, he thought the internet was too easily manipulated.

The morning newspaper was delivered to his door every morning, his downstairs neighbors would take turns doing this, as a thing of honor. When he was done reading he would bring the paper down for anybody else to read if they wished, then it would get recycled.

Quinn owned three books, two of them had dust covers on them, hiding their titles. The third one was the Bible, it didn't need a dust cover as he read it every day. He would pick a book and Chapter at random, or if he had a question he would ask and let it fall open and would find the answer on those pages. He didn't know if this worked for everyone, but it strengthened his faith as it worked for him.

Quinn took Emma's card and pinned it to the wall next to the refrigerator. He stood and studied the card for a few minutes, then went to shave and shower and proceed with his normal weekend routine.

4

Monday morning Dave arrived to work about fifteen minutes early and found Quinn in Jim's office talking about a girl he had met. Quinn wasn't sure if he should call her. He knew he could teach her self-defense, but he felt she wanted more. He wasn't sure if he could maintain a long-term relationship.

"Just teach her and don't assume anything else." Dave said from the office doorway.

Quinn turned his head and said "Good morning, David." He paused, "I was thinking maybe I want her to like me."

"How could she not." Jim put in.

"Exactly! Just be yourself and teach her the best you can and if anything comes of it then it was meant to be. If not then..." Dave opined, ending with a shrug.

"Besides, you told me she knew your name." Jim said.

"Wait, she already knew your name?" Dave asked incredulously.

"Yup, I think she's been stalking him." Jim teased. Quinn blushed and they all laughed.

"Well, that means something." Dave said putting a hand on Quinn's shoulder and giving it a little shake before withdrawing.

Quinn looked at Dave. "I am thinking I will call her after work today." he said, then turned to the boss, "And James, thank you for the advice." Quinn turned and walked to his cubicle. Dave was sure he saw a lightness in Quinn's step as he walked away.

The office was filling up as Dave turned to head to his space. As he passed Amanda's cubicle he looked in to find it empty. 'Curious' he thought, ' she's usually here by now'. He continued on to his cube, sat down and started work.

When lunchtime came around Dave went straight to Jim to ask about Amanda.

"She's fine, she had a death in the family," Jim said, "she'll be back on Wednesday."

Dave was relieved to hear she was alright. He rarely worried about other people, or about anything for that matter, but Amanda seemed to attract mischief and misery. Through no fault of her own, it just seemed to seek her out.

Dave had been through times like that, when things piled up against him for no apparent reason, for months on end. Quinn explained it as Darkness going after those who love the Lord with pure simple faith.

The stronger the faith the harder it comes after you. Dave thought it might be time to share this wisdom with Amanda when she returned to work.

Dave nodded to his boss, then walked over to Quinn's cubicle, "I'm going to the lunchroom, you coming?" Dave asked.

"I'll be right there, I've got a phone call to make." Quinn replied.

"Can't wait 'til after work?" Dave teased, "Don't sit talking and leave me to eat all by myself."

"I won't be long," Quinn said, trying not to smile, "now go." Dave turned and went to the lunchroom.

Dave had prepared his lunch and was about to sit down, when Quinn entered the lunchroom. Quinn went to the refrigerator and grabbed his bagged lunch, then proceeded to their table and sat down.

"Well?" Dave asked, eyebrows raised.

Quinn broke out in a huge grin, "I am meeting her Saturday morning at her bus stop, at ten o'clock." he said.

"Excellent, now just don't be late," Dave instructed, "women hate to be kept waiting."

"Point taken, however I don't drive the bus," Quinn replied, "kind of out of my hands."

"True." Dave said with a nod. With that the two men sat and ate their lunches.

The next couple of days seemed kind of drab to Dave. It wasn't until Thursday that Amanda returned to work, he was surprised at how much brighter the office seemed now that she was back. And he wasn't the only one who felt that way, half of the office went by to see how she was doing.

Dave waited until lunch before going to check on Amanda. As he approached her cubicle, he saw Amanda giving Quinn a big hug, and he was hugging her back.

Quinn wasn't a big hugger, he put up with it when called for, but... not his favorite.

Amanda gave Quinn a peck on the cheek, then he stepped back and said to Dave "I'll be in the lunch-room.", then walked away.

Amanda wiped away a tear as she turned to Dave. "He really is a wonderful person." she said with a warm smile. Dave looked at the desk behind her and saw a couple of CDs of the sort that gave people bonuses.

Amanda, seeing this, raised a finger to her lips and gave a quiet "Shush". Dave nodded and smiled. Amanda smiled back and asked, "Do you mind if I stop by after work Friday?"

Dave looked surprised, "If you don't mind watching me pack, of course, you're always welcome," he said. "There's no problem, is there?" he asked.

"No, no problem," she answered, "I just need to talk to someone I can trust."

"Well, I'm flattered, and I look forward to your visit." Dave said, "and it's good to have you back." Dave gave her a hug and went on his way to the lunchroom, where he found Quinn sitting at their usual table.

Dave grabbed his lunch and as he sat down he said “It’s been a hell of a week, eh buddy.”

Quinn’s normally straight face started to crack into a smile, “I am thinking, it could always be worse.”

5

Friday finds Dave keeping his head down and keeping busy, yet the day just kept dragging on. He punches the keys for what seems like an hour, only to look up to find ten minutes had passed.

It was getting close to lunch when Joe, returning from his lunch break, stopped by. "How's it going?" he asked. Dave looked up at Joe, Joe laughed, "Now you know how Fridays are for me." he said.

"I got jelly brain because I'm going on vacation." Dave offered.

"Nah, it's the anticipation," Joe said, "that's how much I love weekends with my family."

"Never thought of it that way." Dave said.

"Why would you? You're single, all you go home to are this morning's dishes." Joe replied.

"True enough." Dave said as he rose to go on his lunch break.

Joe continued on to his workspace and Dave went

on to meet Quinn. Amanda gave him a smile as he passed. Dave smiled in return, and as he approached Quinn's cubicle he could hear, from Jim's office, Rob arguing about his paycheck.

Jim came to his office door and asked Quinn and Dave to come into his office. The two men looked at each other, smiled, then went in.

Rob sat in a chair, with a red face and even redder ears, obviously embarrassed at having his co-workers brought in.

"Rob, here, thinks it's unfair that I deducted that hundred as an advance," Jim said, "said I should have given him more time to pay it back. I said we made a deal, You two were witnesses."

"I watched you agree to what he said." Dave put in.

"Robart, I heard you offer the deal to James. Almost begging, "Quinn began, "now you're upset that he is treating you like a man." he finished, with a condescending tone.

Rob got up and quickly exited the room, leaving the three men standing there with nothing more that needed to be said. Dave and Quinn left the office and headed to the lunchroom.

"That was kind of sad." Dave said.

"Yes, it was, but he should take himself a little more seriously." Quinn responded.

"But you," Dave said, "you had a little mean streak come out. Have you been practicing that?" he asked with a sly grin.

"No, I must have picked it up through osmosis." Quinn answered, thoughtfully.

As they sat down to eat, Quinn said "I've made an arrangement with Joey to ride home with him on the days I am to water your plants."

"Good thinking," Dave said, "you know that you can stay there if you want, right? Then you could ride with Joe every day."

"I know, and thank you. I may try it one night." Quinn responded. He knew he would most likely not spend the night, he didn't like to be the only person in a building.

"So, have you got everything ready for tomorrow?" Dave asked, after eating most of his lunch.

"What do I have to get ready?" Quinn asked. "You told me to be myself, I don't have to get ready to be myself." he stated.

"That's all true," Dave said, "I was talking more in the 'How do I explain what I do' kind of vein." Dave paused, "You seem a little nervous, that's not like you."

"I am thinking you may be right." Quinn said, with a little laugh at himself.

The two friends finished their lunch and returned to their respective work areas.

As the end of the week arrived Dave straightened up his space, he didn't want people looking at a mess while he was gone. He closed his station and headed to the timeclock. As he got in line to punch out he heard, from behind, Amanda say, "I'll follow you."

He turned around and smiled, "I'll do my best not to lose you." Dave said.

"You don't have to worry about that, I've seen you drive." Amanda joked, "You drive like an old man."

Dave broke into a grin, "True enough." he said.

They clocked out and headed to the parking lot. Dave had arrived early, so he had a spot close to the building. He reached his mini-van and watched Amanda as she walked on to her car.

Amanda drove a small, red sporty type of econo-car. It looked to be about ten years old, but well maintained. She had parked near the outer edge of the parking lot, and Dave watched her all the way to her car.

Dave drove past her, and she got in behind him. She followed him, doing the speed limit, all the way to his house. It took about fifteen minutes to make the trip. Dave pulled into his driveway with Amanda arriving seconds later.

"I could have made that trip in ten minutes." Amanda said as she got out of her car.

"Why not go for it and do it in five?" Dave asked.

"That would be dange..." Amanda stopped and looked at Dave, who was watching to see if she would catch the irony.

"That paper you signed to get your license was you agreeing to obey the rules of the road." Dave explained.

"I just do what everybody else does." Amanda replied.

"Oh, that's a good standard." Dave said sarcastically.

"I see what you mean." Amanda said as they entered Dave's house.

"Make yourself comfortable, can I get you something to drink?" Dave offered.

"Yeah, you got beer?" Amanda asked.

"It's a Jamaican export." Dave said.

"It's beer!" Amanda said with a Jamaican accent.

"That's my girl." Dave said as he went to the kitchen to get the beers.

He returned with the beers, one in a glass and one still in the can. He set the glass in front of Amanda, who was sitting on the couch.

"Oh, you didn't have to go to any trouble, I don't mind drinking from the can." Amanda said, a little surprised at the attention.

"Serving yours in a glass just seemed natural." Dave said, with a smile.

"I guess I can let my 'proper lady' have her day." Amanda said, with a giggle.

Dave sat down next to her on the couch. "Ok, so tell me what's bothering you," Dave asked, looking at her, "It's not your boyfriend, is it?" he asked.

"No, yes, but that's not it." Amanda said.

"Ok?" Dave said, puzzled.

"You heard about the death in my family?" she

asked. Dave nodded.

"Well, it was my Aunt Beth. I used to spend my summers with her and my Uncle Ernest on their ranch. It was my aunt that taught me how to take care of myself, you know, self-reliant." Amanda explained, "Well, my uncle passed away about five years ago and since then I've been going to spend time with her three or four times a week. I figured others in the family did the same, but they didn't. Turns out I was the only one who would visit her."

"They didn't have kids?" Dave asked.

Amanda winced, "She couldn't have kids, but they adopted a girl, we grew up together. She OD'ed more than ten years ago." she said, with a vacant look.

"Sorry, I didn't know." Dave offered.

"That's ok, how would you know?" Amanda replied.

"Anyway," Amanda continued, "after the funeral my aunt's lawyer comes over to me and says that he needs me to come to his office the next day. So I go to his office Wednesday morning and he tells me my aunt has left everything to me, then he hands me a check for one hundred thousand dollars."

"Wow, that's a lot of money." Dave said.

"That's what I thought," Amanda said, almost shaking, "so he hands me this check and says that this should hold me over until the estate is settled."

"Wait, what? What are we talking about here?" Dave asked, confused.

"Upper nine figures." Amanda answered, now visibly shaking.

"That's hundreds of..." Dave mumbled, as he sat blinking.

"I didn't know she had that kind of money." Amanda said.

"I expect your family didn't know either." Dave interjected, shaking his head.

Amanda chuckled, "No shit!" she said, "I mean, she had the ranch and all, so I figured she was comfortable. Like, she never complained about bills or anything. But I never imagined anything like this. I just loved her and liked spending time with her."

"She probably knew that." Dave stated, still blinking.

Amanda finished her beer, and as she got up to get another she checked Dave's can, it was almost empty. She went to the kitchen, opened the refrigerator and saw condiments and beer. She grabbed two beers and returned to the living room where Dave still sat, no longer blinking. She swapped Dave's empty with a fresh one and then filled her glass with the other. She returned to the kitchen and rinsed the two cans and set them on the counter. As she came back into the living room Dave was getting up slowly.

He looked at her and said "You gotta start a foundation or something."

"I already got one of those, but that's separate from my personal wealth." she responded. Dave sat back down with a thump.

"The lawyer gave me a fat file when I was there, turns out it was a list and description of all of my aunt's holdings." Amanda explained, "I spent Wednesday alternating between giggling fits and panic attacks."

"That, I can understand." Dave said, nodding.

Amanda continued "So then, I get back from lunch on Thursday, and I catch Quinn putting two CD's on my desk. He said he knew I missed a lot of time and he didn't want me to struggle." She looked directly at Dave, "He is truly a gem." she said, fighting back tears.

"One of a kind, for sure." Dave said, not surprised that it was Quinn helping people out anonymously.

"So, now you know my problem." Amanda said.

"Yeah, big problem." Dave said, with soft sarcasm. They sat in silence for a few minutes, when Dave sat up and asked "What about your boyfriend?"

Amanda chuckled and said "Oh, Steve. At the funeral I told him my transmission was slipping and I didn't know how I was going to pay for it, and maybe he could help."

"And this was before...you knew?" Dave asked.

"Oh yeah, way before." Amanda said, "So Thursday at work I get a call from him, he says that he doesn't think it was working and we should both move on. What an asshole." Dave stared in disbelief.

"My Aunt taught me that trick. She said that men

thought if it had tits or wheels it's gonna cost money." Amanda offered.

"So, you really must want the woman if you're willing to pay for her wheels." Dave said, "Your Aunt was a smart woman."

"You would have liked her, I told her about you, how you help me with advice and such." Amanda said, "She said you were good for me."

"I just found you easy to talk to, and that doesn't happen too often." Dave replied.

"I noticed you don't really talk to many people, I mean, you're nice to everyone and are willing to chat and stuff. But you don't get close to hardly anyone." Amanda said.

"Probably from growing up in the orphanage." Dave said, thoughtfully.

"Either way, it's part of why I like you." Amanda said, "I know when I talk to you, it's going to stay between you and me."

"Especially this." Dave said, "So, are you going to quit working?" he asked.

"Not right away, I figured a slow transition would be better." she replied.

"The office won't be the same without you." Dave said, with a touch of sadness in his voice.

"I'm not gone yet, so don't be sad." Amanda said with a smile. Dave smiled back.

"You want another?" Dave asked as he got up to get

himself a fresh beer.

"No, thanks, I'm going to head home." Amanda replied.

"Oh, ok," Dave said, "anyway, your secret is safe with me."

"Thanks, I just needed to tell someone." Amanda said, "If you ever need anything you let me know, ok?"

"Believe it or not, I have made myself fairly comfortable through the years. But thank you, anyway." Dave said, as they stepped out onto the porch. "You can do a lot of good with this," Dave said," just remember to keep your trust in God and not your money."

"My uncle used to say that." Amanda said.

"Sounds like you come from wise people." Dave observed.

Amanda turned and gave him a hug, with a full body press, leaned back and gave him a quick peck on the lips. "Hurry back, ok." she said, then turned and walked to her car.

Dave felt his senses go off, like when a woman is trying to get something from him, or maybe he was just getting a boner. He stepped inside and watched through the screen as she drove away.

6

It was just past six a.m. when Joe came through Dave's back gate, to find Dave packing a box into his mini-van.

"Morning Dave." Joe said, with a yawn.

"Morning," Dave said, "one more bag and I'm packed."

"How's that for timing." Joe said with a smile.

"Yeah, we'll be ready to go in a few minutes." Dave said, "You want coffee?" he asked.

"Sure, I'll take a cup, but I was talking about not lifting anything." Joe said, now grinning.

"See how you are." Dave said, trying to look serious.

The two men went into the kitchen where Dave had two travel mugs set out. One was an older type, with cartoon images on it, the other was a newer model, all black and chrome.

"Black, right?" Dave asked.

"What gave it away?" Joe said, looking down at his arms.

"I seem to recall from the last time you had coffee here." Dave responded, acting like he missed the joke. Dave filled both mugs and handed the newer one to Joe.

"Here's the keys, you're driving." Dave said as he handed the keys to Joe.

"Thanks, when do you have to be there?" Joe asked.

"Oh-nine-thirty," Dave answered, "that's military for nine-thirty in the morning."

"I think I got that." Joe said sarcastically, "that gives us more than enough time." he noted.

"I figured on buying breakfast along the way." Dave said as they walked out to the mini-van.

Joe warmed up the van as Dave packed the last bag into the back and then locked up the house.

"Not even six-thirty and we're already on our way." Dave said as he got in the passenger seat. He clicked his seatbelt and said "Feels weird, being on this side. It's my first time, so be gentle with me."

"Don't worry, we'll have plenty of time for breakfast." Joe said, with an evil grin.

Joe slowly pulled out onto the street, and they were on their way south to the base.

7

Quinn woke early Saturday morning, it was five o'clock, too early for the paper to be there. He put on a pot of coffee and sat down to look out the window. After a few minutes he decided to start his morning routine even though it was early.

Routine was one of the things Quinn used to filter the input. The normal filters the brain develops during infancy never occurred in Quinn's brain, he had to teach himself how to filter the overwhelming assault on his perception.

He was just finishing getting dressed when he heard someone coming up the stairs, with his paper, no doubt. Quinn opened the door just as the person got there, "Good morning, William." he said.

Billy took a step back, startled by Quinn opening the door. "Good morning Mr. Quinn." Billy responded. "I have your paper here, I got to bring it today." he said with a smile.

“I thank you for your consideration.” Quinn said, taking the paper from Billy.

“You’re up early today, it seems different.” Billy said, looking a little concerned.

“Don’t you worry, it’s just that I have an appointment... no, a meeting... no, a thing that I must do today.” Quinn explained.

“You seem nervous, must be a girl involved.” Billy said with a beaming grin.

Quinn could feel himself blushing, “No fooling you, is there William.” Quinn said, with a smile he couldn’t control.

“I will let you suffer in silence. You have a good day, Mr. Quinn.” Billy said turning away.

“That is advice I will try to take, thank you.” Quinn replied, as he watched William head down the stairs. He turned around and went back into his apartment and closed the door. “I must be rattled, if I’m that easy to read.” he said softly to himself.

He went to the kitchen to read the paper and have some coffee. On the table was a small gym bag that had been packed the night before. The bag looked well taken care of, but time was catching up with it. It was one of two bags he left the orphanage with, the other was a military-style duffle, which he still had folded up in his closet.

It was nearing eight o’clock when Quinn got up, grabbed the small gym bag and left his apartment. He walked to the corner and waited for the bus to come.

The bus arrived a few minutes later. Quinn could tell who was driving just by how little the brakes squealed as it stopped. The door opened and, without looking up, Quinn said "Good morning, Sharika."

"Good mornin', baby. How you doin' today?" Shari responded. Shari was a pretty, full figured woman, who loved to talk.

"I am doing well today, so far." Quinn answered.

"I hear tell that you're some kinda hero, you know, stopping that trouble before it could go too far." Shari said, with a big smile.

"I didn't do much." Quinn said, a little uncomfortable thinking people were talking about him.

"Oh, no, baby." Shari said, "I saw the tapes. What was that move you did?" she asked.

"I was just thinking, it was something I taught myself when I was a kid." Quinn said as he took a seat.

Shari could tell Quinn didn't want to talk anymore so she let it go and concentrated on her driving. She took a bit of pride in stopping without squealing the brakes.

Quinn sat quietly as the scenery passed and people got on and off the bus. About a block before his stop, he stood up and walked to the line behind the driver.

"Next stop, please." Quinn requested.

"You got it, darlin'." Shari said as she brought the bus to a stop.

"Thank you for the ride, Sharika." Quinn said as he stepped off of the bus.

"You have a good day, baby." Shari said as she closed the door.

After the bus had pulled away Quinn crossed the road and started down the side-street he had seen Emma walk down. He had walked about half of a block when he saw Emma turn onto the sidewalk about four houses up ahead.

Emma smiled and waved when she saw Quinn walking toward her. She walked quickly to meet him.

"Hello Quinn, you are early." Emma said, "I wanted to be there waiting when the bus arrived."

"I was just thinking, the bus was either a little early or a lot late." Quinn said. He felt the 'I was just thinking' slip out. He knew he was nervous, he took a deep breath.

As they walked to Emma's place he noticed that the lot sizes were much larger than in his neighborhood. They stopped in front of a large, ranch-style house, "This is my house," Emma said, "I live here with my parents, I bought the house five years ago. They moved in three years ago."

"It looks like a beautiful home." Quinn stated, as they walked to the house.

"Thank you, we work hard to keep it nice." Emma replied, "Come to the back yard, where you can meet my father."

Quinn followed her, thinking 'parents, I didn't sign up for parents'. As they reached the back of the house Quinn could see a small area set up with gym mats, like they used for wrestling when he was a boy. He also saw Emma's father standing by a table with assorted martial-arts paraphernalia. Her father was wearing sweats and had his back to them.

As they approached, Emma stopped with Quinn about ten feet from her father, she signaled Quinn to stay where he was. She advanced two more steps, stopped and waited.

Her father turned to face them, "Good morning, Emma." he said, with a slight bow.

She bowed her head more deeply, "good morning, father," she said, without lifting her head, "this is Quinn, the man I told you about."

Her father looked at Quinn with a discerning eye, Quinn instinctively bowed in his direction.

"Quinn," Emma said, raising her head, "This is my father, Jonathan Cheung."

"I was just thinking, it is good to meet you, sir." Quinn said nervously.

"Really?" Jon asked, "I always hated meeting the parents of the girls I knew." he said with a chuckle.

Quinn relaxed almost immediately, now knowing the man had a sense of humor.

"I have been studying martial-arts for over fifty years and I would like you to show me what it is that you do." Jon said in near perfect English.

Quinn could detect the remnants of an accent, this made him think that Emma was probably first generation of her family born here.

"I am thinking I should warn you, nearly everything I do is forbidden in the ring." Quinn stated.

"I consider myself warned." Jon said as he invited Quinn onto the mats.

Quinn set his bag on the table, walked to the center of the matted area, turned to Jon and said "Mr. Cheung, if you would, try to move me."

Jon cleared his throat, "Ok then, do you want me to use karate or just grab you?" he asked.

Quinn made momentary eye contact with Jon, "However you feel you will be more successful, sir." he offered.

Jon sidled, karate-style, nearer to Quinn, then exploded with a grab at Quinn's shoulder. As soon as his hand touched Quinn, Quinn grabbed his middle two fingers, stepped on his foot, bowed his arm up and slipped under. Jon folded over, face first, towards the mat when the tension on his arm stopped him, inches from hitting the mat.

Quinn grabbed Jon's shoulder, and as he let go of Jon's fingers, he pulled him upright. "Wow, that was fast." Jon said, "Where did you learn that? Who taught you?" he asked.

"I grew up in an orphanage, I got beat up a lot."

Quinn said, "When I was eight I bought this." He opened his gym-bag and pulled out a book with a dust jacket on it. Jon looked curious.

"Grey's Anatomy," Quinn said, "I read this, it showed me weak points, range of motion, and basically how to dismantle a joint. I thought about it for a long time, while I used these." He reached into the bag and pulled out three different sizes of squeeze-spring grip builders. There were more in the bag, but Quinn figured these would get his point across.

"Ho Ree Clap!" Jon said in amazement, "You mean to tell me an eight-year-old's system just embarrassed me?" he asked incredulously.

"The first time I tried it, the other boy's fingers slipped from my grip. I ended up in a headlock getting my face punched." Quinn explained.

"I can see that," Jon said. "I thought for a moment, if I could free my hand, I could throw you. But it felt like my hand was in a vise." He stood shaking the blood back into his fingers.

Quinn saw a bowl of fruit on the table, he reached over and grabbed an apple. He gave it a quick squeeze and the apple exploded in a spray of juice and bits.

"My fingers were in a vise!" Jon exclaimed. He looked at his daughter, who had been quietly watching. Emma clasped her hands together and smiled hopefully.

She had been watching her father spar with his

friends and opponents all her life and she had never seen anyone do that to him, let alone that fast.

Jon smiled at his daughter, "You have my approval to work with this man." he stated.

Emma gave a little jump and a quiet clap, "Oh, thank you father." she said.

Jon turned to Quinn and gave a quick nod, "My daughter has been studying Wing Chun, with her mother, most of her life. Perhaps you will learn from her as well." he paused for a moment, then said, "I will leave you to it, then." Jon turned and walked to the house and went in.

"So, you didn't need to be saved, did you?" Quinn posed.

"He was a large man, I would have had to work much harder." Emma offered.

Quinn nodded and gave a little smile. He picked up his book by the spine, held the book upright, spine down, and when he opened his hand the book opened itself to the anatomy of the wrist and hand. He handed the book to Emma, "This shows how and where everything is connected, it is good to know." he said.

Emma took the book from him and looked at it with reverence, "I will study, and I will take care of this." she said, looking at Quinn for approval.

"Thank you," Quinn said, "now you should try the grippers, to see how strong you are." He held out one of the smaller springs.

She set the book down and tried the gripper. She was able to squeeze it easily. They went through a few more springs until they found one that offered enough resistance.

"You have a pretty good grip." Quinn said, obviously impressed. He spent the next hour answering questions and explaining different grips. He found her really easy to talk to.

Jon looked out from the kitchen, 'I got a good feeling about this." he thought to himself.

8

Joe turned into the parking lot of a diner, about a mile from the base, at eight-fifteen. "See, I told you we would have enough time for breakfast." he said with a smile.

"That was a nice ride," Dave said, "I'm usually not a good passenger, but I have to say, you're a good driver. A little bit of speeding, but I suppose that can be forgiven."

"Thanks for noticing." Joe responded, "I did a bit of slalom racing when I was younger." he explained as he parked.

"Really, I did too, back when I was married." Dave said, "Got me out of the house, anyway."

As the two men walked into the diner they looked around, there were more tables taken than open.

"This is a good sign." Dave said about the number of customers.

Joe nodded in agreement, "Don't want to be the

only ones in a diner at breakfast time." he replied. They found themselves a table by a window and, as they sat down, a waitress came to the table.

"Morning y'all, my name is Tiffany." she said, "Can I get you some coffee?" she asked as she placed a menu in front of each of them.

Dave looked at her, she was young and pretty. "I'll have some." he said, "Joe?" he asked.

Joe was looking over the menu, "Yes, coffee." he replied without looking up.

As Tiffany walked away Joe and Dave looked at each other, Joe's eyes got big and Dave smiled broadly.

"Oh, to be a kid again." Dave said.

"That's the kind of thing that got me married in the first place." Joe said with wonder.

"I see they have skirt steak and eggs," Dave said, "That's what I'm having."

"Sounds good to me." Joe said, nodding.

Tiffany returned with two mugs of coffee. "You decided yet?" she asked while setting down the coffee. Dave motioned Joe to go first, and the two men put in their orders.

Ten minutes later Tiffany returned with their meals, then came back and topped off their coffees.

The two men engaged in some light conversation while they enjoyed their breakfast. It was ten minutes after nine when they finished eating. Tiffany brought the check and Dave reached it first. "I got this." Dave said.

“Ok then, I got the tip.” Joe responded.

Dave looked at the check and pulled out fifty dollars, “It’s forty-six and change.” he said.

Joe pulled out fifteen dollars and set it on the money Dave had set down. “My wife was a waitress for a while, tips are important.” Joe said in response to Dave’s look at the large tip.

“You’re right, my bad.” Dave said, feeling a little stupid.

Tiffany came by to get the payment, “Was everything good for you?” she asked.

“All good.” Dave said as he handed her the money.

“Keep the change.” Joe said as he stood up.

Tiffany looked at the money, “Thank you so much.” she said, smiling.

The two men walked out of the restaurant and headed to the mini-van.

“I’ll drive onto the base.” Dave said.

“Fine with me.” Joe said as he tossed the keys to Dave.

Dave drove the remaining distance to the base, pulling up to the gate a few minutes later. An armed guard stopped them and approached the window, Dave lowered his window.

“Driver’s license, and reason for being here.” the guard requested.

“David Smith to see Mr. Peters of the Diplomatic Corps.” Dave said as he handed him his driver’s license.

"I've got 'you, plus one' on the list," the guard said, after photographing his license. "And this is..?" he asked, motioning to Joe.

"Joey Coleman, sir." Joe answered.

The guard wrote Joe's name on his clipboard. "You're cleared to go." he said, motioning them through the gate.

"Excuse me, but could you tell me how to get to where I need to be?" Dave asked.

"Of course," said the guard, and he gave him a series of instructions to get them to the proper Admin building.

"Thank you." Dave said, then proceeded through the gate. "Did you get all that?" he asked Joe.

"I think so," Joe said, "I'll let you know if you miss a turn." he offered, sounding a little worried.

They reached the Admin building without incident and Dave found a parking spot near the entrance. There weren't many cars in the parking lot and Dave didn't see the embassy car anywhere. 'Maybe it's on the other side of the building' he thought.

Dave looked at the time, "Nine-twenty-three." he noted.

"If you're not five minutes early, you're late!" Joe said, "That's what my daddy taught me."

"Smart man." Dave said as he opened the door. "Wait here, please." he requested as he got out.

"Won't move until we talk again." Joe said.

Dave nodded and closed the door, then headed towards the building entrance. He was about five yards from the entrance when it opened and three men came out.

"Dave!" one of the men said.

"Jimmy Peters, it's good to see you again." Dave said, extending his hand. they shook hands, then bro-hugged.

"Dave, I would like to introduce you to the ambassador, Mr. Linehouse, Mr. Ambassador, this is Dave Smith." Jim said. Dave shook hands with the ambassador. "And this is Lt. Bozman, Lt., Dave Smith."

The two shook hands and Dave said "Nice base you got here." The lieutenant smiled and said nothing. "I don't see the embassy vehicle anywhere." Dave said, looking around.

Jim put his hand on Dave's shoulder and said "About that, I may have been confused." Dave looked at him with a thousand questions on his face. "The government flew the limo down to Belmopan." Jim explained.

"Don't worry, the deal is still the same. It's just the vehicle that's been changed." the Ambassador interjected.

"Wait. What?" Dave asked, flabbergasted.

"I need someone to drive my teenage son's van to Belmopan, he's not old enough for that kind of trip." Mr. Linehouse explained.

"Ok then, so what am I driving?" Dave asked.

The ambassador opened his briefcase and pulled out two envelopes, One large manila and one small white one. He closed his briefcase and offered the envelopes to Dave.

"The big one has all the paperwork you will need, insurance, permission, etc. The small one has your expense card and numbers you can call if you have a problem." the ambassador explained.

Dave took the envelopes with a nod, "And the keys?" he asked.

Jim reached into his suit coat pocket and retrieved a set of keys with a chrome Playboy rabbit fob. He handed the keys to Dave and pointed to a brown, early nineties, full size Chevy cargo van. It had clearly seen better days.

Dave took the keys from Jim, "It's like bait and switch." he said with a smile.

"It's been nice meeting you, Dave." the ambassador said, "I must go." He turned and entered the building with the Lt. close behind.

Dave turned to Jim and said "Rather terse for a diplomat."

Jim chuckled, "He's busy with the move, a lot of stress." he said, "So the van's all gassed up and ready to go."

"Well, thanks for everything," Dave said, "I'll give you a call when I get back."

They shook hands and Jim returned to the building

while Dave walked back to his mini-van, which was two spaces away from the brown van.

As Dave approached Joe got out of the mini-van, "So, what's up?" Joe asked.

"There's no limo, I'm driving that." Dave answered, pointing at the brown cargo van.

"That giant turd looking thing?" Joe asked in disbelief.

"Yup," Dave said as he unlocked the van, "let's get it loaded." As Dave opened the door the air inside hit him in the face. "Oh no, it smells like feet and farts." he said with a grimace.

Joe carried a couple of boxes to the open cargo door of the van, "Damn! Feet and farts with a side of cat piss!" he said, with a laugh.

"What's so funny?" Dave asked, knowing the answer.

"Just the idea of you spending a week inside that thing." Joe replied, still laughing.

"Yeah, yeah. Real funny." Dave said, trying to not laugh himself, "Let's get this done."

They loaded the van in short order, and as they finished Joe said "Wait a minute." Joe ran back to the mini-van and retrieved a small mint tin from his lunch cooler. "Here you go." he said, handing the tin to Dave.

Dave opened the tin to find several joints and a couple of mints. "Thanks!" he said.

"Don't worry, they don't check for drugs going into

Mexico, just leaving." Joe said with a smile, "Just have them gone by time you get to Belize."

"Don't you worry about that, I'll probably use them as incense or air fresheners." Dave said with a grimace.

"Maybe stop and buy a couple dozen of them little pine trees." Joe said trying to not laugh.

"There goes my budget!" Dave said, finding less and less humor about the situation. "Anyway, thanks for helping out, and be careful on the drive home, ok." he said.

"Anytime, my man, anytime." Joe said, meaning every word, "and you be careful, remember, you ain't in the good ol' U.S A. anymore."

"I'll keep that in mind," Dave said, "I'll see you when I get back." he said as he shook Joe's hand.

"Drive safe." Joe said as he walked to the mini-van, "I'll follow you out."

Dave climbed into the van and started it up, it seemed to run ok. He rolled down the windows, 'maybe a cross-breeze would help' he thought. He was just glad it wasn't the middle of summer, he did not want to find out what the a.c. smelled like.

He let the engine warm up for a few minutes before looking over at Joe and giving a nod. He put the van into drive and pulled away slowly. Joe got in behind him and they drove to the gate, where the guard waved them through.

As Joe followed Dave to the highway, he noticed

that the van Dave was driving looked like it was 'doggy-walking'. That meant Dave would have to keep extra pressure on the steering wheel in order to go straight. That would be exhausting after a couple of days.

When they reached the highway Joe went north and Dave headed south. Dave looked at the time as he entered the highway, it was five after ten. He figured about an hour to the border.

Joe got up to the speed-limit as he merged with traffic. He settled into driving before lighting up a joint.

He had finished the joint about three minutes prior when flashing lights appeared behind him. He looked down at the speedometer, it read seventy-six. He quickly lowered all the windows as he slowed and pulled onto the shoulder.

Joe came to a stop on the shoulder with an unmarked squad car in close behind. He turned the van off and put his hands out the window. He could see the officer in his side mirror, the cop visibly relaxed when he saw Joe's hands and took his hand off of his gun as he approached the window.

"License, registration and proof of insurance, please." the officer requested.

"Sure thing, officer." Joe said as he opened one of the overhead compartments and pulled out Dave's registration and insurance card, then handed them to the patrolman. Then he reached onto the dash to retrieve his wallet. He pulled out his driver's license and his own insurance card and handed them to the officer.

"Wait here, please." the cop said as he turned to return to his squad car.

Joe watched the officer get into his car before saying out loud, "Friendly sort."

After about ten minutes Joe heard the cop's door close, so he put his hands out of the window again.

As the officer approached, he told Joe he didn't have to put his hands out, then he handed him a clipboard. "Sign here, please." he said, pointing at a blank line on the form with a pen.

"Of course, officer." Joe said as he took the clipboard and pen.

The officer bent down an inch or two, "This is a ticket for doing eleven miles an hour over the speed limit." he said, emotionless.

"I'm sorry about that, officer," Joe said, "It's just that this is the first time I've driven my friend's car and I didn't realize it's cruisability." He finished signing the form and handed the clipboard and pen back to the cop.

The officer took the clipboard with a smile, "I know what you mean," he said, "sometimes I have to drive my wife's mini-van, and I must admit it's easy to cruise along and end up speeding. But, I was doing seventy-three when you passed me like you were in your own little world." he explained as he folded the paper and handed it back to Joe. "Here's your copy, sir."

"Again, I'm sorry." Joe said as he accepted the ticket. The cop smiled and nodded as he turned and walked back to his car.

Joe pulled away as soon as traffic would allow. He got up to the speed limit and engaged the cruise-control. He did not want to get another ticket.

"I guess Dave was right." Joe said out loud, with a chuckle. Dave had explained how white people hate getting pulled over by the cops too, but the secret is compliance. Just smile and do what you're told, don't complain, and definitely do not reach for anything unless you are told to by the officer. He also said it helped to admit your mistake, if you know you were wrong. If you didn't think you were wrong do not argue with him, save it for court. Joe came up with putting his hands out the window himself. He figured that it couldn't hurt.

He had to admit to himself that it sure made things go a lot easier. He didn't even feel that his color had anything to do with it. "Compliance, who would've thunk it." he said out loud with a chuckle. He drove the rest of the way without incident.

Two hours later he was pulling into Dave's driveway. He parked and locked the mini-van and walked down the alley to his home. "I hope no-one saw me driving a mini-van." he said as he entered his kitchen, where his wife was sitting at the table.

"Don't want to ruin your rep, now do we?" his wife teased.

"Hey now! Don't be joking 'bout that. That's some serious shit." Joe said, keeping a straight face. "That mini-van stuff don't wear off." he said as he hugged her from behind, while she remained seated.

9

As Dave approached the border he decided to stop at the duty-free store before he crossed the border. He parked near the door and thought about leaving the windows down but decided to lock the van. 'Better safe, and smelly, than sorry.' he thought.

He noticed a currency exchange next door, 'Good, I can get some pesos before I cross' he thought as he entered the duty-free shop.

Dave looked around for a moment, then walked to the liquor section and grabbed a bottle of Kentucky bourbon. 'This should get me to Belize' he thought. He looked around a bit more and decided to buy a couple of cartons of cigarettes. He hadn't smoked cigarettes in a long time, but he figured that they may come in handy.

He pulled a cold soda out of a stand-alone cooler while he waited in line to get the cigarettes and to pay for everything. He took a drink from his soda as he waited his turn.

Finally through the line, Dave stashed his booty in the van and proceeded to the exchange. There wasn't much of a line in there so he was in and out in minutes, with a hundred dollars' worth of pesos. He liked to use cash for tips and such.

He climbed into the van, started it up and headed to the border crossing, where he got into line to enter Mexico.

Before long he was pulling up to the gate on the Mexican side. He stopped where the guard told him to, then another guard approached his window with a clipboard in hand. "Reason for coming to Mexico?" the guard asked, in near perfect English.

"Just passing through." Dave said, with a smile.

The guard did not look amused, he set his pen down on the clipboard and gave Dave a stern look.

"I'm sorry sir, I mean I'm driving this van to Belize for the American ambassador." Dave said, hoping he hadn't pissed-off the guard.

"So, this is not your vehicle?" the guard asked, deciding just how much grief he was going to give the gringo.

"No sir, it is not." Dave said as he reached over to retrieve the envelope he received at the base, "I have some paperwork here authorizing me to drive this thing." he said as he pulled several papers from the envelope.

He found the registration, proof of insurance and

the letter of permission, then handed them to the guard, who took them and started transferring info to his clipboard. Dave looked down into the envelope and saw an envelope with an official looking Mexican seal on it. He took the envelope out and saw it wasn't sealed, it contained a letter from a local General.

The letter granted Dave passage, unmolested, through Mexico. Dave handed the letter to the guard, who, after reading it, returned all of Dave's paperwork to him and said "You have a safe trip, sir."

Dave took the papers and said "Thank you, now, could you tell me how to get to administration building number one, zero, eight?"

The guard, now smiling, told Dave it was about three blocks away. Then proceeded to give Dave a short list of directions.

Dave drove to the admin building without missing a turn. He pulled into the parking lot and found a space away from the door near a couple of Jeeps.

As he got out of the van he noticed a few soldiers sitting at a picnic table under a tree. He overheard one of them say, in Spanish, "Looks like a rolling donkey-turd." The soldiers all laughed at this.

Dave, who spoke fluent Spanish, smiled and waved at the soldiers as if he didn't understand what they were saying. He went into the building and spoke to the person at the information desk. The info-officer told him his escort was outside waiting in the parking lot. He then handed Dave an envelope with some official looking papers in it.

"You'll need this to cross into Belize." the officer said. Dave took the envelope, said thank you and left the building.

As he approached the soldiers he asked, in English, for Sgt. Ramirez. One of the soldiers stood up and said "I am Sgt. Ramirez. Are you the person we are to escort?"

"Yup." Dave said offering his hand to shake, "I'm Dave."

The Sergeant shook hands and said "I thought we were escorting an embassy limo. What happened?" The other soldiers laughed when he asked this.

"It caught an earlier flight." Dave responded, "Hey, I'm just as thrilled to drive that thing as you are to escort it."

"I wouldn't be too sure about that." the sergeant said with a scowl. He turned to his men and said, in Spanish, "Move it, this is who we are to escort."

As the men went to the Jeeps, Dave said to the sergeant "It's the ambassador's son's van. You want to check it out?"

The sergeant looked at him and said "That's ok, I think I can smell it from here." the sergeant laughed as he sat down in his Jeep.

Dave climbed into the van and started it up. The Jeep with Sgt. Ramirez passed in front of him and the second one waited for Dave to pull out. He got in line between the Jeeps and they all headed south into Mexico.

They had gone about fifteen miles when the first Jeep pulled off the road into a gas station. Dave followed, as did the Jeep behind him. They all came to a stop and the sergeant got out of his Jeep and walked over to Dave's window. As he neared Dave could hear the other men saying that it was embarrassing to be seen near this van.

"This is as far as we go." Sgt. Ramirez said, in English.

"But, I thought you were going to be with me for fifty miles or so, at least to the first checkpoint." Dave said.

"Don't worry, man. No-one will want to steal your van, you will be fine." the sergeant replied, then turned and walked back to his Jeep.

"Don't want to be seen with a rolling donkey-turd, right?" Dave said, in Spanish, but with a smile.

The sergeant looked back at Dave and returned the smile, then shook his head and got in his Jeep. The two Jeeps pulled out and headed back to town. Dave watched as they drove away, then he pulled back onto the highway and headed south. He had gone another fifty miles when he came upon the first of many Army checkpoints.

He stopped where they told him to and put the

van in park. A soldier walked up to his window, "Turn off the engine." he said in English. Dave immediately turned the van off and got out with the paperwork he would need.

"Open the back doors." the soldier said, almost demanding.

"No problem, sir," Dave said, as he opened the rear doors, "and, if you would sir, I have some papers you need to see." The soldier in charge took the papers and started looking through them.

"This says he is to be allowed to travel 'unmolested'," the soldier said to the others, in Spanish. He looked at Dave, "I think you are being molested by that smell." he said in English. "You are free to go, amigo." He handed the papers back to Dave.

Dave closed the back of the van, got in behind the wheel and started it up. He looked over at the soldiers and gave them a wave as he turned onto the road.

He passed through three more checkpoints before stopping for the night at a relatively new hotel in a small town. He was just happy to have indoor plumbing. He ate and slept and got up early to start it all over again.

On the third night he stopped about twenty miles from the border with Belize. Another half days drive and he would be away from the smell, he figured. He found a nice looking hotel and pulled into the parking lot. It wasn't very busy, but then the busy season had ended a few weeks ago. He had been noticing that the closer he got to the coast, the more Americanized everything seemed to be getting. So, he expected this place to be modern. He walked to the check-in desk and, in Spanish, asked about a room.

"We have plenty of accommodations, would you like to see a room first?" the woman at the desk asked, in perfect English.

He glanced at her name tag, "Dot, I think that would be fine." Dave said, in English, with a big smile. Her speaking English caught him off-guard after speaking nothing but Spanish for the previous three days. He was starting to think in Spanish, hearing English again was a bit of a relief.

Dot came from behind the desk and motioned Dave to follow. "Your Spanish is excellent," she said as they turned down a hallway, "but something told me you were American."

"Thank you, but what gave it away?" Dave asked, curious because most of the way he wasn't questioned. "Too white?"

"No," she said, opening a door to one of the rooms, "We can let you have this suite for the price of a single room." The door opened to a beautiful three-room suite.

"I think this will do," Dave said, "kinda makes me want to stay more than one night." he said as he gave her a quick once over. She was a good-looking woman who seemed to be approaching middle-age with grace. She also looked to keep pretty good care of herself, physically.

"Well, maybe we can convince you to extend your stay." Dot said, with a coy smile, as they returned to the front desk to complete the transaction.

Dave thought 'this girl is flirting with me', then thought better of it. 'She's just trying to make sales' he concluded. "So, Dot," Dave said as he signed the credit slip, "What's the best food within walking distance?" he asked as he handed her the pen.

"Any of the restaurants on main street, that you could walk to would be ok." she replied.

"And where would you go, like for a special occasion?" Dave asked.

"That would not be on the main drag." Dot answered, looking him in the eyes.

"No? and why not?" he asked, his interest piqued.

"It's where downtown was years ago." she said, with a look of disdain. Then she smiled, "I get off work in half an hour, I could show you where it is." she offered.

Dave paused for a moment, "That would be great, but I'll have to follow you." he said, "You do not want to get in my van."

"Don't be silly, you can ride with me. And I'll have you back here whenever you want." Dot said.

"Ok then," Dave said with a smile, "I'll go get cleaned up."

"I'll come to your room when I'm off work." Dot said, smiling back.

Dave went out and moved the van closer to his room, then gathered his personal items and returned to his suite to get ready for dinner.

It was ten minutes after seven o'clock, as Dave put on his sandals, when a knock came on his door. He opened the door to find Dot standing there, she had changed out of her hotel uniform into jeans and a t-shirt. She looked beautiful, and Dave told her so.

"You look great!" he stated.

"Thank you, you're too kind." Dot said, almost blushing, "we should get going."

"Sounds good." Dave said as he locked his door, He followed her out to her car, it was a late model Toyota that appeared to be well taken care of. "You girls really take good care of your cars." Dave said as he got in the passenger seat.

"I bought it new a couple of years ago, and it's going to have to last a long time." she explained as she started the car. She let it warm up for a few minutes before heading out. She drove down main street for about a mile before turning onto a side street. It became noticeably less 'touristy' as they left main street behind.

"This is where the good stuff always is." Dave said, noticing that the neighborhoods seemed less well lit.

After a few turns she pulled into a well-lit parking lot of a restaurant called 'Maria's'. The parking lot was still almost full, even after the dinner hour. Dave took this as a good sign. Dot parked near the door and they went in the restaurant, Dot was greeted warmly by several of the employees, "This place is owned by my aunt and uncle," she explained, now speaking Spanish, "but still, I have to say, they have the best food in town." Dot led him to a table near the kitchen. He was holding her chair out for her when an older woman came out of the kitchen and gave her a hug.

"This is my Aunt Maria, and Auntie, this is Dave, he's staying at the hotel." Dot said, by way of an introduction.

Dave responded in Spanish, "At your service, madame." he said, with a bow.

Maria held out her hand, which Dave shook gently, "You don't sound like a gringo." she said to Dave.

"Which means I look like a gringo." Dave said with a laugh. Maria laughed, and so did a couple of people in the kitchen who were obviously eavesdropping.

Maria turned to Dot and said "Your brother is in town." Just then the kitchen door opened and a tall muscular man came out and Dot ran over and gave him a, what looked to Dave like a long overdue, hug. After a few seconds she let go and said "Carlos, this is Dave. Dave, my brother, Carlos."

The two men shook hands and Carlos asked "So, what brings you here?"

"Your sister," Dave said, "I was just looking for

something good to eat and your sister said she could fill that order." Carlos looked at Dave with a confused gaze, almost threatening.

"That didn't come out right." Dave said nervously.

Dot laughed and told her brother not to worry, "He seemed nice so I thought he would like the food here." she said.

Carlos looked Dave up and down, as if sizing him up. He motioned to his sister to follow, and he walked back into the kitchen.

"Have a seat," Dot said, "I'll be right back."

Dave sat down and watched her follow her brother into the kitchen. As the door swung closed he couldn't hear them, but he could see them talking. Carlos seemed quite animated as he spoke to his sister, a lot of pointing and poking his finger into his opposite palm. Dot looked over at him a few times during the conversation, but Carlos seemed unconcerned with him at this point. Their conversation ended with a hug and Dot returned to the table.

"Sorry about that." Dot said.

"Did I do something wrong?" Dave asked, feeling worried.

"No, not at all, my brother told me that he heard that the cartel was trying to get a foothold in the area. He just wants me to be careful." she explained.

"That looked like an awful lot for just a warning." Dave said, still a little worried.

"Well, it wasn't about you, so don't worry, ok." Dot said, trying to ease Dave's mind.

"Ok, if you say so." Dave said, with a smile.

"The food will be here soon, do you want a drink?" Dot asked.

"Food?" Dave said, confused, "We haven't ordered yet, and I'll have a margarita, thank you."

Dot put her hand up, making a 'V' with her fingers, then switched to the A.S.L for 'M', then lowered her hand.

A couple of minutes later a young waitress showed up with two margaritas. As she turned to leave, Maria came out of the kitchen carrying a tray of chips and salsa. The waitress took the tray and distributed the chips and salsa on the table.

"Thank you." Dave said as he reached for a chip. The salsa was hot and the margaritas were cold, and they sat making small talk until the food started to arrive. And arrive it did.

There were several more places set than people at the table, but one of everything were placed on each side of the table, all served 'family style'.

Carlos and another gentleman came out of the kitchen and sat down next to Dave, with his friend sitting down on Carlo's other side. Then Maria came out and sat next to Dot.

Dave looked around the restaurant to see that it was nearly empty, except for their table. The waitresses came out with platters of various types of meat, squeezed them onto spaces on the table, and then took their places at the table. Then the cooks, having washed up, came out and sat down.

As the remaining customers got up to leave, the bartender walked them out then locked the door behind them. He returned to the bar and retrieved two earthen jugs filled with margaritas.

As the man was setting the pitchers down, Dot said to Dave "This is my Tio Juanito, he owns the place."

Juanito gave Dave a nod and Dave said, "Mucho gusto." nodding back.

Juan took his place at the head of the table, standing as everyone took hands around the table, and proceeded to give thanks for the meal and blessings for everyone at the table. Juan sat down and the food started flowing.

Juan looked at Dave, "So, what brings you to our little town, when there are no other tourists?" he asked.

Dave smiled and told them the story of the original deal, what the deal turned out to be, and of the unrelenting smell.

"That must be why you didn't want me in your van." Dot said with a laugh.

"Now you know my secret." Dave replied. Everyone at the table got a good laugh, at Dave's expense. It was all very good natured, and Dave enjoyed the evening immensely.

When they were finished eating and everyone had a cup of coffee, there were a few very relaxed conversations going on, Dave leaned over to Dot and quietly asked "What do I owe for the meal and drinks?"

"You just ate with my family, you don't owe anything." Dot replied.

"Well, you all have my gratitude and respect." Dave offered.

"Thank you for that," she said with a smile, "Now, you look tired, you ready to go?"

"I do believe that I am." he said, rubbing his belly.

Dot announced that they would be leaving and went around the table getting hugs from everyone, Dave got a few handshakes and a hug from Maria.

On the ride back to the hotel Dave again thanked her and told her that he would like to stay on one more night. When they got to the hotel she went into the lobby with Dave. She punched some keys on the computer, a paper printed out and she handed it to him, "Sign here." she said.

Dave signed the paper, got his receipt and walked Dot out to her car. Before she got in she turned to Dave, "Aren't you going to ask me to your room?" she asked, coyly.

"No, I can't do that," Dave responded, "as much as I would like to, I made a promise, no more out of wedlock sex. So, I look at you as a sister, a beautiful, young, little sister." he explained.

Dot reached up and kissed him on the cheek, "I knew you were a nice guy." she said as she got in her car. "I will see you tomorrow." She then drove off.

Dave waved as he stood there, watching her leave, 'That was close' he thought. Fifteen years ago he would have been trying to get her in bed, but since he had become 'born again', he had to change how he approached life. He smiled at himself, returned to his room and had a really good nights sleep.

10

It was mid-morning on Monday, when Jim noticed an increase in inter-office electronic chit-chat. He walked over to Quinn's workspace and stuck his head in, "Quinn, there seems to be something up in the office today. Do you have any idea what's up?" he asked.

Quinn motioned Jim over to his desk, "It's Robart, looks like someone beat him up pretty good." he said quietly, "People are betting on who did it, and why."

"What's the general consensus?" Jim asked.

"Most believe it was the husband of someone he fooled around with." Quinn posed.

"Nah, he's not the type a married woman would risk her marriage over." Jim explained.

"That makes too much sense." Quinn said, with a smile.

"See if you can find out what happened, would you?" Jim asked, "I'm kind of curious now."

"I will give it my best, sir." Quinn answered.

Jim turned and walked back to his office, trying to get a glimpse of Rob as he passed his aisle. He was unsuccessful in his attempt to see Rob, however, Amanda saw him and asked if he had a moment.

"Sure thing, let's go into my office." he said, motioning her to precede him. Amanda walked into the office and turned so she could close the door behind him.

"This isn't bad news, is it?" Jim asked as he sat down behind his desk.

"No, not really, but maybe." Amanda said, sounding a bit confused, " I wanted you to know that my situation has changed some and I'm not sure how much longer I'll be working." Then her eyes got big, "But I'll be sure to give you plenty of notice before I leave," she said, "You have been really good to me."

"Oh no, I hate to lose you." Jim said, "Tell me, what's going on?" he asked.

"Remember last week, when I went to my Aunt's funeral?" she asked, "Well, she left me some money," she paused, "no, a lot of money. Anyway, enough that I don't have to work, ever again." she explained.

Jim sat and stared at her, "Well, that's good for you, anyway." he said.

"I guess, but it's going to take some time for everything to get settled and I thought I would keep working until then," she paused, "unless you have someone that needs the job." she said.

"You can stay as long as you need. I'll consider this

your official notice, so you don't have to worry about offending me." Jim said, "You've made me too much money for me to get mad. Besides, everybody here likes you. You kind of keep things in harmony around here." He smiled warmly.

Amanda got up and gave Jim a peck on the cheek, "You are a dear." she said as she turned to leave.

"Now go out there and make me some more money." Jim said, trying to look stern.

"You got it, boss." she said as she headed to her cubicle. She felt better knowing Jim was understanding about her situation. She pretty much expected him to react the way he did. He had always treated her with respect, and he had a good sense of humor about himself, but it felt good to have that conversation behind her.

When lunch time arrived, Amanda went to the lunchroom to find Quinn about to sit down with Rob. She found a seat within earshot, so she could listen in.

Rob was sitting by himself when Quinn sat down at his table. "What do you want?" he asked, visibly annoyed at Quinn sitting down.

"To eat lunch," Quinn responded, "and to say that the big money is on you getting your ass beat by your girlfriend." He added, without emotion.

Rob shook his head. He had one hand in a splint, two black eyes, a couple of cracked ribs and he was in no mood to talk.

"Maybe it was a jealous husband?" Quinn asked, needling him.

Rob, getting aggravated, stared and said nothing.

"Or, my favorite, you hustled someone strange to you." Quinn pressed, knowing it was getting to him.

Rob was on the verge of getting angry, "You can leave now." he said quietly.

Quinn got up slowly and as he turned, Amanda could see him smiling. She was proud of Quinn for needling Rob. She had seen Rob repeatedly torment Quinn, and Quinn rarely did anything in response. It was kind of fun watching Quinn get back at him, if only a little bit.

As Quinn left, Rob looked over at Amanda. She didn't say anything but gave him a sincere 'what happened' look. He gave a small shrug and said "I owed a guy some money. I was supposed to pay him Saturday, but my check was short."

"Seems counter-productive to break your hand." she observed.

"Ya think? I don't think I can make quota this week." Rob opined as he rose from the table. "Later." he said as he walked away.

Amanda watched as he walked away and decided she was going to help him. After she finished her lunch, she went to her cubicle to retrieve the two C.D.'s Quinn had given her last week. She walked over to Rob's cubicle to find him sitting and staring at his computer screen. "Ahem" she said to get his attention.

Rob looked at her, "What now?" he asked.

Amanda handed the C.D.'s to Rob, "Just pop them in and hit 'enter'. she instructed.

Rob took the C.D.'s, "What are these?" he asked.

"About a hundred to one-fifty each." Amanda replied, "They should help you out."

"Cool, that could help." Rob said as he turned back to his screen.

Amanda stood there for a moment, blinked, then turned and walked toward her cubicle. She had always gotten a bad vibe from Rob, but always tried to ignore the feeling and give him the benefit of the doubt. Now she wasn't sure that was the right path to take with this guy. She walked past her space and went on to Quinn's cubicle. She stopped at the door and tapped with her fingernail.

Quinn looked up and smiled, "What brings you to this part of town?" he asked good naturedly.

"I just wanted you to know that I gave those C.D.s to Rob. Amanda said, hoping he would be ok with it.

"Why would you have done that?" Quinn asked, confused.

"After you left him in the lunchroom, he told me that he got beat up because he owed someone some money and his check was short. I thought I could help him with the C.D.'s." she explained. "He didn't even say 'thank you'."

"I thought it was just me," Quinn said, "he and I have never gotten along."

"So, you're not mad?" she asked, tenetively.

"Of course not, I gave those to you to do with as you pleased." Quinn said, putting her at ease. "It is not my place to be mad."

"You are such a dear." she said, "I owe you a big hug." She added as he turned to go back to work. She could see Quinn smile at the thought of her hug.

"So, he owed some money, must not be your average friendly banker." Quinn mused.

"You got that right." Amanda said, "What kind of person does that to another human being?" she asked.

"Well, you've asked the right question." Quinn said. "Probably a professional." he added under his breath.

"I've got to get back to work," she said, "bye for now." She gave Quinn a small wave as she left. Quinn nodded and returned to his work.

As everybody was leaving, Quinn stopped by Jim's office. He knocked on the open door and waited for him to invite him in. Jim finished what he was doing on his computer and looked up at Quinn and signaled him to enter.

Quinn entered the office and sat down across from Jim, "I have an idea of what happened," he said, "I think it was a bookie." he posed as he told Jim what Amanda had found out. "You don't get beat like that for owing a friend." he said.

"So, a gambling debt." Jim said, "That would explain Friday."

"Yes, he was rather stressed," Quinn said, "he knew the beating was coming."

"I wonder if he tried to duck out." Jim said.

"That would explain the severity of the beating." Quinn offered.

"Well, we can't be sure, we'll just have to keep an eye on the situation," Jim said, "see if anything changes."

"Sounds like a plan." Quinn said as he rose to leave, "I'll see you tomorrow." Jim nodded, as Quinn left, then returned to his computer.

11

Dave slept in past sun-up for the first time in a long time. As he woke he thought ‘now it’s feeling like vacation’. This brought a big smile to his face. He did his morning routine at a leisurely pace, and it was after eight o’clock when he walked across the street to have breakfast.

He finished breakfast and got back to his room about an hour later. He decided to go sit by the pool and have some coffee. By time he finished his cup of coffee it had started to warm up, so he went for a dip in the pool. He was getting out of the water when he saw Dot pulling into the employees parking area.

She saw Dave by the pool and gave him a wave as she walked in to start her shift. Dave smiled and waved back, then went back in the water.

He had just emerged from under the water when he heard what he told himself must be firecrackers. He had a feeling that it was gunfire in the distance, and if it was, it sounded like two armies going at it, but that didn't make sense. It had to be firecrackers.

The popping stopped after a couple of minutes, with the occasional 'pop' being heard for another minute.

Two young ladies came out to sunbathe, followed by a young waiter. The waiter came to Dave and asked if he wanted more coffee. Dave declined but told the waiter to see if the ladies wanted anything. The ladies both had water bottles, and so declined gracefully. They gave him a 'thanks anyway' wave. He waved in return, then sat back to catch some rays of his own.

About ten minutes later he felt something behind his chair, "Enjoying the view, I see." came a familiar voice.

Dave looked up to see Dot standing over him, smiling. "Why not, it just keeps getting better and better." Dave replied, returning the smile. "Thanks again for dinner last night, that was an experience I will never forget,"

"You're welcome back tonight, if you'd like." Dot offered.

"How could I pass that up? Of course, I'd love to." he replied, visibly happy at the invitation.

"See you after seven, then." she said as she turned to go to work.

"Looking forward to it." he said, watching her walk away. He sat a few more minutes before figuring he had enough sun for one day. He gathered his things and made his way back to his room. He showered and got dressed, then headed to the lobby to find something to do with the day. He found a rack of brochures, featuring a variety of options. Everything from animal rescue farms to zip-lines.

Dave was considering his options when an arm reached around him and picked out a tour pamphlet and handed it to him. "You should try this one." came that familiar voice again.

He turned around to find Dot standing almost too close to him. "You think this will pass the time equitably?" Dave asked, not backing up.

"You will see all of the interesting places we have to offer." she said, finally moving back a bit.

"You think you could make the arrangements for me?" he asked, giving her the 'puppy dog eyes' look.

Dot laughed, "Of course sir, right away." she said and went to the desk to make the call.

"It will be about half an hour 'til he arrives." Dot said, returning from the desk, "you could wait in the bar until then." she suggested.

"It's a little early, but then I'm not driving." he said, with a grin. He went to the bar and ordered a margarita. He noticed there was a table with all sorts of munchies, he got a plateful and got to his table the same time as his drink. He was enjoying the tapas with his drink when the girls from the pool entered the bar. Dave gave them a salute with his glass as they passed. He could hear them giggling to each other and assumed they thought he was interested in them.

A short time later a gentleman came in and, looking at the girls, asked for the party waiting for the tour.

"Over here." Dave said, and gave a wave.

The man, obviously disappointed, looked at Dave and said "If you would like to get started." Then motioned to the door.

Dave took the last sip from his drink, got up and headed to the door. As he passed the driver, he handed Dave a leaflet with options and prices.

When they got outside Dave saw a late model, well maintained, Continental waiting in the parking lot. He studied the options and said "I'd like to go on the 'Ruins and Historic sites' tour, if I may."

"That would be fine," the driver said, "however, one of the stops, north of town, isn't open at this time." he explained.

"I guess I'll have to see it next time," Dave said, "I'm sure the tour will be just as good."

"Thank you, sir." the driver said as he opened the rear door to the limo.

"I'd like to sit up front, if you don't mind?" Dave asked.

"I'm sorry, sir. the insurance company won't allow that." the driver replied.

Dave climbed into the back of the limo and found it very clean and comfortable. The driver closed the door, then got behind the wheel and took off from the hotel parking lot.

"My name is Jose'," the driver offered, "If you want to stop and get out to check out any of the sites, let me know. We can stop anytime, anywhere. No extra charge."

"Well, Jose', we'll just have to wing it." Dave said, as he sat back to enjoy the ride. Dave spent the next two hours being shown every building that was over three-hundred years old and several Mayan ruins, both in town and out.

Dave got out and explored the Mayan ruins whenever they came up on the tour. He had always found ancient ruins fascinating, he was amazed at their building techniques. As they neared the end of the tour Dave asked "Your info said something about a blood sacrifice temple. Is that coming up?"

"I am sorry, sir. That is the site that's closed." Jose' explained, hoping that this wouldn't eat into his tip.

"It is what it is. I'm sure you didn't close it just for me." Dave said, smiling.

When the tour ended and they were back at the hotel, Jose' handed Dave a bill for what would have been about seventy-five dollars U.S.

Dave produced a one-hundred-dollar bill and handed it to Jose'. "Keep the change." Dave said, "I had a wonderful time."

"Thank you very much, sir." Jose' replied, obviously

happy with the situation.

When Dave got back to his room it was around four o'clock. He turned on the radio and found an oldies station, then climbed into bed for a nap.

Dave woke with a start, He looked at the clock, it was after six. 'Slept too long' he thought, it left him with an uneasy feeling. He turned on the T.V. and put on the local news, it seemed to have been an uneventful day, for the most part.

Dave puttered around the room, getting things ready for the next day's drive. It was around seven-thirty when he came upon his last joint, so he left his room for a short walk around the back of the parking lot. The walk did as much good as the joint in dispelling the uneasiness he felt when he got up. Feeling much better, he headed back to his room.

He entered he hotel from the back lot, and as he turned the corner to his hallway he could see Dot approaching from the opposite end.

She got to his door a few seconds before him and stood tapping her foot, trying to look put off.

"You're early." Dave said, emphatically.

"I'm hungry." Dot responded, with a grin, "So, you were out admiring the scenery?" she asked.

"Just out catching a fresh of breath air." he explained as he passed her to unlock his door.

"Oh" Dot said as she smelled the marijuana on his breath, "I didn't expect that."

"Well, I can't be everything you expect, now can I?" Dave said, "Besides, what would be the fun in that?" he asked.

"Oh, don't worry, I don't mind." she said, trying to put him at ease, "At all" she added, with a smile.

"I don't worry about anything." Dave said, reassuringly, "It's kind of a rule with me."

"Good, now grab what you need and let's go eat." she said, with a look of impatience.

Dave went to the bedroom and grabbed a mint, some cash and his I.D.s and was back to Dot in under two minutes. "Let's go," Dave said, "Whatcha waitin' fer?" he asked as he opened the door for her.

They arrived at the restaurant in good time, but Dave noticed that the parking lot was much emptier than the night before. "Not so busy tonight, huh." Dave said.

"I don't recognize any of these cars." Dot noted. There were only three cars in the customer parking area, if she didn't know them, then they weren't local.

She parked the car and they went into the restaurant to find it a bit subdued. There was an older couple just finishing their meal, and two younger couples, having tapas and drinks together. But no locals, "That's strange." Dot said, looking around. "Grab us some drinks, I'll be right back." she said as she headed to the kitchen.

Dave went to the bar and ordered two margaritas,

He noticed a tip jar on the bar, so he slipped a fifty-dollar bill into it when he thought no-one was looking. He didn't want to insult anyone, but he knew the employees all relied on their tips.

Dave paid for the drinks, even though he was told not to. He took a table near the kitchen and sat down and waited for Dot. He took a sip from his drink as he watched the old couple get up and leave while the young couples ordered more drinks.

Dot emerged from the kitchen and Dave stood up to get her chair. "What a gentleman," she said, "no-one does that anymore."

"Everything all right?" Dave asked, concerned.

"Oh yeah, everything is fine. Tio's not feeling well today, so none of his friends are here to take advantage." Dot explained. "It's still early, so it's just us for dinner." she said, looking a little disappointed.

"I guess I'll just have to settle." Dave said, looking at her like he had won a prize.

Dot smiled, "I didn't mean for it to sound like that." she said.

"I know," Dave said, "let's order, I'm hungry too."

Dot nodded and raised her hand, pointed at the ceiling and made a circle. The waitress went into the kitchen to place their order and came out with more snacks for the young couples.

They sat enjoying their drinks and making small talk, when Dave got this strange feeling he should tell her a joke. Just as he was about to tell the joke, Maria came from the kitchen and sat down with them. He figured, 'what the hell', and started his joke anyway.

Dave looked at Dot, "Do you know the difference between light and hard?" He asked, in English.

Maria looked at Dot and shrugged, then Dot said "No, tell us."

"I can go to sleep with a light on." Dave said with a straight face.

Maria started giggling immediately, and it took Dot a few seconds before she laughed out loud. Maria slapped Dave's leg, "I like this man." she said in near perfect English.

Maria looked over to the bar and gave an almost imperceptible nod to the bartender. A minute later a waitress brought her a glass of wine.

The food arrived and Maria stayed and ate with them. She told them stories of what her grandbabies were up to, and of her past, when she was young. Everyone was eating and laughing, and it was a really good time.

The two young couples stayed until nine o'clock, having received their check and given last call. Maria got up and walked over to their table, "It's closing time, you are going to have to leave." she explained to them.

One of the men pointed at Dave and Dot, "What about them?" he asked.

"They are my family, I hope you can understand."

Maria said apologetically. When a cook came out of the kitchen the man grunted and threw a wad of pesos on the table.

"That should do." the man said as he motioned for his friends to get up. They complied, and they all left the restaurant.

Maria watched as the two men got in one car and the girls got into the other. They drove away in the same direction, parting ways at the edge of town. When they had gone from sight, Maria went into the kitchen and came out with Carlos and her husband. Carlos had his arm in a sling and Juan had some bruising on his forehead and hands.

Dave looked confused, "I thought," he said, when Dot cut him off.

"We weren't sure of those couples, we think they're with the cartel." Dot explained.

"What's going on?" Dave asked, still confused.

Dot looked at her brother and nodded in Dave's direction.

"We had a run in with the cartel this morning." Carlos said.

"The firecrackers" Dave mumbled to himself.

"What?" Dot asked.

"I'm sorry, I said 'firecrackers'," Dave explained, "I heard something earlier and told myself it had to be firecrackers, because I didn't want to imagine the alternative."

"Well, it was the alternative, unfortunately." Carlos said, "One of our cooks got killed, and me and the other cook got shot."

"Two other families each lost someone," Juan interjected, "but it should be quiet for a while."

"If what I heard was gunfire, then it was more than a run-in." Dave said, looking at the two men.

"If there is no-one left to report back to the bosses, then it takes them longer to return," Carlos explained, "there is no-one within fifty miles who is not on our side."

"So any investigation gets misdirected." Dave surmised.

"They will send couples and small groups all over, to try and pick up any chatter."

Dot said, with Juan nodding in agreement.

"And you conveniently supply the chatter." Dave said, understanding, "But how did all this get started?" he asked.

"Long version, or short?" Juan asked.

"Short, we have to go soon." Dot said quickly.

Juan smiled, "Ok, my brother was working in the U.S., he had his green card. He met a woman, a U.S. citizen, married her and had two kids. One day they decided to come down to visit, they were shot by the cartel, for something stupid, no doubt. Anyhow, the parents died and the kids lived." he said motioning to Dot and Carlos.

"So we lived here with our aunt and uncle," Carlos

continued, "When I turned eighteen I returned to America and joined the army. I spent fifteen years in Special Forces, and did several tours overseas."

"When Carlos got back, the cartel was trying to move in," Dot said, "Carlos talked to all the major families and organized a force to repel the invaders, and that's where we are now."

"So, how long before they return?" Dave asked.

"About four weeks has been the average, then they send a squad to the area to reconnoiter. If we catch them, they never return." Carlos answered, "Then we have another four or five weeks of peace."

"And if we miss them, they come back in a week with more guns and try to move in." Juan said, "That's what we were dealing with today."

"Wow... so how long has this been going on?" Dave asked, with keen interest.

"I've been back for six years now, so, six years." Carlos mused.

"Anyway, enough of that," Dot said, "We have to get going." Dot went around the room getting hugs and saying her good-byes.

Dave looked at Carlos, "I wish there were some way I could help." he said, "I have money, if you need it."

"The season just ended, we're flush with money," Carlos said, "It's supplies that are short."

"Again, I wish there was something I could do." Dave said.

"Thanks for the thought, anyway." Carlos said, putting a hand on Dave's shoulder.

Normally Dave didn't like being touched, but this had a real familial feel to it and he didn't mind so much. 'Maybe I am changing in my old age.' he thought, with a smile. Carlos let go and Dave shook hands with the man.

Dot had made her rounds and they left the restaurant and headed back to the hotel. Not much was said on the drive back. Dave's mind was racing, trying to incorporate all he had learned, and Dot was afraid if she tried to talk she would start crying.

They pulled up to the hotel and Dave looked at her, "We probably won't see each other before I leave in the morning." he said, with sadness in his voice.

"I know, I just hope to see you again." Dot replied, then she leaned over and gave him a hug and a kiss on the cheek.

"Who knows what the cosmos has in store," Dave offered, "you never know." He hugged her back as they said their good-byes. He got out of her car and watched her as she drove away. Before she was out of sight he turned and went to his room for the night.

12

It hadn't been a full week and Quinn was getting used to the routine of going to Dave's every other day. Monday, Wednesday and today he took a ride, after work, with Joey. He always got a good feeling being around Joey, and he enjoyed getting to know him better on these rides.

Weekends he planned to take the bus, it would give him the chance to catch up with the drivers. Today, though, on the way to Dave's, Quinn suggested that Joey just drive to his house and he could walk to Dave's through the alley.

Joe appreciated that Quinn noticed he had to go out of his way to drop him off, just because of the way the subdivision was laid out. Joe agreed to Quinn's suggestion and drove straight home, to find his wife working in the back yard.

Joe parked in the driveway and they both got out and closed their doors in unison, this made it louder than usual and Joe's wife gave a little jump.

"Quinn, I would like you to meet my wife, Rebecca." Joe said as they neared her.

"You can call me Becky." she said and reached out to shake hands.

Quinn shook her hand, "Rebecca, now I see why Joey is always so anxious to get home."

Becky looked at Joe with a questioning look. Joe shrugged, "I know, he always uses everyone's given name. It's like O.C.D. or something." he said to his wife.

"Could just be that it's their name." Quinn offered as an alternative. "Of course, though, you are right. sometimes my brain has more control over my mouth than does my mind." he said, with a blank stare. He snapped back to reality a second later, "I'm thinking I should go now." he said, a little nervous at opening up to her.

"Quinn, it has been a pleasure meeting you," Becky said, "and don't worry, your secret is safe with me." she added as she shook hands with him again. Joe gave him a nod as he turned to leave. Quinn left through the back gate and disappeared.

"So, that's Quinn," Becky said, "I don't know what I expected, but it wasn't that."

Joe laughed, "I know, you wouldn't think he was one of the smartest people I ever met." he said, with bewilderment. His wife took his arm as they went into the house.

Quinn walked slowly down the alley, he had never been this way and he wanted to take it all in. After a couple of minutes, he arrived at the back gate to Dave's house. 'That felt like a short-cut' he thought. He knew that didn't make sense, but he also knew that it meant it was safe.

He walked up to the back door, and noticing he couldn't see the street, he continued on to the front door and entered there. He felt better, seeing what was out front.

Once inside, Quinn set about checking all the plants to see which ones needed water. He knew which ones liked to stay moist and which ones liked to dry out between waterings. A few of the plants looked much better since he had started to take care of them. Dave had told him to water every two to three days and everything would be fine, but look, less than a week and already there were improvements.

Quinn had rearranged a few of the plants, so they would receive more appropriate sun light. He spent a few minutes with each plant, talking to it and checking soil conditions, removing dead leaves and even dusting a few of them. The plants seemed to like it, judging from their response. Quinn tended to the plants for about an hour, then locked up and headed to the bus stop.

He didn't have to wait long, after arriving at the bus stop, for the bus to pull up. Quinn climbed onto the bus and greeted the driver.

"Hello, Stephan," Quinn said, "How are the roads this evening?" he asked.

"Q.T., The streets are flowing like a swollen river." Steve answered, with a grin.

Quinn had only known Stephan for about four months, and was slowly getting to know him. He thought that Stephan drove well enough that he could relax and think about other things, but found Stephan would ask him a lot of questions. It could be annoying at times, however, Quinn didn't let it phase him, he just kept answering.

Quinn took a seat across from the driver and watched out of the front of the bus, to see the traffic and the buildings go by.

"So, do you think that trouble-maker will go to prison?" Steve asked, without taking his eyes off of the road.

"Prison is for really bad people," Quinn answered, "someone like that might end up there sometime, but for what he did, he probably won't even go to jail."

"You don't want him in prison?" Steve asked.

"Prison is like bad-guy college," Quinn stated, "they come out more dangerous than when they went in. They work out and become monsters, they compare notes and become better criminals."

"You got that right. But what can be done?" Steve wondered.

"I was thinking prison should be a Lazy-boy, a five

thousand calorie a day diet, and nothing but positive programming on the television." Quinn opined, "then when they get out, ain't no six-hundred-pound man going to be going out committing crimes. Plus, you have the added benefit of ordinary citizens losing weight because they don't want to look like they were in prison."

Steve started laughing, along with a few passengers within earshot. "I can almost see that working." he said, still chuckling.

"I think it would be better than what we have now." Quinn responded.

"I don't know where you come up with this stuff, but I like it." Steve said, "I think your stop is coming up here, Quinn."

"Yes it is, thanks." Quinn said as he moved to the door. The bus pulled over and Quinn exited and walked down his street. He was walking slowly, not for any other reason but that he liked sunset, it was his favorite time of day. The breezes started to cool and the sky often danced with color. It gave him a sense of completion, like he made it to the prize at the end of the day.

He sat down on the front steps of his building, to watch the last little bit of day. To see the trees reaching up for that final ray of sunshine. As he sat watching the trees, Billy came out and sat down next to him.

"Beautiful sunset today." Billy said.

Quinn nodded, "Yes William, it was a beautiful end to a really good day." he said.

13

Dave woke before sun-up and had the van packed and was ready to go by the time the sun lit up the hotel. He reached in and started the van, standing outside of it while it warmed up. After a couple of minutes, he got in and pulled up to the hotel lobby. He parked and went to check out. Paperwork done, he returned to the van and proceeded to the border. He passed through the final checkpoint without incident and arrived at the border after a half of an hour.

He pulled up to the inspection station and dug out all the papers he had. Two men walked around the van, and one of them checked under the van with a mirror. Dave handed his paperwork to a third man who had a clipboard. The man looked through the papers, looked up at Dave, then went into a building to the side. A few minutes later he returned with a rather official looking gentleman. Dave, seeing the men approach, got a little nervous, 'This guy looks pissed' he thought.

The official looking man came up to the window and looked at Dave, caught a whiff of the van and stepped back a step, "How far did the escort travel with you?" the man asked.

"About fifteen miles, they seemed embarrassed to be seen with me." Dave answered, "Or maybe it was the van." Dave smiled and gave a shrug.

"Thank you for your co-operation." the man said to Dave, "You can go now."

Dave blinked, started the van, got his paperwork back from clipboard guy, and drove into Belize. He made it! He was finally here. He went through the checkpoint on the other side of the border like a breeze, and he was on his way.

He stopped in Belize City for lunch, he found a booth on the shore that had some of the best seafood tacos he had ever had. Satisfied, he continued on his way south. He arrived in Belmopan shortly after two o'clock and had no trouble finding the embassy. He unloaded his stuff from the van and happily turned it over to the ambassador's son. He called for a taxi, which arrived in minutes, and he was on his way to the rental cabin.

They pulled up to the cabin and Dave could see his rental car was there, waiting for him. He unloaded and paid the cabbie, adding an extra ten dollars for the tip. The driver seemed grateful, said thanks, and drove back to the city. Dave went into the cabin and unpacked, arranged everything to his liking, then got into the shower to wash off the smell.

With the last remnants of the drive washed down the drain, Dave turned to the stack of brochures and maps, left for him by the travel agent to help with his stay. After dividing the pamphlets into two stacks, 'no-way' and 'look at again', he decided to take a walk and check out the neighborhood. A walk around the block should do for starters.

He walked out to the street, first he looked down the street, then he looked up, if he started downhill and circled the block he would end his walk going downhill, besides he was only a few houses from the cross street, down to the east.

He was enjoying his walk, he got a few waves from people in their yards, and he got some stares from people who didn't expect to see a white man walking around their neighborhood. At the top of the west run he turned the corner to head across to the downhill part of his journey when he caught wind of a familiar scent. The aroma stayed with him until he neared an alley. When he reached the alley, he looked down it to see three men, standing around a car in an open garage, sharing a joint.

Dave walked towards the men, and as he got near the largest of the three looked at Dave, "You lost?" he asked, threateningly.

"I was until I found Yeshua!" Dave said, then smiled broadly.

The man studied Dave for a moment, then broke out in a deep laugh, "That's cool, mon." he said, "You're alright. You must be the one renting Arbol's place." he said pointing down the alley towards his cabin.

"That's right, I guess," Dave replied, "to tell you the truth, I caught wind of your libations, there, and I thought I would take a chance. By the way, my name is Dave."

"And a chance you did take." the large man said, with a wicked smile. "Lucky for you I know the man who owns the place you're staying, so we were expecting to see someone new in the neighborhood." The man put his hand out to shake and said "My name is Jody, and these are my friends, Mike and Mike."

Dave shook hands with Jody, when one of the Mikes said "Yeah, someone new, and you don't look like a local." The three black men got a good laugh at this, and so did Dave, as they handed him the joint.

"So, besides you guys, who else is worth knowing around here?" Dave asked, passing the joint to Jody.

"Your neighbor to the east, Nessa, she keeps up on all that's important, if you have a problem or need something special, you talk to her." Jody offered.

"And Wall." Mike said.

"Yeah, Wall." the other Mike chimed in.

"Wally?" Dave asked, confused.

"No, just Wall." Jody replied, "His name is Demitri, but everybody calls him 'Wall'. You'll know why if you ever meet him."

"He's six foot ten and three hundred pounds of pissed-off muscle." the first Mike said, eyes wide.

"And he don't particularly like white folk." the other Mike added.

"Sounds like a man who demands respect." Dave said, "If I meet him, I shall try to not piss him off."

"Good strategy," Jody offered, "If that doesn't work, try praying." he said with a smile.

"Well, thank you for your hospitality, gentlemen, but I shall be on my way." Dave said, as he was about to leave. "Maybe we can talk about some of that, later." he asked, nodding in the direction of the joint.

"I'm here most days, in the afternoon. I'll see you around." Jody said, invitingly.

Dave smiled and waved as he continued on his walk. He walked downhill to his cabin and, turning into the driveway, he saw a young man looking in his rent-a-car.

"Try the door before you break the window, I'm pretty sure that it's not locked." Dave said as he approached.

The kid jumped, upon hearing Dave. "I didn't touch anything, I was just looking." the kid said, trying to explain his actions.

"You could probably make more money working for me than you could stealing what little I have here." Dave offered, figuring better to make a friend than an enemy.

"I wasn't stealing anything," the kid said, "but, what

are we talking about?"

"What would you charge to keep the thieves away from here?" Dave asked.

"At least ten dollars a day." the kid said.

"My name is Dave." He said, offering his hand.

"They call me 'Little D' " the kid said, shaking Dave's hand.

"Little D, huh, why, you're taller than me." Dave said, "How 'bout a hundred a week, just to keep an eye on things when I'm not here. If I need you for anything else, I'll pay you extra." he paused, "But I don't put up with any bullshit.... you be straight with me and I'll be straight with you."

"Deal." Little D said, "When do I get paid?"

"At the end of the week, every seven days, but here's a signing bonus." Dave said, handing him a twenty dollar bill.

"Twenty, what's this for?" L.D. asked, suspicious of the white man, taking the bill.

"To see if I'm dealing with a man or a boy." Dave said as he walked past him to go into his cabin.

Little D put the twenty in his pocket as he watched Dave go in. He shook his head and walked out of the yard to head up the street.

Dave watched out the window as the kid left, 'I guess I'll find out tomorrow.' he thought. "Oh, damn." he said out loud, "I should have had him get me some food." He started looking through the food pamphlets and found one that delivered. He called and soon had food being delivered to his doorstep. He ate dinner and watched the local news. When he had finished eating, he watched some local gameshows until he fell asleep in the recliner. He woke an hour later and shuffled off to bed.

Dave woke early the next morning and found a brochure for a local grocer. He called and placed an order for pick-up. He grabbed the entertainment pamphlets and went to sit on the porch to study them and enjoy his coffee. He heard a noise and looked up to see Little D walking up his driveway.

"Is there anything I can do for you today, sir?" L.D. asked, hopefully.

"First, stop with the 'sir', my name is Dave, ok." he said, "and yes, there is something you can do. I placed an order for groceries at the 'Mayan Grocery' this morning, I would appreciate it if you could pick that up for me."

"Can do, Dave." Little D said, tenetively.

"Look, L.D., you have got to relax, the only difference between you and me is that I have been around long enough to have made a little bank, otherwise... pfft." Dave said, hoping the kid would understand.

Little D looked at Dave as if he had never heard that combination of words before. 'This guy isn't like any of the white guys my dad talks about.' he thought.

Dave could see the kid thinking, like there was

some sort of conflict going on in his head. “I started out working for pennies when I was a kid.” he offered.

“I guess everyone starts somewhere.” L.D. said.

“Right, now, my groceries.” Dave said with a smile.

“Gotcha.” L.D. said and turned to go pick up Dave’s order.

L.D. returned shortly with Dave’s groceries and brought them into the kitchen. He placed the two bags on the counter and looked at Dave, “What kind of work did you do for pennies?” he asked, kind of disbelieving.

Dave handed him a ten-dollar bill, “When I was about six, me and a couple of others from the orphanage would stand outside the grocery store and ask everyone who came out if they needed help carrying their bags.” he explained.

“You’re kidding, right?” L.D. said, blinking in disbelief.

“It was a long time ago, and no, I’m not kidding. I’ve been doing all kinds of work all my life. I believe a man should be able to provide for himself, without relying on, or taking from, others who are just trying to get by themselves.” Dave explained further.

“I get what you’re saying,” L.D. said, understanding at last, “Like, earn your own way, and not owing anybody.”

“You’ll end up feeling a lot better about yourself.” Dave said.

“So, like, you didn’t have parents?” L.D. asked

rhetorically, “I can’t imagine life without Mom and Dad.”

“You’re lucky, remember that.” Dave said emphatically, “Especially when you’re giving them a hard time about something stupid.” he added, with a grin.

Did you need anything else done today?” L.D. asked, changing the subject.

“No, not that I can think of, thank you.” Dave replied.

“Then I’ll see you later.” L.D. said as he turned and walked down to the street.

“Yup, later.” Dave said to the kid’s back.

Dave spent the next week taking local tours and peoples recommendations for places to eat. In the mornings he would see L.D. and would try to have some chores to do. Whether he had chores or not, he and the kid would sit and talk for about an hour each morning. Little D. was a curious sort and Dave enjoyed teaching him things he knew. Turned out that each enjoyed the others company.

At the end of the first week Dave paid L.D. one hundred dollars. L.D. took the money and brought it home to his mother, like he had been doing all week.

“That’s a hundred and eighty dollars you made this week.” his Mom said smiling, “Your Dad will be home soon, we’ll see what he thinks about that.” Little D. went outside and found some chores to do while he waited for his father to get home from work. A short time later he heard his father's truck pulling into the driveway. His dad got out of his truck and gave L.D. a wave as he went into the house. L.D. nodded to his father, then finished the job he had started.

Finished with what he was doing, he went in and found his parents sitting and talking quietly. With the money sitting on the table, between them.

"L.D., I have a few questions." his Dad said.

"Sure Dad." L.D. replied.

"Who you workin' for?" his Dad asked.

"His name is Dave, and he's a tourist from America." L.D. answered.

"What did you have to do for this much money?" was his Dad's second question, knowing what his wife had told him.

"I get a hundred a week for keeping the guys from messing with him and his stuff, the rest I earned running errands and doing odd-jobs." L.D. explained.

His Dad sat and looked at him for a minute, "Thank you, son, for helping out," Dad said, "this will help a lot. I know you have a date tomorrow, so, thirty enough?" his Dad asked holding out the money.

"We can have a good enough time on twenty." L.D. said pulling a twenty from his Dad's hand. He knew his Dad had just put a bunch of money back into his business, and money was tight.

His Dad smiled "You're a good son." he said, kind of amazed.

"I just want to have a positive impact." L.D. said, "Like what Dave told me, a man does what he says, watches out for family, and always tries to leave things better than he found them." His Dad smiled, these were things his son wouldn't listen to when he tried to tell him.

"Maybe I should talk to this 'Dave' person." his Dad said, with a stern look.

"I'm sure he'd like to meet you." L.D. told his Dad, while not being sure at all.

The next morning Dave was sitting enjoying a fresh brewed cup of coffee when, suddenly, the room went dark. Dave looked over to the front door and saw there was no-longer any sunlight coming through. It was as if someone had put up a wall. His eyes adjusted and he could see L.D. standing at the front door with someone behind him. "Hey, there L.D." Dave said, motioning for them to come in.

"Morning Dave," L.D. said as they entered, "I want to introduce you to my father, Dad, this is Dave."

"Dave Smith" he said, putting out his hand.

"Demitri Freeman" the large man said, reaching out. Dave's hand disappeared inside Demitri's hand as they shook.

"A pleasure to meet you," Dave said, "your son quotes you often."

"And a pleasure to meet the man who got my son telling me about integrity and dignity," Demetri said, "he didn't seem to want to hear it from me."

"He listens a lot more than he lets on," Dave replied, "We've had some pretty good conversations, he's a smart kid."

"Excuse me," L.D. broke in, "is there anything you need done?"

"If you would like, you could clean up the yard. There was a lot of wind last night." Dave offered.

"Don't I know it, I'll get that done for you right away." L.D. said, then went out to take care of the yard.

"I like that, you askin' him instead of telling him." Demitri said, "I think I know why he likes you."

"Well, Demitri, I think your son was well on his way to becoming a proper man long before I showed up." Dave said, "He earned my respect right away."

"Wall, you can call me Wall," the big man said, "It's what my friends call me."

The two men sat and got to know each other, spending the next hour talking, when L.D. came in and announced that the yard was done and that it looked great. They both looked at each other and got up to check. They looked around for a minute, "Your report was accurate." Dave said, pulling out thirty dollars and handing it to L.D.

"Thank you." L.D. said, accepting the money.

"And thank you for your diligence." Dave said, then turning to Wall, "And it's been real good talking with you, but I heard you didn't like white people."

“Who told you that?” Wall asked.

“A man I met a week ago, name’s Jody.” Dave answered, hoping he wasn’t starting something.

Wall laughed, “He was trying to scare you, or something, I don’t know, “he said, “Truth is, I don’t much care for anybody. Black or white, don’t matter, most of them are fools.”

“Well, it worked. When you blotted out the sun, I must admit, I had a moment of concern.” Dave said, eyes wide.

Wall got a good laugh at that. “Jody is my cousin, I guess he’s just trying to keep the myth alive.” Wall said, as they made their way to the door. Dave walked them to the door and they said their good-byes.

Dave was left with the impression that he had just made an important friend.

14

At the top center of his computer screen, Curtis watched as a small red square appeared and started pulsing. He moved his mouse to click on the pulsing square.

Curtis had been with C-Tag for only two months and the training period was still fresh in his mind. 'Anything unusual on the screen and you are to click on it and the computer will give you instructions that are to be followed to the letter.' the instructor had said, several times, several ways, during the three day training period. It seemed more like indoctrination to him, but what the hell, at least he was working.

The computer screen changed and gave him a list of key stroke combinations to go through before ending with instructions to gather everything involved with this file and bring it to the C.E.O.'s office, and to not discuss it with anybody. Curtis followed the instructions to the letter and, as he was returning to his workspace, the guy at he next workspace, Bill, stopped him and asked if he had found a BB.

"A BB?" Curtis asked, confused.

"Yeah, a BB." Bill said, "You know a 'brown blinker'. I got one of those a couple of months ago. They told us it is a gold box, but everyone thinks it's more brown than gold."

"Yup, a brown blinker." Curtis said, not wanting to reveal anything, "What do you suppose they mean?"

"I heard it's because the sample got contaminated," Bill said, "that's why they're so rare, we're good at what we do."

"Yeah, that makes sense." Curtis said as Bill turned his back and returned to work.

Curtis knew that wasn't the reason, at least not for what he had. His was a 'red blinker'. When he got home he wrote down everything he could recall from the file. When he finished writing it all down, he got a strange feeling that prompted him to hide the file. He was strangely proud of how much he remembered, he didn't have a 'photographic memory', but he could usually remember anything he had concentrated on. It was just that this felt different, somehow. He wondered what triggered the red square, and what happened to the file after he turned it over.

The secretary had an emotionless expression on her face as she took the file from Curtis and wrote his name on a post-it and attached it to the file. She said 'thank you' and stared at him until he turned and went back to work.

When Curtis had left the office, she got up and went into her boss' office. "Mr. Matthews," the secretary, Janet Birch, said as she entered his office, "I think we have what you've been looking for." She closed the door behind her, she was hoping the good news would mean some attention for her. They had been having an affair for a couple of years now, but she had realized early that he would never leave his wife, the source of his money.

Martin Matthews had inherited the company when his father died of heart failure in his early fifties. That was when Martin found out the condition was genetic. After he took over the company, he also found the research his father had been doing to try to correct the flaw.

His father, Michael, had been involved in the decoding of the D.N.A. of the 'ice man' that had been found in the Alps. Everyone that saw the 'ice man' swore he was in his late twenties to early thirties. When it was determined that he was in his eighties, Michael thought there might be a chance to remedy his situation.

He isolated the gene he was interested in by comparing it to the D.N.A. of thousands of everyday modern people. It turned out that virtually no-one had this gene sequence, but he did find one. He got in touch with this man and paid him handsomely for some of his blood. He then transfused the blood into himself, causing some relief in his symptoms. This resulted in him buying more blood and experimenting with delivery methods to increase the results and trying to make it permanent. Whatever improvements he gained faded after about a week, then disappeared. Leaving him back where he started.

Michael hired the man the third time he needed blood. He told him he would be traveling throughout Europe, to collect D.N.A. samples from different populations to build profiles for comparison. Six months later Michael contacted the man's next of kin, to tell them that he had died in Eastern Europe. What really happened to the man was that Michael tried a complete transfusion and he ran out of blood.

Martin took over the company at the age of twenty-five, learning that he was already middle-aged. It was quite a blow, he had married only a year before, into money, and was looking forward to the free life for a while. Responsibility and duty weren't his strong suits, but with help from his wife, he turned a genetic research lab into a profitable enterprise.

And, behind the scenes, he continued his father's research. Using the data he collected to build an international network of people, dedicated entirely to himself. This was aside from the people out in the field collecting samples, which the company actually did.

This network ran under the name 'Martin Services',

posing as a security provider. Most of the employees Martin had found by hacking into the governments criminal D.N.A. databases. Whenever C-Tag received a sample from a felon, looking to find out their ancestry, and they had certain skills, he would hire them. The rest received their results with no side effects. He also employed some mercenary types and some disaffected techies, all without criminal records, to front the operation.

They did a few jobs locally, from personal bodyguards to secure transport of goods. But most of their money came from overseas, providing muscle for people with money looking for power. It was lucrative.

Janet was still bent over his desk, with him still on top of her kissing her neck.

"Join me in the shower?" Martin asked quietly. They both finished removing their clothes and got in the shower.

After three minutes, long enough to get his back washed, Martin said "I'll need to talk to Edgar Dhu." Janet got out of the shower and dried off, got dressed and returned to her desk to arrange the call to Martin Services.

15

Quinn was on his way to Emma's for the third Saturday in a row. He found her to be an excellent student, and he enjoyed her company. He arrived at the Cheung residence a few minutes to nine and was greeted at the door by her father.

"Good morning, Quinn. Emma's in the study, playing with her computer." Jon told Quinn.

"Video games? Doesn't seem like her." Quinn responded.

"I said playing with, not on, her computer." Jon explained.

"My mistake, I didn't listen." Quinn offered as an apology, "I get distracted when I'm to see Emma."

Jon smiled, "I'm the same way with her mother, even now, after all these years." Jon said, warmly.

"I was just thinking, I should see Emma now." Quinn said, nervous at the direction of the conversation.

Jon led Quinn to the study, "I'll leave you to your

lessons." he said as he opened the door to reveal Emma, deep in concentration over her computer.

"Thank you, sir." Quinn said as he entered the study. Jon closed the door behind him and returned to what he had been doing. "You ready for another lesson?" he asked, as he approached her desk.

Emma quickly raised a finger, to ask for a second, then returned to typing furiously on her keyboard. After another two minutes of typing, she stopped and looked at Quinn, "Machine code programming, I needed to finish or it would take me forever to get into thinking like that again." she explained. "I'm writing a program to destroy the computers of anyone who tries to infiltrate my computer with ransomware." she said with a grin.

"How did you solve the problem of seeing the malware without turning it on?" Quinn asked.

"That was the hard part." Emma replied.

"I know, that's why I asked." Quinn said, trying to not sound sarcastic.

"I had to create, like, a glass hallway for anything coming in, to have to travel through. Then, when it sees some malware, it re-routes the program into, like, a closet that it doesn't know it's in. then it reads where it's from and sends death and destruction to their computer." she told Quinn, proudly.

"Do you need to test it?" Quinn asked.

"I don't have a spare computer to test it on, but I'm

fairly certain it will work." Emma said with confidence.

"I have an old computer at home that we could use." Quinn offered, "I could try to infiltrate your system tomorrow, or whenever you'd like."

"It would be great if I could test it at least once, just to see what kind of damage will be done." Emma said thoughtfully.

"I will use the latest version of ransomware that I have." Quinn said.

"You have different versions?" Emma asked, a little confused.

"I have four different versions, the latest is definitely the most sophisticated." Quinn stated, "The second one was more sophisticated than the third." he added, with a puzzled look.

"How did you get all that?" Emma asked, as they made their way to the back yard.

"That's how many times they've attacked me." Quinn replied, "Something inside me tells me something is wrong with a particular e-mail, so I don't open it. Instead, I break into the program and find out what its intentions are."

"How do you know which ones to examine?" Emma asked, curious.

"Can't say, I was just thinking it may be sub-conscious." Quinn answered, suddenly uncomfortable with the question.

"Sorry," Emma said, noting his discomfort, "I

shouldn't have pushed."

"You should use a disposable computer, in case it gets through." Quinn said, pushing past his discomfort. "I could bring one over tomorrow, if that would be convenient for you."

"Seeing me two days in a row. What will people say?" Emma teased.

"I have overheard a lot of conversations through the years, and it's pretty rare that someone would talk about me." Quinn said, straight faced.

Emma blinked, "No,... she started, "it's just..." Quinn slowly smiled and Emma said "Got me." She smiled, slightly embarrassed thinking he needed anything explained to him.

"How long have you been programming?" she asked, changing the subject.

Quinn couldn't help but find her adorable. "How long have computers been around?" he asked in response.

"Most of my life, I'd say." Emma replied.

"Yeah, mine too. But I started when I was about ten, or so." Quinn told her.

"You must be older than you look." she commented.

"It's been thirty-five years since I was dropped off." Quinn said.

"Dropped off?" Emma asked, curious over his choice of words.

"I was dropped off at an orphanage when I was an

infant." Quinn related, "I was labeled 'Quinn', I don't remember much of that time."

"So you don't even know your own birthday?" Emma asked, rhetorically.

"No, but I'm here, able to contribute." he stated, with some personal pride.

"I'm sorry, I shouldn't have said that." Emma said with regret.

"Don't worry about it," Quinn said, "I think we are friends, so I am not offended when you want to know about me." he added, looking her in the eyes.

Emma melted into his gaze, then broke contact, shaking. "Thank you, I think we are friends also." she said relieved and happy. She gave him a big hug, then led him outside.

Quinn hugged back, "Have you been practicing?" he asked.

"I have leveled up two grip springs since we started, and I'm still studying the book." Emma answered, "And my father helps by letting me twist him up." she added with a grin.

"And he is impressed with the mechanics of it." came a voice from the side.

Quinn looked over to see Emma's mother approaching from the garden.

"Mother, this is Quinn, Quinn," Emma started.

"You can call me 'Mrs. C.'." Emma's mother said, as she extended her hand.

"Yes, ma'am, pleased to meet you." Quinn said as he shook hands gently.

Mrs. C. nodded to Quinn, "It is a pleasure to meet the man my family has been talking about."

"I was just thinking, I see where Emma gets her beauty." Quinn said nervously.

"Why thank you." Mrs. C. said, then turned to Emma, "I like this guy." She smiled as she turned to go to the house.

"Nice meeting you, Mrs. C." Quinn said as she walked away. Mrs. C. gave a wave as she entered the house. "She seems nice." he said to Emma.

"She has her ways." Emma said, without explanation.

"Shall we get on with the lesson?" Quinn asked.

"Yes, let's." Emma replied. They spent the next hour and a half talking about different techniques and going through moves, over and over, to improve muscle memory. They also covered a lot of subjects not related to fighting. At the end of the lesson, as Quinn readied to leave, Emma stepped up to him and gave him a big hug. Quinn could feel her lower body pressing into his. He wasn't quite ready for this, but returned the hug the best he could.

Quinn thought about that hug the entire bus ride to Dave's, where he had plants to take care of.

16

Dave spent the second week of his vacation teaching L.D. how to do a variety of household repairs, and even helping when it required more than two hands. Always making sure he was taking direction from L.D. when he was helping L.D.

On Saturday, when L.D. showed up to work in the morning, Dave came out and said "I'm taking today off, so I guess you are too." He reached into his pocket and pulled out an envelope and handed it to the kid.

L.D. looked in the envelope and saw an extra fifty dollars. "You already paid me for yesterday." he reminded Dave.

"I know, that's a bonus for making this place more comfortable for me." Dave explained.

"Thank you." L.D. said, "Oh, my dad wanted me to invite you to our Sunday barbeque. I hope you'll come, you can meet my girlfriend."

"That sounds like a good time," Dave said, "besides

I haven't had any 'sore thumb' time in hours."

"Sore thumb time?" L.D. asked.

"Yeah, think about it, I pretty much stick out like a sore thumb around here." Dave explained.

"Got it." L.D. said, laughing.

"Tell your dad that I will be there." Dave said, "What time, and do I need to bring anything?" he asked.

"Any time after ten-thirty, but we usually start eating around one," L.D. said, "and no, you don't have to bring anything."

"You sure? I'd feel funny showing up, for the first time, without some sort of gift." Dave explained. "Is there something special your mother would like?"

"Told you, you don't gotta bring anything." L.D. said as he turned to walk home.

"See you there." Dave said, wondering what he should bring. He had been hoping L.D. would have given him a clue.

L.D. gave a wave as he turned onto the street, then disappeared around the corner.

Dave turned around and went back in to get another cup of coffee and look through the tourist pamphlets again. He had already done most of the things to do in the immediate area and was considering heading north for a few days. He found one leaflet from a park that bordered a large wildlife refuge. It boasted of high cliff trails and some of the oldest ruins in Central America, it had his interest. He had toured all of the ruins around town and, though impressive, they seemed manicured somehow. He wanted to see ruins still held by the forest, and that was what was offered at the end of a long trail. He figured the harder it was to get to, the less messed up by people it would be. This was a trail he wanted to hike.

The maps showed about a two-and-a-half-hour drive, if he left early enough he could make the hike in and get his camp set up before sunset. He could spend the next day exploring, then hike out on the following morning. He thought he should spend a night in the local village, to see anything else in the area. Then he could spend the day after that taking his time driving home, seeing whatever was along the way. 'Sounds like a plan' Dave thought. 'Now, to the problem at hand' he thought. What was he going to bring to the Freeman's tomorrow? There was no-way he was going to show up, especially for the first time, empty handed. He had no idea what their interests were, if either collected anything, if they needed anything....no idea! He battled with his dilemma for a good half-hour, to no avail. He considered going to town and walking around until something caught his eye, maybe he would find inspiration in some shop window.

As he readied to go to town, he walked by the window and caught sight of his neighbor, Nessa, coming up the hill from town. 'Of course,' Dave thought, 'if anyone would know what to bring, it would be her.'

He had spoken with her several times, over the fence between them, during the past two weeks. It had been mostly niceties and small talk, so far.

Nessa appeared to be a late middle-aged woman, in good shape for a woman of her age. She held a matronly status among the local people, both for her wisdom and for her uncanny ability to know everything happening in the area. Dave had seen through the fence that Nessa was a smoker, so he got a carton of cigarettes from his luggage and headed to Nessa's house to see if she could, or would, help.

It was a short walk to Nessa's house and as he turned up her walkway, he could see her come to the front door. She was waiting behind the screen door as Dave made his way onto her porch.

"And what brings you all the way down here?" Nessa asked, smiling.

"I come seeking advice." Dave said, with a bow. "I have a small dilemma that I believe you might be able to help me with." he added, straightening up.

"Come in, young man," Nessa said, as she opened the screen door, "If I can't help, then you are in trouble."

Dave entered her home and looked around, noting several beautiful antiques. "You have a beautiful home." he said, impressed with the quality of craftmanship demonstrated in the construction of her home. "Some of these pieces are museum quality." he noted.

"Thank you, these pieces have been in my family for

a long time." she said proudly. "My grandfather, along with my father and his brothers, built this house with their own hands." she said, beaming. "Now, what can I do for you?" Nessa asked, curious.

"First, I'd like to keep this between you and me." Dave requested.

"Done." she replied.

"Thank you... oh, this is for you." he said as he handed her a bag with the carton of cigarettes in it.

"The man brings gifts, I like it." Nessa said, with a wry grin.

Dave gave a slight bow, "I've been invited to Wall's tomorrow and, though they said I needn't bring anything, I don't feel right showing up empty handed." he explained.

"An old school gentleman," Nessa quipped, "I see your dilemma, you want to respect their wishes, yet show your appreciation." She paused to think, "I got it! A good, aged Scotch whiskey." she recommended.

"Free booze, who could say no to that." Dave said, jokingly.

"It would be something he could set aside for later." Nessa explained.

"Sounds like a good idea, I believe I shall take your advice." Dave said, "Now, that settled, could I talk you into a tour of your home?" he asked.

"It would be my pleasure." Nessa said. She spent the next half-hour telling Dave stories about each room and the people that had occupied them over the years.

After the tour Dave walked down to find the oldest bottle of Scotch in town. He liked the walk into town, even though it was uphill for the return trip. He had become acquainted with the closest liquor stores and a pretty good idea which one would have what he was looking for. The one that catered to the tourist crowd.

"Mayan Empire Liquor and Package Goods" Dave read aloud as he approached the store. He went in and asked where the dusty bottles were kept.

"And what, exactly would you be looking for?" one of the two men in the store asked.

"I'm looking for an aged Scotch," Dave replied, "the older the better."

"Right this way." the other man said, as he led Dave deeper into the store. He stopped in front of a closed cabinet and opened it to reveal the high-end products, none of which were dusty.

Dave saw a bottle of forty-year-old Scotch by a maker he recognized. "How much for that one?" he asked, pointing to the bottle of Scotch.

"That is the oldest, and it is two-hundred and seventy dollars, after taxes." the man said, expecting that to end the conversation.

"You won't find anything older in town." the other man said from the front of the store.

"You can check around if you like, it will probably

still be here when you get back." the man next to him said.

"And we won't even raise the price." the other joked, from the front.

"It's like I'm being tag-teamed here," Dave joked, "But I think I'll take it now and save myself the extra walk." he said, pulling out his wallet.

One of the men carefully wrapped and bagged his purchase while the other took his money. Purchase complete, Dave returned to his cabin feeling pretty good about the situation.

17

It was the Sunday before Dave's return and Quinn was headed to take care of the plants. He got off the bus and was walking up the street when he noticed a large, black SUV parked a few houses down from Dave's. Quinn couldn't see who was in the vehicle, but he could tell there were two men sitting in it. Quinn walked past the SUV and then continued past Dave's and turned the corner, something didn't feel right. He walked to the alley so he could enter Dave's house unseen from the street. As he walked down the alley he slowed down, he hadn't approached Dave's house from this direction before and he wanted to see what it had to offer.

Reaching Dave's, Quinn went through the gate and entered the house from the side. Once inside, he got to work tending to the plants. He had been working about ten minutes when he noticed his neighbor, Dan, leaving his house. He watched as Dan walked toward

Dave's and turn up his walkway.

Quinn opened the door as Dan opened the screen door to knock, he waved Dan into the house and closed the door behind him. "Hello, Daniel," Quinn said, "What brings you over?" he asked, as he stood back from the window to watch the SUV.

"I saw you come in from the back and I thought I would come over and keep you company." Dan explained.

"How long has that black SUV been there?" Quinn asked, staring out the window.

"It was there when I woke-up this morning." Dan answered, wondering what was bothering Quinn.

"There are people in it." Quinn stated.

"Are you sure? I didn't see anybody and I've been up since five." Dan argued.

"It's past ten now, that's a long time to sit in a vehicle." Quinn posed.

"Are you sure you're not being paranoid?" Dan asked, trying to lighten the mood.

"I like being paranoid." Quinn stated, "It means, by definition, that it is not really happening. So when you stop being paranoid, that means that it's really happening." he explained.

Dan blinked several times thinking, 'No wonder he always takes my money.' "I'm not sure if that was absolute truth, or extreme bullshit." Dan finally said, shaking his head.

"It, like life, is what you choose it to be." Quinn posed. "Have you ever given thanks for being how you are?" he asked, glancing at Dan's eyes for a moment, then back out the window.

Dan paused for a minute, jolted by Quinn's' glance, "Yes I have, but it was a process, I tell you what." he finally said.

"Someone is getting out of the SUV..., he's headed this way." Quinn reported.

"No problem, I'll get the door." Dan offered, and headed toward the door. A loud knock on the door gave Dan a start, Quinn stood silently staring out the window. Dan opened the front door "Can I help you?" Dan asked the man at the door.

The man at the door showed an official looking badge, "Agent Johnson, with 'Natural Resources Department', we're looking for 'David Smith'. he said, looking threatening.

"Well, he's not here, I live next door and my friend, over there, is here to take care of the plants until his return." Dan explained.

"I'd like to see some I.D.s." the agent demanded with authority.

"We'd like to see a warrant." Quinn responded.

"I'm sorry, what?" the agent scowled.

"A warrant, you know, so we know what this is about." Dan said defiantly, as Quinn came to his side at the door.

The agent started to reach for the door handle, "You are not welcome here." Quinn stated, as the man pulled on the door, which Quinn had locked behind Dan when he came in. The agent pulled the door open and reached for Quinn. As soon as he touched Quinn, he found himself with his face about three inches from the floor. "You are not welcome here. Did you not hear me?" Quinn repeated.

Quinn stood the man up, still holding his fingers, and walked the agent down the porch stairs. He saw the passenger door open on the SUV and another man, similarly dressed, exited the vehicle. Quinn spread the agents fingers a bit, and said "Tell your partner everything is ok, and that Dave is not here." The agent did as he was told, and his partner returned to his seat in the SUV. Quinn released the man, "You should tell us what this is about." he said.

The agent, rubbing his hand, said "It's a private matter." He walked to the SUV, got in and drove away.

"That was weird," Dan said, "and what was that thing you did to him?" he asked.

"I've never heard of any 'Natural Resource Department', have you?" Quinn asked, trying to figure out what had just happened.

"I guess you weren't paranoid, after all." Dan said, shaking his head.

"I am thinking it would be better to be paranoid." Quinn responded.

"I think we should call Dave." Dan said as he took out his phone and dialed Dave's cell phone. "It's going to voice-mail," he said, waiting for the beep, "Dave, this is Dan, someone was just here looking for you. There were two men in a black SUV, one of them tried to touch Quinn. He drove them off, it was awesome. Call me when you get this." Dan said to the machine. "Now what do we do?" he asked Quinn.

"I don't think the police can help," Quinn said, "They'll tell us to call if they come back."

"Did you get a license plate number?" Dan asked, knowing Quinn was very observant.

"No plate on the front and the rear looked fake, like a cover over their real plate." Quinn replied.

"So, we have nothing to give them. You're right about the cops not being able to help." Dan said, "Still, we would have a report, you know, an official record."

"We need a plan, in case they come back." Quinn stated, staring out the window. Dan, also staring, nodded.

18

With address in hand, Dave walked up the street, and as he approached Wall's home he could hear the sounds of festivities coming from the back yard. He considered walking up the drive and joining the party, but since this was the first time at their home he walked up to the front door and rang the bell.

The door was answered by a very attractive, middle-aged woman, who obviously took very good care of herself. "Hello, welcome, you must be Dave." the woman said as she opened the screen door. "Come on in." she said, taking his arm.

"Thank you, and yes, I am Dave. David Smith at your call." he said.

"I'm Wall's wife, Roxanne. You can call me 'Roxy'. She said, by way of an introduction.

"Well, it's a pleasure to meet you, and this is for you and Wall." Dave said, handing her a bag with the Scotch in it.

Roxy accepted the package and, looking in, seeing the neck of the bottle, said quietly "Nothing like a forty-year-old single malt to get a 'come back again'...." She let out a chuckle and looked at Dave, "Thank you very much." Roxy said as she led Dave through the house, "There's the facilities, if you need them, when the door is open." she said, pointing at a closed door at the end of a short hallway. They continued on to the back porch, "There's Wall," she said, pointing at her husband, "you have a good time now, ok." she said as she returned to the house.

Dave walked over to where Wall was standing, talking with two men, one of which Dave recognized as Jody. "Hello Wall," he said as he neared the men, "and hello to you gentlemen."

Wall turned, upon hearing Dave's voice, "Dave! Glad you could make it. I believe you already know Jody, and this is his brother, Jamie." Wall said, with a big smile.

Dave shook hands with all three men, and for some reason he felt that he had seen Jamie before. "I brought you a gift, I left it with your wife." Dave said, pointing back towards the house.

"So I've heard." Wall said, straining to not laugh.

Dave looked at Jody and Jamie, who were also trying not to laugh. "Did I miss something?" Dave asked, trying to not be annoyed.

"Everyone knows that when I drink, I only drink

Jamaican beer." Wall explained, pointing at the kitchen window. Dave turned and looked through the window to see Nessa pouring herself a glass of the Scotch he had brought. The three men burst into laughter and Dave just looked at the ground and shook his head. After a moment Dave started laughing also, and looked at Wall and shrugged, as if to say, 'how was I supposed to know?' Wall stopped laughing long enough to say "Don't feel too bad, she's gotten just about everybody at some point."

"Well, I think we should all do a shot before it's gone." Dave suggested, "Hell, I've never tasted a forty-year-old Scotch, have any of you?" he asked. The three men looked at each other and shook their heads. Dave fell in between Jody and Jamie, behind Wall as they paraded onto the back porch.

"Wait here." Wall said as he entered the house.

The three men stopped on the porch and Dave got a better look at Jamie. "You were at the liquor store, weren't you?" Dave asked. Jamie grinned and gave a little shrug. Dave chuckled, "Now I get it." he said.

The screen door opened and Wall emerged carrying a tray with four glasses, each half-filled with liquid gold. "Gentlemen" Wall said as he set the tray down on the table.

The men each took a glass and, after a lot of sniffing, each took a sip.

"Oooh, that's good." Wall said, as his eyes almost

rolled to the back of his head.

"I think I've just been spoiled." Dave said, amazed at how smooth it went down.

"Nessa talked us into buying that bottle three years ago." Jamie offered. The other three men looked at Jamie, then all four burst into laughter. They finished their drinks and Wall took the empty glasses back into the kitchen. He returned a few moments later.

"Come on, I'll introduce you around." Wall said. Wall led Dave around the yard and introduced him around, most were family and a few were local growers. The two men stopped for a moment, while Wall spoke with one of the growers, when L.D. approached.

"Excuse me, Dad." L.D. said, then waited to be acknowledged, "I would like Dave to meet my girlfriend."

Wall looked at Dave and raised an eyebrow, "Make yourself at home." he said as he waved across the yard, in a welcoming gesture.

"I think I can do that." Dave said, then turned and followed L.D. to a table near the back of the yard. The table was occupied by a few young people, in the middle of which sat a young lady that caught Dave's eye. She was absolutely the darkest human being he had ever seen.

As they reached the table, L.D. said "I would like you to meet my girlfriend, Sarah." The young lady that caught Dave's eye looked up at Dave, "Dave this is

Sarah, Sarah, Dave." L.D. said.

"Sarah, it is my pleasure to meet you." Dave said, waiting for her to offer her hand to shake.

"L.D. has told me about you, he talks of little else." she said as she raised her hand.

As Dave shook her hand he noticed that her skin was nearly perfect, and her features were in excellent proportion. 'This girl is beyond beautiful.' he thought to himself.

"Sarah is going to the Olympics with the track and field team for Belize." L.D. said proudly.

"I've got a good chance to make the team," Sarah said, "Nothing's settled yet."

"Oh, she'll make the team." a voice came from behind Dave.

"Hi Gramma." Sarah said as Nessa walked up beside Dave.

"Hey, darling," Nessa said to Sarah, as she took Dave's arm, "If you kids don't mind, I am going to steal this man away." she said, tugging at Dave gently.

"Sarah, it was amazing to meet you." Dave said as Nessa pulled him away. "Your granddaughter is absolutely beautiful." Dave said to Nessa when they were out of earshot of the kids.

"Yes she is, and she is starting to realize it." Nessa said, sounding worried. "Her parents were killed in a plane crash, almost five years ago, we've been taking care of each other ever since." she said with a warm smile. They walked a few more steps "All that aside, I have an issue with you." she said with a scowl.

Dave was taken aback, "I can't imagine what I could have done to upset you." he said with sincerity.

"It seems Wall has developed a taste for good Scotch. After you convinced him to try it, he came back and put the bottle up. Lucky for me I had just refilled my glass." Nessa explained, "All you had to do was buy a thirty-dollar bottle of Scotch and I could have drank all night." she added, almost smiling.

"Here, and I thought I was doing something special." Dave responded.

"Well, I did get to try a forty-year-old Scotch." Nessa said in contemplation.

"It was good, wasn't it." Dave said, "But now, I could use a beer. How about you?"

"Thank you, but no." Nessa answered, with a smile, "I think I'll go back to my place in the kitchen." She turned and walked back to the house and went in.

Suddenly Dave found himself standing alone in the middle of the yard, he realized, for the first time, that he was the only white person there. He looked around and saw Jody near the house. He walked over to find Jody and Jamie preparing the grills for cooking. "Is there anything I can do?" he asked, wanting to be of use.

"Just sit back and enjoy the magic." Jody said with a big smile.

Dave retrieved a beer from a cooler and found a perch near-by, to sit and watch and occasionally tossing out some directions, just to keep it interesting. Dave watched as the two men brought five, of the seven, grills to life. The three men laughed and joked with each other until the fires were ready, that's when Wall and his son came from the kitchen carrying trays with different kinds of meat.

"We have beef hot dogs and hamburgers, chicken, three kinds of fish, and steaks." Wall said proudly.

Dave found himself extremely entertained as he sat with L.D. and watched the three men working the grills like professionals. They worked together with an efficiency that comes from years of working with one another. The aroma was magnificent as the food was getting ready to be served. They piled the meat on platters as the women brought salads and side dishes out from the kitchen. They lined the food up, buffet style, on two long tables and the people lined up to eat. Dave walked to the end of the line and found himself just ahead of the kids.

"Don't worry, There's always enough. At least until the kids go through the line." came L.D.s' voice from behind.

"I never worry," Dave said, turning to L.D., "But just smelling all that food is making my mouth water."

The line moved quickly and soon Dave was standing over some of the best smelling, and looking, food he had come across in a long time. He tried some of everything he didn't recognize, passed on the hot dogs and burgers, and took a piece of each type of fish with a steak to top it off. Wall walked by and pointed Dave to a seat at his table, then walked to the back of the line. Dave walked to the table with his plate and sat down. Everyone waited until their table filled up then gave thanks and started eating. As soon as Wall sat down, his wife, Roxy, gave thanks. As soon as the 'Amen' was said Wall stood up and everyone in the yard got quiet.

"Here's to our new friend, Dave. The most laid-back white man I have ever had the pleasure to meet." Wall said, raising his beer. The yard erupted in cheers, catching Dave by surprise.

Dave raised his beer in return, "Thank you for allowing me to be a part of this." he said, taking a big swig of his beer. Dave ate his food in the midst of joyful conversation and even went back for some chicken and a hamburger.

When the eating was done, people formed groups according to their liking. There was a table where a card game was starting, another where several gentlemen, and a few ladies, were enjoying after-dinner cigars. Dave found a seat at a table where Jody was about to fire up a joint with a few of his friends.

"So, how you likin' our little country here?" Jody asked, after exhaling.

"The only thing better than the scenery I've seen,

are the people I've met." Dave said, "This, so far, has been the best vacation I've ever taken."

"How much longer you planning to stay?" Jody asked.

"Another week, I'm scheduled to leave next Sunday afternoon." Dave answered, starting to wish he could stay longer.

"Any big plans for your last week here?" one of the others asked.

"Mike, right?" Dave asked, recognizing Jody's friend. Mike nodded in response. "I've got plans to go north tomorrow." Dave said, "There's a trail up there that I hear is one of the best."

"The Mayan sunset trail," Jody said, "I know it, it can be dangerous. Especially after a rain." he warned.

"I figure to hike in, spend a couple of nights, then hike out and spend a day wandering back here." Dave explained, "I should be back here by Thursday."

"It's well worth the hike." Jody said, reassuringly, "I did it when I was younger."

"I just got to let L.D. know to keep an extra eye on the place while I'm gone." Dave said, as if thinking out loud.

"Don't you worry, we'll handle everything while you're away." Jody offered, to ease Dave's mind.

"That would be greatly appreciated." Dave said, as he pulled out a joint of his own.

As the evening approached the crowd thinned down

to core family and close friends. Wall started a fire as it grew dark, and they talked and partied until almost midnight. Dave walked home feeling pretty good, he had a mellow buzz going and the cool night air felt good on his face. He walked down to his cabin, went in, set his alarm and went to sleep.

19

The drive north to Evans, Utah took several hours. Agent Johnson was still shaking his hand when they arrived.

"Hand still bothering you?" his partner asked. Agent Johnson just glared at him. "Sorry, I won't mention it again." his partner said, not wanting to piss him off.

They got out and went into the building, his partner going straight to his office and Agent Johnson went to the office of his boss.

"What happened?" Edgar asked, "You were supposed to bring him here."

"There were two guys there that said Smith wasn't around, he was on vacation or something." the agent explained. "I tried to check if he was there, but one of them stopped me."

"One of them stopped you?" Edgar asked, looking at the agent. Agent Johnson was one of those animals Quinn had talked about. "How did that happen?" Edgar wanted to know.

"I don't know, I just touched him and suddenly my face was inches off the ground." Agent Johnson replied, "I'm not sure what happened." He stood, rubbing his hand, looking confused.

"You know my boss wants him here, right?" Mr. Dhu said, watching him rub his hand.

"I'll try to get some intel on him and work it out." the agent offered.

"You do that." Edgar said, "Now, get out."

Agent Johnson went to his own office to make plans for his next effort. He would not go in blind this time, he had resources at his disposal, He did not want to disappoint his boss again.

20

Dave was up before his alarm went off, he felt excitement like a little kid, with the anticipation of seeing one of his dreams come to fruition. He packed what he needed into the car and headed north. He was on the road before six a.m., ahead of schedule, and he had a feeling that it was going to be a good day.

He arrived at the park later than he expected, having been lost three times on the way there. His 'good day feeling' had dissipated while he was lost for the second time. He paid the entry fee, and extra for secure parking until he returned. After parking, as he was putting on his gear, he noticed a few people coming out of the jungle trail. 'It's getting late to be starting out.' he thought, but he was determined. He rolled the windows up, but left the car unlocked. There wasn't anything to steal, except a box of tissues and a gallon of water, and he didn't want a window broken to find that out. The car was a rental, and so more trouble than it was worth to steal, but insured, just in case.

Backpack secure and walking stick in hand, Dave headed to the trailhead, stopping to sign in and give a destination. "Here we go!" Dave said aloud as he started up the trail. He was feeling better already, just being out of sight of the parking lot. He loved how lush and green everything was.

The trail rose at a comfortable rate and was relatively flat and wide for the first mile. That was when he came to the base of a waterfall, where there were many people playing in the plunge pool. The trail narrowed after that and started up a series of switchbacks that had Dave huffing and puffing. At about the three mile point the trail came to an ancient rockslide area and turned back to the east. The trail seemed different somehow, a little wider maybe, but the jungle was just as thick. Sometimes it seemed that the jungle would reach out and grab or push at him. After a half-mile of backtracking the trail turned back to the west and settled in about fifteen feet below the ridgeline.

Every now and then Dave would come across a place where the water had washed the dirt off of the trail and exposed what looked like worked stone. Dave figured it was probably the park service repairing the trail, but he liked to let his imagination run wild with theories of who made them and when.

He was a bit distracted as he crossed a stone patch, when a branch reached out and hooked his backpack.

He tried a quick pull to free himself, when the branch recoiled and threw Dave backwards against the side of the mountain. He bounced off the rock, his rear end hit the edge of the trail and he started tumbling down the mountainside.

He pinballed between the rocks and the trees for the first two-hundred feet down, when a particularly sharp rock separated him from his backpack. He immediately missed the padding it had provided as he tumbled down, with ever increasing speed. He could no-longer differentiate between the sound of breaking branches and his bones breaking. His head went straight into a tree and everything went black, with occasional bright flashes of light when he hit extra hard or somewhere tender. It seemed like he was falling for twenty minutes, when in reality it was less than one. He landed in a small outcropping in the side of the mountain. Slipping into unconsciousness, Dave reached out with his bloodied hand to find a handhold, when he hit a worn spot on the wall. He saw a bright light as he fell unconscious to the ground.

21

Traveling to work on monday Quinn paid particular attention, looking for anything out of the ordinary. He was still edgy from his encounter the previous day, and he didn't want to be caught off-guard. He made it to work without anything setting off his senses, and was able to relax a bit.

Quinn waited until lunch to tell Joey about what happened at Dave's on Sunday. Amanda sat with them and listened intently to Quinn's story.

"If they were willing to force their way in, this could get dangerous." Amanda said, worried.

"They must not know he's on vacation." Joe said, wondering who 'they' might be.

"If they come back we should keep Dave away from them until we find out what they want." Amanda suggested.

"Dave gets in Sunday, I'm thinking he can handle it." Quinn said.

"So, who do you think they were?" Joe asked. Quinn shrugged, as he watched Rob enter the lunchroom. Rob walked by and sat at a table by himself.

Quinn thought for a moment, "I don't think they were government," he said, "They didn't have that G-man smell."

"Oh, you can smell cops?" Joe asked sarcastically.

"Yes, they always have a background smell of gun-oil and Murphy's leather soap." Quinn explained.

"And you can smell that?" Joe asked in disbelief.

"And you can't?" Quinn responded.

"I guess I never considered smelling people." Joe said, in wonder.

"Try not having a choice in the matter." Quinn stated flatly.

"Anyway, did you try to get a hold of Dave?" Amanda asked, bringing the subject back to Dave.

"Dan called and left a message." Quinn recalled, "Amanda always smells good." he added, out of the blue.

"Why, thank you Quinn, my Aunt taught me that perfume should entice, not overwhelm." Amanda said, warmly remembering her aunt.

"Nothing to do until we hear from Dave, just wait and see if the bad guys show up again." Joe opined.

"Right, Joey," Quinn said, "you could check tonight, or we could wait until tomorrow when I take care of the plants."

"We can do both," Joe said with a smile, "I'll call you tonight if they are there, and you call me if they are there tomorrow." he suggested.

"No bad guys...no call." Quinn clarified.

"Not much of a plan, but I think it will do for now." Amanda said, giving her approval.

They finished their lunch and returned to their respective workstations.

On the bus ride home that evening, Quinn held his phone in his hand. He didn't want to take the chance of missing the call, it never came.

The next day Quinn rode home with Joey, so he could take care of Dave's plants. He went into Dave's by the side door and looked out the front, to see if there was anybody watching the house. There was no-one in sight, so Joey didn't get a call either.

On Wednesday, Amanda and Quinn were sitting together at lunch when Joe came in and sat down with them.

"You ever get the feeling that you're being watched?" Joe asked as he unpacked his lunch.

"I'm sure everybody feels like that at some point." Amanda offered. Quinn smiled and didn't say anything.

"As I was leaving the house, this morning, I had the distinct feeling someone was watching me." Joe explained, "the feeling went away as soon as I started driving."

"Then it wasn't the cops, they're more likely to

watch you when you drive." Quinn said, joking about his driving.

"Oh, first Dave and now you." Joe said, defensively, "You may find yourself back on the bus." he added, trying to look serious.

"Amanda, I need your 'puppy-dog eyes' here." Quinn said, knowing it was a facial expression he had yet to master. Amanda and Joe burst into laughter as Quinn rolled his eyes up and blinked a couple of times. He looked more like he had been maced than looking like a puppy.

After a few minutes of laughing and joking, Amanda asked "Still no bad guys?"

"Nope," Joe said "no bad guys."

"Has anyone heard from Dave?" Amanda asked, sounding worried.

"No word yet." Quinn responded, also worried.

After work Quinn did not receive a phone call from Joey, and still no word from Dan, who was waiting for Dave to respond.

Thursday, after work, as Joe and Quinn walked to Joe's car, Quinn stopped at the back of Joe's car. "Have you touched your fender in the last two days?" Quinn asked, looking at his car.

"No, why? What do you see?" Joe asked, curious about what Quinn had found. He walked back to where Quinn was looking, "I don't see anything." Joe said.

"Look here." Quinn said, pointing at a spot on his fender. "It looks like someone put their hand right here, like they were on the ground." Quinn got down on his knees and looked at the undercarriage. "There's a clean spot on the frame." he pointed out.

"What are you saying?" Joe asked, slightly confused.

"I am thinking you had a tracker on your car." Quinn stated.

"A tracker? Why would anyone want to track me?" Joe asked, really confused.

"Not sure," Quinn replied, "I am thinking, bad guys at work." They got in the car and Joe drove home. Quinn walked down the alley to Dave's house, and after looking for the black SUV and not finding it, went about the business of taking care of the plants.

On Friday, Quinn and Joe got to the lunchroom to find Rob sitting next to the only open table in the room. Joe sat down at the table while Quinn retrieved their lunches from the refrigerator. Amanda came in and joined them at their table.

"Dave gets home this weekend, doesn't he?" Amanda asked.

"Sunday night, if he's not having too much fun." Quinn replied.

"I hope it's sooner than later," Amanda said, "It's not that I don't want him to have a good time, it's just that I miss him."

"I miss him, too." Quinn said.

"I'm wondering why he hasn't returned any calls." Joe said.

"He probably turned his phone off when his vacation started." Quinn offered.

"Sounds like Dave." Joe agreed.

"Then he should turn it on before he heads back." Amanda said, thinking out loud, "If he does, he'll call."

"Then, at least, we'll know when to expect him." Joe said.

"Looks like more waiting." Quinn stated.

On his way home, while still on the bus, Quinn's phone rang, it was Joey calling. "Hello Joey." Quinn said, answering his phone.

"Quinn, they're here, they're about two houses down from Dave's. But I'm sure it's them." Joe said excitedly.

"Are you sure that they're in the vehicle?" Quinn asked, trying to calm Joey down.

"Couldn't see in, windows were too dark. But it has to be them, I mean a black SUV, who else could it be?" Joe responded, confident in his assessment.

"You are probably right." Quinn acquiesced, "I'll call you tomorrow, if they're there."

"Ok, talk to you then, bye." Joe said.

"Bye, Joey." Quinn responded as he hung up. Questions started pouring into his head, questions he didn't have any answers for at this time. He knew the only way to start to figure this out would be to sleep on it, and let his sub-conscious have at it. He could bounce some ideas off Emma in the morning. This was enough of a plan to allow Quinn to relax and enjoy the evening.

The next morning, Quinn was explaining everything that had happened at Dave's, Emma seemed anxious to get involved. "This could become dangerous. why would you want to risk anything over this?" he asked.

"Because my life is boring," Emma stated, "and since we became friends, it's not so boring."

Quinn couldn't help but smile at this, "I thought the goal of Eastern philosophy was to have a boring life." he said. "Isn't it a curse to say 'may you live in interesting times'?" he asked.

"That may be true, but boring sucks." Emma said, looking exasperated.

"You are welcome to join me today, when I take care of the plants." Quinn offered, finding himself wanting her to come along. He was enjoying her company to a point that even surprised himself.

"Oh, thank you," Emma said, excitedly, "We can take my car." she offered.

"You have a car?" Quinn asked, surprised, "I've always seen you riding on the bus."

"I love driving, and driving to and from work would ruin that." Emma explained, "Besides, I'm not the best driver. But I'm getting better at it all the time."

"I don't drive, they don't want me on the road." Quinn stated, matter-of-factly, "I couldn't get a license if I tried." he added with a smile.

Emma started to apologize, then saw Quinn smiling and let it go. "Let's go out back, I want to show you what I have been working on." she said, as she led Quinn outside to the practice mats. "Thank you for your help with my program last week," Emma said as a side note, "I've got it installed and I'm just waiting for some poor fool to try to mess with me." she added with an evil grin.

"I'm glad you're on my side." Quinn said, feigning fear.

"Now, let me show you what I came up with." Emma said, "I figured out how to make someone smash their face into their own knee on their way down. I know you're not supposed to hit someone when they're down, but this is on the way down. And they're doing the hitting." she explained, "I think it's kind of ironical."

"Sounds like a technicality," Quinn replied, "but one I'm willing to live with."

They spent the next hour refining her moves. He was surprised at how much her grip had improved and impressed at the fluidity of her movements. He thought about how graceful she would be kicking someone's ass. Quinn understood that he moved more like a precision machine, and she looked more like a big cat, with millions of years of built-in instincts, he enjoyed watching her.

When they were done with the lesson Emma said "Wait here, I'll get my keys." and ran off into the house. She returned a few minutes later, having changed out of her sweats into a cute top and some 'Daisy Dukes'.

"Nice legs." Quinn said, with a smile.

"So, you do notice that kind of thing." Emma said, returning the smile.

"I notice most everything." Quinn replied, as his smile faded.

"I'll go warm-up the car." Emma said, heading to the garage. About three minutes later she pulled out of the garage in a '72 Datsun 240Z. Quinn felt a twinge of nervous excitement at the thought of being a passenger in a car like this. "You going to get in?" she called out the window, as Quinn stood looking at her car. "Or you ascared?" she teased.

'Oh great, now she's pushing buttons' he thought to himself as he walked around to the passenger side. "This car is beautiful." Quinn said as he sat down.

"It's all original, even the paint," she said proudly, "It's a little faded, but I like the way it looks."

"Like I said, this car is beautiful." Quinn repeated. He gave her directions to Joey's as she rolled down the driveway to the street, then they were on their way to Joey's house.

22

Agent Johnson's men had learned where Quinn worked, they watched him and figured out that he arrived at Dave's through the back. They traced him back to Joe's and tracked him to where he worked. They watched Quinn and checked out anyone he talked to. That's how they found Robart Bott.

It didn't take much to find out that he owed money, and who he owed it to. They bought his debt for more than he owed, just to make it disappear from their memories. Rob was now a tool.

Rob told them everything that he knew about Dave and his friends, he did not want another beating like he received before he met these people. These people looked like they were professionals and could do a lot more damage to him, and he had had enough pain for a while.

Agent Johnson wasn't sure about the information they were getting from this 'Bott' character. He was told that Bott seemed the type to say anything to save himself, and some of the things he said seemed made-up. But he was sure about some things that could be verified through the reports he had received, and that was enough to start with. The agent wasn't sure if he would ever trust this guy, but as long as Bott proved useful he would use him to his advantage.

The agent now had an idea of who he was dealing with, particularly the guy Bott called 'Quinn'. He took a lot of crap from the guys over his first encounter with Quinn, and it was not going to happen again.

Mr. Dhu received a request from his boss to retrieve a sample from this Quinn person, he passed the request on to agent Johnson.

Agent Johnson did not relish getting that close to Quinn again, but figured this time he would be better prepared. He called his partner to let him know they would be heading south, again. He had wanted to wait until Smith was back from vacation, but the request from his boss took precedence, so it would take two more trips. He did not want to stay in Arizona because he knew there were still warrants out on him, from his previous life.

It had been just over six years ago when he had been contacted by Martin Services, and the statute-of-limitations would soon make his life a lot easier. After prison there weren't many opportunities for employment, so his life of crime continued. Now he didn't want to jeopardize the life he had built here.

The next morning agent Johnson went to his partner's house for breakfast, then they headed south to complete their mission.

23

Dave was slowly regaining consciousness, he could make out that he was in a square room. His walking stick was in the corner, 'I didn't expect to ever see that again' he thought, and his backpack was next to him on the bed he was in. There were no windows and only one door, leading to the dark. He felt that there was someone else in the room, but was having a hard time focusing on him. There was little light in the room and it didn't seem to have a source, it seemed to emanate from the entire ceiling. He couldn't sit up, a blanket held him down that conformed to his body. It reminded him of the Vac-U-Form toy that had been advertised when he was younger. His arms were free, and he retrieved his cell phone from his pack. He used it to light up the room and saw that there was a man sitting in the room.

"You're awake, good." the man said, "About time."

"Where am I?" Dave asked, starting to see more of

where he was. The walls were stone, and there weren't any decorations, artwork, or even any warning labels. This was not a hospital, of that he was sure. The light increased in the room and he turned the light on his phone off, then subtly switched on the voice recorder and set it down on the bed beside him.

"You stumbled into one of our entrances, you would be dead if you hadn't. It is extremely rare that someone gains access to our village." the man said.

"I don't understand, where is this? And why can't I move?" Dave asked, starting to get frustrated.

"Relax, the repair machine will be done soon." the man said, "What do they call you?" he asked.

"Dave, Dave Smith," he said putting his hand out to shake. "And you are?"

The man did not get up to shake hands, "I am the person they sent to talk to you." he said, "You can call me Bob."

"Bob?...ok, Bob, where am I?" Dave asked, for the third time.

"You are inside the mountain you fell off of." Bob said, matter-of-factly.

"Inside?... I remember falling." Dave said as the blanket withdrew to his waist. It seemed to draw into itself as it retreated, it looked very odd to Dave. The bed then raised him to a sitting position. "You said I found a door to your village." Dave said, "Your village, inside a mountain? Who are you people?" he asked.

"We are the Olmaya," Bob answered, "we have lived in this area for over fifteen-thousand years."

"Fifteen thous..., and you just happen to speak English, like you were born to it?" Dave asked, head reeling.

"I am one of several in my tribe that can speak to you." Bob said, "We have been allowed to remain here on the condition we do not interfere with the outside world. So, we keep to ourselves, and we are left alone."

"Are you the only ones that stayed?" Dave asked, not quite believing what he was hearing.

"Heavens no." Bob stated, "There are more than a dozen places that are still occupied, either by us or them."

"Us or them? What...?" Dave muttered, even more confused.

"Human and other than human," Bob said, stone-faced.

"What is 'other than human'?" Dave asked.

"Serpentine, insectoid, and mechanical." Bob answered, "And the Others."

"The Others, serpentine, and what?" Dave said, still not knowing what to believe.

"Think of the Earth giving birth, sending life out into space. It's happened several times before, first it was the serpentines. They evolved from the dinosaurs, a long time ago. Their technology seems like magic, even to us." Bob explained, "Then it was the insectoids, then it was our turn. We humans have sent two waves into space, and looks like we're going to go again, soon."

"Wait... dinosaurs in space?" Dave asked in disbelief.

"Our mythology holds that the serpentines created the insectoids through genetic manipulation, and that's why their civilization was destroyed. But they deny it, totally. Bob said, shaking his head.

Dave tried to pull at the blanket that had him pinned, to no avail. He was getting antsy and wanted out of this place.

"Easy, now. It will retract when you are done being healed." Bob offered, trying to ease Dave's mind. "Most of us thought you would only be here a day. We didn't expect you to be so damaged when you got here. It has taken longer than we thought for you to be healed."

"Wait... how long have I been here?" Dave asked, suddenly aware that he didn't know what day it was, let alone what time.

"Three nights have passed since you came through our door." Bob stated.

"That means it's Thursday," Dave said, gaining perspective, "I should be on my way home by now." He knew that everything would be ok for an extra day, but any longer than that might cause some to worry. "When can I get out of here?" he asked, hoping for the best.

"Outside of the injuries caused by the fall, you were in pretty bad shape for a man half my age." Bob said, looking directly at Dave.

Dave returned the look, "I'm eighty-six years old, I know I don't look it but it appears to me that we're the same age." Dave said, defiantly.

Bob started laughing, "I am two-hundred and ninety-six, you're younger than I thought."

Dave started looking around the room for hidden cameras, this had to be some kind of set-up. There was no-where to hide a camera in this room, no mirrors, nothing on the walls, no furniture except for the bed and Bob's chair. Nowhere to hide a camera of any size, everything was pointing to this being real. He pushed at the blanket some more, still with no effect. "So, you're almost three-hundred years old?" he asked.

"That is correct." Bob replied.

"And you live in a mountain?" Dave asked.

"Most of the time, yes." Bob answered.

"And you were sent to talk to me?" Dave wondered, "And who tells a three-hundred-year-old man to do anything?"

"The village elders said I was to be here on a certain day at a certain time." Bob explained, "So I did as I was asked, and here I am."

"How did anyone know when I would be here?" Dave asked, still trying to make sense of his situations.

"About seven months ago a young woman had a dream of you arriving on a certain date and at a certain time. She told the elders that I should be there to greet you. I got there ten minutes before you, I didn't expect you to be in such bad shape when you got here, though." Bob explained.

Dave sat, trying to absorb the information, when he heard the sounds of someone coming down the hall. The hall outside the door lit up moments before a young lady came into the room. She was rather plain looking, not as dark as Bob, and wore what appeared to be a toga. She started speaking to Bob in a language that he thought resembled the sounds made by the aborigines of the Kalahari Desert in Africa. When Bob answered the girl he spoke in English, at least that's what Dave heard. "Who is that, and what did she say?" he asked.

"This is the woman I told you about," Bob answered, "And she wants to know who your father is."

"I don't know who my father was, I was orphaned as an infant." Dave replied.

Bob turned to the woman and said "He doesn't know his father, he was an orphan."

"I just said that." Dave said, looking at Bob.

"She doesn't understand your language." Bob said.

"But she understands when you speak it?" Dave asked, confused.

"She does not hear what you hear, when I speak." Bob explained.

"Wait...what?" Dave asked.

"I speak in tongues," Bob revealed, "Whatever your native tongue is, that is what you hear when I speak. I also hear in the same way."

"I thought speaking in tongues was when you babbled while praising God." Dave said.

"That is 'prayer language', It's different, and should be kept private." Bob said, as they watched the woman leave the room.

"You know about prayer language?" Dave asked.

"Of course, we are all believers in the Messiah, here." Bob replied, "We keep the old stories alive, so we will be ready when He returns."

Dave studied Bob, trying to sense what he could about the man. Bob was dark-skinned and had thick lips, he looked more African than South American. He stood about five-foot-six inches tall, maybe a hundred and thirty pounds. He had good muscle-tone and little body fat, basically the body of a forty-year-old man, that took care of himself. That was when Dave noticed that Bob's lips didn't sync with what he heard. It was like an old kung-fu movie, and a little disconcerting to see in real life.

The young woman returned, carrying what looked like a golden tray. She stopped at the foot of his bed, held the tray level and tapped the side of the tray with her finger. She studied the face of the tray for a minute, tapped the side some more and studied it again. She looked up at Dave and studied his face for a moment, then broke out in a series of clicks, whistles, and pops, with the occasional vowel or consonant thrown in.

"What's she saying?" Dave asked.

"There's no record of who your father is, or was. She checked back six-hundred years, and your paternal D.N.A. sequences have no match." Bob said, a bit astonished at this.

"Six-hundred years, are you sure that's enough?" Dave asked, sarcastically.

"Should be, we rarely live past six-hundred." Bob answered, ignoring the sarcasm.

The woman said something to Bob, while tapping on the tray. Dave looked at Bob, waiting for a translation of what she said.

"It bothers her that she cannot find your family line anywhere in the records, so, she is recommending that you not be welcome here." Bob translated, "She does not want you to be here."

"Yeah, well, I didn't ask to come here, so just let me go and I'll pretend this never happened." Dave offered, irritated at the implications of not being welcome.

"You can go when you are healed." Bob said, matter-of-factly.

"Oh, yeah, thanks for all that you guys did for me." Dave said, "I know I probably wouldn't be here without you, seriously, thank you."

The woman glared at Dave for a long moment, then turned and left the room without saying good-bye. Dave found that to be rude in any culture, not even a nod to indicate you were worth the effort.

“She’s just full of warmth.” Dave said, with more sarcasm.

Bob ignored Dave’s remark, “You will be here for another hour, do you have any questions you’d like answered?” Bob asked.

“Yeah, all of them.” Dave said, “But how about you tell me the story of your people.” he requested. It was then that he heard a beep from beside him on the bed, he had forgotten his phone and now it was shutting down, battery dead. “You wouldn’t happen to have a charger around here, would you?” he asked, looking at Bob, helplessly. Bob looked as if he had never heard of such a thing.

“We humans were created about four-hundred-thousand years ago, by the Almighty, and protected from the effects of in-breeding for forty-nine generations. We spread across the globe as we were told. We would have occasional contact with the serpentines, they follow the brightest of the Others, and it never ended well.” Bob started.

“Others?” Dave interrupted.

“The Others were created, full grown, when He spoke the word that created the universe. They were on this planet before us, and some did not like us being put here.” Bob explained, “They are beings that can exist in two places.”

“Two places? You mean two places at one time?” Dave asked, hating to interrupt again.

"No, two different dimensions. But only one at a time." Bob clarified, "They can be dangerous, well, not like they used to be, but, still. Many of them showed up about sixty thousand years ago, demanding to be worshipped. Some taught us things in return, but most used us for their pleasure. The humans that were eager to bow down to them, received technology. It was like magic to us, and we hadn't earned the right to possess it, so we left and came here. We created our own technology, it took a long time, but we earned it. We paid the price for doing it ourselves, and we were allowed to keep it. It's knowing when to use it, that's what's important.

The Others that showed up here once worked for the Master, but disagreed about the humans. They were told to serve us, and they didn't believe we deserved anything. They believe we are a lower form of life and should serve them. They come in many forms, the higher ranks, their leaders, tend to look most human, except for the glow. Others resemble different animals and others are hard to describe. All have power according to their station, and so, are dangerous.

We rejected them, and they wanted to destroy us, but the Master protected us. They were told to leave us alone, and we keep to ourselves.

The Master left for a while, although we could still feel his presence, somehow. He returned around thirteen-thousand years ago, He didn't look to change anything, He just wanted a garden where He could relax. He tried his best to ignore what had become of his creation, what the Others had done.

He made his own humans, to help around the garden and for company. The man seemed incomplete, so He made a female for him. It was her that the serpentines targeted, they sensed a weakness in her. The one the serpentines follow believed he was as powerful as the Master, which, of course, he isn't. This angered the Master, and He closed the garden to everyone but Himself. He, still, would come out and commune with the new tribe He had created. We didn't know at the time that he had a plan, we believe, now, that everything was determined by which word He spoke to create the universe. We believe that word was 'Yeshua', but spoken in His language.

The new tribe grew large and some mixed with the other humans, and some were lured away by the Others, who experimented with this new strain of D.N.A. Soon, there was so much corruption in the human race that the Master brought the flood, to start over. This time with new rules for the Others. No longer would they be allowed to inter-mingle with us. They are supposed to remain in their own dimension, which overlaps our own, and not interfere with us.

We were allowed to build this refuge and wait out the flood, so were some others around the world. Like down south, they built a city at the top of the world.

They stayed above the water the entire time, it was kind of amazing. Most built underground refuges, to wait out the flood. We were underground for almost six months, when we emerged, almost everything had been washed away. Only a few temples survived, and the bases of several others could still be seen, but there was little trace of anything else.

About two-thousand years ago, one of us was seen entering one of the old temples to retrieve a piece of technology. It was a terrible mistake, they were seen putting a drop of blood on a door sensor. The people tried to open the door, first by cutting themselves, then by cutting others. They built temples over the bases of the old places that had doors and poured blood over the sensors, to no avail. Eventually they forgot why they were sacrificing people, and starting killing hoping to influence the future." Bob related.

"You mean to tell me that the Incan and Mayan sacrifices were originally trying to open doors?" Dave interrupted.

"Yes, and at some point some fool thought more blood would do it, it just got worse from there." Bob replied.

"This is all kinda hard to believe." Dave said, not wanting to insult.

"You asked for our story, this is it." Bob said.

"I'm sorry, it's just kind of...overwhelming." Dave said, apologetically.

“We have chosen not to interfere, others have chosen differently.” Bob explained.” There are enclaves which have conspired with various governments through the years. These can be dangerous, they have agendas.”

“So that’s how the government can say they’re not dealing with extra-terrestrials, because they’re from here.” Dave interjected.

“Sounds like something that a government would say.” Bob said, with an understanding smile.

Dave sat quiet for a few minutes, trying to assimilate all he had heard.

“You will be healed soon, we will take you to the waterfall and let you go.” Bob said. “I can’t tell you not to tell anyone about us, but I think you would be better off forgetting about us, just tell them you’ve been lost.” Bob instructed as he motioned at the bed.

Dave started to speak, but when Bob waved his hand, he fell unconscious.

24

Dave slowly regained consciousness, everything around him was a green blur. He gained his footing, with his head spinning, he found himself on a narrow animal trail and could hear the waterfall a short distance to the east. He did a quick inventory of his possessions, which should have been littered down a mountainside, to find everything was there. He did a check of his physical condition, he knew he had broken several bones during the fall, there was no trace of any of the damage he had incurred. He also noticed that the chronic problems he had, like his knees and his shoulder, were not to be found.

He had many scratches, like he had been pushing his way, or been dragged, through the jungle for days, His clothes matched the damage to his body. There weren't the massive blood stains on his clothes that he remembered seeing on his way down the mountain, just traces of blood where the jungle appeared to have reached out to grab him.

Dave finally felt confident enough to head to the waterfall, he grabbed his walking stick and started down the game path. He struggled along the path, which had been made by animals much shorter than he, until he came to the pool at the bottom of the waterfall. It was mid-morning and there were several people at the site, enjoying the water. He pushed his way out of the brush, startling a few people and causing everyone to stare, got his bearings and headed down the trail to the parking lot.

He arrived at his car to find a red notice, tucked under the wiper, informing him that he owed another night's fee. Dave retrieved his wallet from his pack, grabbed the notice, and walked over to the attendant's booth. He paid the fee and gave the young man a large tip, for watching over his car. The young man smiled broadly, it reminded Dave of Bob's smile.

Dave got into his car and headed down the mountain towards civilization. It was noon when he reached town, 'I'm pretty close to my new friends in Mexico, I could be there in an hour.' he thought. He headed to the border and then on to see Dot and her family. Dave reached Dot's town in good time and he noticed many of the stores were now closed for the summer. He made his way to the resort where Dot worked and parked in front of the main door.

Dot was behind the desk when Dave pulled in, she

looked up and recognized him immediately. She went to the door to greet him. As he was getting out of his car, he saw the main door open to reveal Dot standing there, with a big smile. "I didn't think I would ever see you again!" She said, excited.

Dave walked up to her and gave her a hug, "I was in the neighborhood and couldn't help myself." he said, "I can only stay one night, I have to get back by tomorrow evening." he explained.

Dot took his arm, "Come on, we'll get you checked in." she said, "You're looking good, vacation agrees with you."

As she took his arm, Dave noticed a bandage on her arm. "What happened to your arm?" he asked.

"Didn't you get my brother's message?" Dot asked, as they reached the front desk.

This made Dave realize he had been neglecting his phone. It had been at least two weeks since he checked his messages, and it died yesterday. "You wouldn't happen to have a phone charger I could borrow, would you?" he asked.

Dot reached down and retrieved a box of chargers, "You should find what you need in here." she said, then returned to his paperwork.

Dave quickly found an appropriate charger, "I'll have this back to you in a couple of hours." he told her.

"Keep it," she replied, "people leave them behind all the time."

"So, what happened?" he asked, "To your arm." He pointed, with a nod, at her bandage.

Dot, finished with the check-in, looked at Dave, "Somebody shot at me yesterday," she stopped Dave from interrupting with a finger, "they missed. It was at the restaurant, a drive-by. A guy, that my uncle hired last week, pulled me out of the way. That's when I hurt my arm, hitting the ground. It's a small gash, not much of a problem, it'll be healed in no time." she explained, handing him his receipt and key, "Same room."

"Thanks," he said, taking the paper and key, "and thanks for the charger." He turned and went to park his car by his room. Once in his room he plugged in his phone, then turned and went to take a shower, it lasted about forty minutes. When he was done with his shower he checked his phone, it was charged enough to retrieve his messages. He found that he had eleven messages, waiting.

The first message, the oldest, had been left by Joe. He made it home safe, with only one ticket, and his van was home without a scratch.

The second came from Amanda, who said she wanted him to have fun but come home soon, she missed him.

The third message came from Quinn, telling him about Emma, how the lesson went and about meeting her father.

The fourth one was Amanda again, with updates on

the office and that she missed him. Dave enjoyed hearing her voice, somehow it made him feel like he was family.

Message number five was Quinn reporting on the condition of his flora. It seemed a little extreme juice was welcomed by all of the plants.

The sixth message was from Dot, inviting him back for vacation. She said she would make sure he would remember it fondly. 'I'll bet she would' thought Dave, with a warm smile.

The next message was Amanda, again. She hoped she wasn't bothering him, but she really missed having him to talk to. Dave got the feeling that she had hoped to talk with him, he felt bad about missing her call.

The eighth message was from Dan saying something about people looking for him, and Quinn chasing them away. This had to be some kind of joke, they were setting him up for a laugh. Why would anyone be looking for him, especially a week ago.

Message nine was from Quinn, telling him about what happened with some men at his house, and how he couldn't figure why they would want him.

Number ten was from Amanda telling him she was worried by everything Quinn and Joe had told her about the strangers that were looking for him. She said she would try to find out who they were.

The last message had been left late last night by Carlos, who said someone had taken a shot at Dot. She was shaken up but was ok.

After hearing his messages, he made a call to L.D. to let him know he was ok, and that he would be back tomorrow evening. The second call he made was to Dan, where he left a message that he was ok and would be back Sunday evening. That done, he turned on the TV and sat back to watch the news. It seemed there were a lot of killings all over the area, and the authorities suspected the cartel, but couldn't prove anything. The local police, however, were truly investigating and had caught a couple of the killers. This made them targets for the cartel, everything seemed to be headed out of control.

As evening came his phone rang, it was Dot asking if he was ready for dinner. He went outside and got in her car, and they made their way to the restaurant. As they walked into the restaurant Maria saw them and went over to greet them. She gave them each a hug, "Good to see you again." Maria said to Dave, with a big smile.

"Good to see you, too," Dave replied, "but I really came back for the food." he teased.

Maria slapped Dave on the arm lightly, then went back to work.

Dot ordered them drinks as she led Dave to a table near the kitchen. The drinks arrived at the same time as Carlos emerged from the kitchen, with another man.

"Didn't think I'd ever see you again." Carlos said, as he offered his hand.

"Good to see you again," Dave said, "I was in the neighborhood, so, you know, here I am."

"I want you to meet Jesus," Carlos said, "Jesus, this is Dave, Dave...Jesus." Dave shook hands with the man and got a very dark feeling from him, but didn't let on.

"Actually, I was hoping to tour the temple I missed last time I was here." Dave explained, "It was closed then, remember?"

"Yes, of course. I think Dot can handle that for you." Carlos offered.

"I would love some company," Dave said, "I think you all should come with, on me."

"I'm free in the morning." Carlos said, accepting Dave's offer.

"I can take a day off, I'll be there." Dot said.

"I got a friend, Miguel, who'd love to see a 'Blood Sacrifice Temple'." Carlos put in.

"What about you, Jesus, you ever been to a temple?" Dave asked, noting that Jesus seemed a bit unsettled.

Jesus shook his head as a no and gave a little shrug.

"Ok, then it's settled, you're coming with." Dave stated, "So, they tell me you're the one that saved Dot." Dave said to Jesus, changing the subject.

"Yes, Jesus saw a car coming with a gun sticking out the window," Carlos explained, "got to my sister just in time."

"I just reacted." Jesus said, with a shrug.

"It seems the cartels have sent their soldiers out to

kill people at random," Dot explained, "It's happening all over down here. We don't know why they're doing this, we don't have enough of anything to make this worth it."

"Well, thank God Jesus was there." Dave said, looking at Jesus, "Thank God you weren't hurt in the effort."

"I'll make the arrangements, five for the temple tour." Dot said as she pulled out her phone. A few minutes later she announced that it was set for eight-thirty the next morning, and if they wanted breakfast, they should be here at seven.

Carlos and Jesus went back to the kitchen and Juanito came over from the bar, "You're going to see the temple in the morning?" Juan asked, rhetorically, "I know the farmer that owns the land where the temple is located, I think I can arrange something special for you." Juan returned to the bar and made the call to his friend. The restaurant was emptying out and Juan chased his friends from the bar and closed the doors, their meal started shortly after.

The next morning, Dave arrived at the restaurant five minutes before seven and found everyone else was there, except Jesus. He went to the table and sat down to a family style breakfast. "I'm not sure about the new guy, Jesus." Dave stated.

"Neither are we." Carlos said, "So be careful what you say around him."

"Yeah, I figured that, even yesterday." Dave

responded, "Do you think he'll show?" he asked.

"Pretty sure," Dot said, "I think he likes me."

"I think he liked you landing on top of him." Carlos said.

"So, he kept her between himself and the bullets." Dave noted.

"I hadn't thought of that," Dot said, "kinda makes him even creepier."

"You're right about that," Carlos said, "but enough about him, let's eat." Everyone took hands and Juan said grace, then the food got passed around the table.

Jesus showed up about ten minutes later, he sat down and had all the plates passed to him, until he had some of everything. The conversation was light, mostly Maria talking about her grandchildren, and filled with humor.

The tour bus showed up a little early, the driver came in and Maria insisted he have some breakfast. He made himself a breakfast sandwich and led the way out to the bus.

The ride out to the temple took about half an hour and Carlos mainly talked about the farmers along the way, and how the weather affected their different crops, and how hard it was to turn a profit. That was why the restaurant only used locally grown produce, they figured every little bit helps, and the money stayed local.

They pulled up to the gate to the attraction and were let through, without having to pay. The bus stopped in front of the path to the temple, which you could see the top of from the parking lot. They were greeted by a stately looking, elderly gentleman.

“Roberto, it’s good to see you.” Carlos said with affection, “Everyone, this is our host, Roberto. Roberto, this is my sister, Dorothy, and her friends.”

Roberto bowed and shook Dot’s hand, then nodded to Dave and the other two men. “Shall we get started.” Roberto said as he turned and started up the path towards the temple. He led the group up the path at a leisurely pace, explaining how the people, in the past, used the different plants that they were walking by.

Dave had always enjoyed learning how ancient cultures used what was around them to handle all of their needs. He thought this part of the tour was way too short, he was about to suggest making a side trail when the path opened up to the courtyard of the temple, revealing the splendor of the temple. It took his breath away, and he forgot all about the path behind him. “This is magnificent!” he said, after staring for a few moments.

Roberto smiled broadly, “You haven’t seen anything yet.” he said, raising expectations among the group. He then started up the steps and motioned for everyone to follow him to the top of the pyramid.

Dave watched Roberto as he climbed effortlessly up the stone steps, he also noticed that it seemed easier for him as well. He wasn’t feeling the pain in his knees that had been chronic previous to his fall. They reached the top of the structure after several minutes of climbing. Carlos and his friend didn't look winded at all, however Dot was taking a few deep breaths and Jesus looked like he barely made it, gasping for breath. Jesus sat down immediately upon reaching the top, a couple of minutes after the rest.

"We'll give you a minute to catch your breath before we continue." Roberto said to Jesus, then turning to Carlos, "You're still as fast as when you worked for me as a kid." he noted. Carlos just smiled.

"I'll sit here for a while, you can go on without me." Jesus said, between deep breaths.

"Are you sure? We only go halfway down and back up, all on the inside." Roberto tempted.

"Yeah, I'm sure. I'll be fine right here." Jesus replied, not wanting to do anymore climbing that day, or possibly ever.

"I'll stay with him." Miguel offered.

"You don't have to do that," Jesus said, "I'll be fine."

"That's ok, I don't like tight spaces," Miguel explained, "I came for this view, I'm good."

"I guess it's just us, I can't wait." Dave said, motioning Roberto to lead.

Roberto led the three around to the different rooms used by the priests, and to where they prepared the sacrifices. Then he brought them to where they performed the sacrifices, it was a seven by four-foot slab of basalt, about three feet thick. The top sloped gently towards the center, where there was a rust-colored circle, from which there was a channel leading to the edge and down the side. They could see where the blood had flowed down the side of the alter and across the stage it was sitting on.

"Now, the really cool stuff." Roberto beamed, as he led them to a massive steel gate. He unlocked the gate and motioned his party through, then locked the gate behind them. "Don't want any unexpected visitors." Roberto said as he took the lead down a hall to some extremely steep stairs.

The hall was about four feet wide, with a twelve-foot-high ceiling. The stairs were the same, but the steps themselves were taller than normal, making the descent very steep.

Dave fell in behind Roberto, followed by Dot then her brother. As they climbed down, Roberto told them about how most of the temples were built on top of older temples, and that the identities of the builders of the original temples had been lost to time.

After descending about a hundred steps, they came to another hallway, which turned and led them out to the top tier of a much older temple. They were facing an empty wall, where they could see where the blood had been channeled to flow down that wall. The dried blood had plugged the channel from above and had long since been forgotten.

"No-one knows that we have found this," Roberto said, "and I hope it can stay that way." All three agreed they wouldn't say anything, unless he gave the ok.

Dave led the way to where the blood ran down the wall. The trail of dried blood was over an inch thick and ended on the floor in an uneven half-hill. Dave noticed a small, raised spot under the trail going down the wall.

"Do you mind?" Dave asked Roberto.

"Do I mind what?" Roberto asked in return.

"If I knock some of that crust off." Dave explained.

"Oh...no, go right ahead." Roberto replied.

Dave looked over to the edge of the dig and found a fist sized stone. He walked back and tapped the dried blood on the spot he had noticed before, a slab of dried blood and dust fell to the floor with a thud. Dave used his sleeve to wipe the spot clean, it was smooth as could be. It wiped clean with no snags, but when he ran his hand across it, he felt something stick his palm, like a needle.

The raised spot retracted an eighth of an inch, then, a second later, a portion of what had appeared to be solid rock began to retreat. It pulled back and swung out of the way, revealing a passageway into the wall in front of Dave.

Roberto looked at his companions, eyes large, and said "This is new!"

Dave led the way into the newfound passage, they had gone about twenty feet when the hallway opened up into an ancient crypt. The room was thirty feet across and fifteen feet wide, and the ceiling was twelve feet high. The room had several tables surrounding a stone slab, upon which was an extremely old skeleton. The tables had a large assortment of jewelry and figurines, all made of gold and encrusted with gems. The skeleton was adorned with the finest of the jewelry, turquoise and red jasper held together with fine gold wire. The craftsmanship was amazing. In the middle of the skeleton's chest laid a gold tray.

"Was he expecting tapas in the afterlife?" Carlos posed, upon seeing the tray.

"I think I've seen something like this before." Dave said, as he delicately lifted the tray from the remains. Dave could feel the device come to life when he pressed his finger to the side of the tray. It had a sheen to it that wasn't there before, and there were several red spots along one edge. When Dave turned, the red spots rotated on the edge to always be on the edge facing north.

"May I see that?" Dot asked. Dave handed the tray to Dot, and it immediately shut off. "What happened?" she asked, hoping she hadn't broken it.

"Here, let's try this." Dave said as he pressed her index finger to the side of the tray, then he slid his finger above hers and pressed. The device came back to life, and stayed on when he let go, and remained on as long as she held her finger to the side of it. There were several red dots along three sides of the face of the device, and a few were very bright. Dave looked at Roberto, "You have some valuable stuff here." he said with a smile.

"Most of it will stay where it is," Roberto stated, "but I will take a couple of small pieces for my museum. I don't want them thinking I have a lot of gold here." he explained.

"I don't know if you'll be able to get back in here when I'm gone." Dave said, knowing that Roberto could blast his way in here if he wanted to.

"I don't need to come back here, it is a place of the dead." Roberto said, "However, the tray responded to you, I think you should have it." he offered.

"Wow...thank you very much." Dave said as he looked over at Dot, who was turning the tray this way and that, lifting it to eye level, then over her head. She stopped when she realized everybody was watching her.

"I think this thing is trying to tell me something." Dot said, as she held the tray vertical and faced the back of it towards Roberto. "I see an outline of Roberto, surrounded by a green glow, but when I turn it upwards there is a red blotch on the screen." she explained, as she brought the device back to eye level. She turned the tray towards Dave, "Now it's showing Dave, surrounded by a greenish-blue glow, with gold flecks." Dot said, curiosity growing.

Roberto, after retrieving a few small pieces of jewelry from a side table, turned to the others and said "I think we should be leaving this place."

"I have to agree with Roberto," Carlos said, "we've been here too long." He turned and headed back to the passage that had brought them there. Carlos led the way with Roberto bringing up the rear, behind Dave. As soon as Roberto passed through the exit it closed behind him, leaving no trace of the door. Roberto brushed the floor by the wall to eliminate their footprints, then had them walk over the spot to make new prints.

"There is no reason ever to go back in there." Roberto stated, relieved to be out of the grave.

"Maybe someday I can come back and we do a complete inventory of what's in there." Dave offered, curious as to what else might turn on when he picked it up.

"I don't think so." Roberto said, as he wiped some sweat off his brow.

"Never say never." Dave quipped, turning to follow Dot up the steep stairway. They were about two-thirds of the way up when Dot asked to take a break. She stopped and turned to face Dave.

Dave, two steps down, noticed she wasn't breathing hard and wondered if she just wanted to have her crotch in his face for a while. He had to smile, he had definitely been in worse positions in his life.

After a minute's rest, and upon seeing Dave smile,

Dot said she was ready to continue. They climbed the rest of the way to the top and Roberto unlocked the gate, they went into the side room while Roberto locked up.

"I can see Jesus and Miguel sitting outside." Dot announced.

"That wall is three feet of solid rock." Roberto said, pointing at the wall.

"Look!" Dot said, as she held the device out in front of her. They all looked to see Jesus, glowing red, and Miguel, glowing green, sitting on the stone railing outside of the temple.

"I think you were right about that thing trying to tell us something." Dave said to Dot, "Look at the north edge." There were many red spots along the edge facing north, "Somebody up there doesn't like you." he said, looking worried.

"The people in the background look beige." Carlos commented, looking over his sister's shoulder. "Let me try." he said, asking his sister for the device. Dot handed the tray to her brother and it immediately turned off. "What the hell?" Carlos said, annoyed.

"Here, let me help." Dave said as he repeated with Carlos what he had done with his sister. It didn't work. "Maybe if I start off with it." Dave said, trying the procedure from the beginning. It still shut off when he let go of it.

"I guess it's just you and me." Dot said, with a sly grin.

"I guess so." Dave agreed, holding the device up and scanning around the room. He saw Roberto, Carlos, and Miguel, outside, with a green glow. Jesus had a red glow, and Dot glowed greenish-blue. He turned back towards Jesus and Miguel. "I'm kinda thinking red means 'not a friend'. Dave posed.

"I wasn't sure about him from the start." Carlos said, "Uncle Juan said he showed up looking for work, but when he was offered a job washing dishes, he didn't look too enthused. Like he felt it was beneath him, but he ended up taking the job. What kind of drifter hesitates when offered a job that comes with meals?"

"I see your point," Dave said, "you think it was all a set-up, to get inside and find out if you have anything to do with anything."

"We can't kill him, whoever sent him knows where he is and if he doesn't return they'll be all over us. And we don't want that." Roberto said, thinking aloud.

"No, we can't kill him, but knowledge is power." Carlos said, drifting into deep thought.

Dave handed the tray back to Dot, who immediately touched her finger to the side and was relieved when the device activated.

"Put that in your bag," Carlos told his sister, "we don't need Jesus telling anyone about what we have."

"We're just simple townsfolk, who don't know anything important." Dot said, "Just like we've been all along." she added as she put the device out of sight in her shoulder bag.

Dot reached over and started pulling cobwebs off of Dave, that's when they all realized they were covered in dust and debris. They were dusting each other off as they walked out into the sunshine.

Miguel saw their condition and looked both disgusted and relieved, Jesus grinned broadly thinking he made the right call.

The climb down the steps of the pyramid was filled with talk of how close and dangerous it was inside the temple, and that they didn't see much future in that part of the temple. Roberto assured them that he would keep digging until they found something that would pay off.

"Maybe you should get some anthropology students, from the college, to dig it out for free." Dot suggested, still pulling cobwebs from her hair.

"Yeah, some college girls running around here might help this place." Carlos joked.

"They dig with teaspoons!" Roberto exclaimed, "I would never see the end of them."

"Well, maybe a few of their ends." Carlos quipped, giving everyone a good laugh.

Roberto grinned and nodded, "Never say never." he said, looking at Dave.

"That's what I've been trying to tell you!" Dave said emphatically.

They reached the bottom and made their way down

the trail to the parking lot, where the van was waiting to take them back to the restaurant. They all thanked Roberto for his hospitality, then climbed into the van for the ride home.

During the ride back, Carlos would tell them that he was sixteen when he worked there and thirteen when he worked here, in between talk of whether the tourists would keep flying over them, to spend their money on the coast, and hopes that the cartel would settle whatever they were doing and stop killing people at random. When they arrived at the restaurant Carlos invited everybody in for lunch.

"I think I should get back before the locals panic." Dave said, "But thank you for the offer, and for setting up the tour."

"It was my pleasure," Carlos responded, as he and the other two men turned to go in and eat, "see you next time." he said, over his shoulder.

Jesus waved good-bye to the odd white man as he turned to go and eat with these people, who reminded him of the people in his village, before the cartel moved in.

Dot remained behind with Dave as the others went to eat, she walked with him to his car. "Here's the tray." she said as she reached into her bag.

"No....you keep it, just keep it secret and be discreet in using it." Dave told her, "I don't think I could get it out of the country anyway. I'll be back around to see if it helped." he said as he opened the car door. She reached up and gave him a hug and a kiss on the cheek. "If it keeps you safe, it's worth it," Dave said, as he returned her hug, "Just be careful." He got into his car and started it up.

"People will want to steal it just because it looks like gold." Dot said in a moment of realization.

"Right," Dave said, "now, I've got to be moving along, but I will be back. And thanks for everything."

"Drive safe." Dot said, as she watched Dave pull away, wondering if she would, indeed, see him again.

25

It was midafternoon when Dave pulled into the drive at his cabin, everything looked to be in good order. L.D. had proved to be worth the money. 'That young man deserves a bonus.' Dave thought as he unpacked the car. He was just finished putting things away when he heard L.D. approaching, talking to someone. The young man turned into the yard accompanied by his girlfriend, Sarah.

"Welcome back, Mr. Dave. We were starting to worry." L.D. said, "I brought Sarah with in case you needed some housecleaning done." he explained.

"L.D.,...z'up?" Dave said, as he came off the porch, "And it's good to see you again, Sarah. I have to say, it's good to be back, but it's a little dusty in there. If you would like, you can dust and vacuum for me."

"Sarah's trying to..." L.D. started to say when Dave cut him off.

"No explanation necessary," Dave said, "but I could

use some food, if you wouldn't mind."

"Glad to, Mr. D." L.D. said, "Anything special?"

"Nah, chicken or beef and a veg. And if you want to eat with me, get enough for all, ok." Dave offered.

"You got it," L.D. replied, "I'll be back soon."

Dave watched as he left, then sat down to have a little smoke on the porch. He could hear Sarah as she cleaned the cabin, she was humming pleasantly as she worked, as if she were enjoying herself. She poked her head out and asked if he wanted the bathroom cleaned.

"No, not today," Dave answered, "but I would like for you and L.D. to clean this place when I leave."

"Sounds ok with me." Sarah said, as she started back in.

"What was that song you were humming? I've never heard it before." Dave asked.

"It's something L.D. wrote for me on his guitar." Sarah said with a smile, "We were trying to come up with some words for it, but haven't yet."

"You should consider leaving it an instrumental, I think it's beautiful and speaks for itself." Dave offered.

"Maybe that's why we haven't been able to come up with anything." Sarah said, as if she already knew it, "Thanks Mr. D." she said as she turned to go back to work.

When Sarah started to vacuum Dave got up and began to clean out the rental car. He had a small bag of empty bottles and food wrappers when he was done, and he was walking to the trash can when L.D. came around the corner.

"I could've taken care of that for you." L.D. said

"You spoil me, to the point I'm getting fat." Dave joked in response.

L.D. laughed and brought the groceries into the house to put them away. Dave finished his trip to the trash can and then followed L.D. into the kitchen a minute later, to find L.D. staring at his girlfriend's rear-end as she worked. With a start, L.D. went back to putting groceries into the refrigerator.

"It's perfectly natural....and understandable." Dave said quietly to L.D., "Just don't be getting a boner in here." He could see the young man blush as he finished putting the food away. "Besides, if there is to be any sex here, I WILL be involved." Dave joked.

"There goes any chance of a boner, and my appetite." L.D. said with a grimace.

Dave let out a laugh, "So, what am I having for dinner?" he asked, eagerly changing the subject.

"I know you said chicken or beef, but when I got there they were delivering the fish for tomorrow, and there were some really good looking fish." L.D. explained, "And I got corn and baby yams for us."

"I don't mind fish, it all sounds good to me." Dave said, with a smile.

The vacuum turned off in the other room and Sarah came into the kitchen, she looked in the refrigerator to see what they were having for dinner. "Oooh, fish. I love fish." she said.

Dave looked at L.D. and smiled, "I guess I'll go start the grill." he said, as he turned to go outside. L.D. looked down, with a wry grin on his face. Dave went out to the grill and got the coals started. As he waited for the coals to be ready, he sat on the back porch and watched the shadows getting longer. He could hear the two in the kitchen, chatting as they prepared the food. He was amazed at how open and honest they were with each other, 'These two have real potential' he thought.

L.D. came to the door, "Is the fire ready yet?" he asked.

"Two minutes and it will be perfect." Dave answered.

A minute later L.D. came out, carrying a tray with the prepped veggies, followed by Sarah, with a tray of glasses and a pitcher of fresh lemonade.

"You've cooked for me a few times, so I would like to cook for you this time." L.D. said, with a hopeful look on his face.

"Ok, buddy, show me what you got." Dave said, as he sat back. He watched L.D. prep the grill with oil, then put on the corn. When the corn was half-way done, he put the sliced yams on.

"My dad taught me it's important that everything is done at the same time." L.D. explained, "It makes the meal better, I think."

"You're right," Dave said, watching the young man

work the grill, "there's definitely an art to it."

While L.D. cooked, Sarah had set the table then came over and sat with Dave and watched L.D. as he worked.

"How long you two been together?" Dave asked.

"I was nine when I came to live here, the other kids would tease me and push me around, because I looked different from them. One day some of the big kids were hurting me, and this little kid comes out of no-where and beats two of them up, the other three took off running. We became friends right there. A few years later, puberty, and the realization that I really liked him, we've been a couple ever since. He's grown considerable in those years." she explained, "No-one ever bothered me again, after that day."

"He was your knight in shining armor." Dave said, "That is amazing."

"That was the day everybody started calling him Little Demetri" Sarah revealed, "after the fight he looked just like his dad, when he was mad."

"So, what is his name?" Dave asked, confused and curious.

"His real name is Elijah." Sarah said smiling, "I like it."

"Does he answer to it?" Dave asked.

"I don't know, it's been so long since he heard it." Sarah replied, with a chuckle.

"Let's find out." Dave said, turning to L.D., "Hey,

Elijah, when's the food gonna be ready?" Dave could see the young man freeze for a moment, then he turned to look at both of them and broke out in a huge grin.

"Long time since I heard that name," Elijah said, "only when I got in trouble."

"I think it's a great name," Dave said, "we could call you Eli."

"I gotta say, that's been in the back of my brain for a while now." Eli said.

"You haven't said anything to me about it." Sarah said.

"I guess it hadn't got to the talking part of my brain yet." Eli posed.

"So, the food?" Dave asked.

"Oh, yeah, it's ready now." Eli answered, taking the food off of the grill and bringing it to the table.

After giving thanks, they sat and ate and talked and laughed for the next hour and a half. When they were done eating, Dave gave each of them an envelope and a letter.

"This is for today, and the letters are invites for your parents and your grandma, Sarah, to come to dinner tomorrow." Dave explained.

"I'm sure they would," Eli said, "I'll give them a call."

"Let's find out." Sarah said, as she got up and walked to the fence, "Hey, Gramma" she called to the house next door. A moment later the door opened and Nessa walked out onto the porch.

"Hey sweetie, everything ok?" Nessa asked.

"I have a letter for you, from Dave." Sarah replied, with a coy smile.

Nessa came off of the porch and to the fence where Sarah gave her the letter, she opened and read it. With a big smile, she looked up at Dave, "It would be my pleasure to dine with you." she said.

"I will be grateful for your company." Dave said from the patio, with a bow.

Nessa laughed and walked back to her house, fanning herself with the letter the whole way. Sarah rejoined the guys on the patio and finished clearing the table, with Eli.

"You guys know you're invited too, right?" Dave said, wanting to be clear.

"Wouldn't miss it for the world." Eli said from the kitchen. A few minutes later, he and Sarah rejoined Dave on the patio.

"I won't be needing you tomorrow, but I would like for you and Sarah to clean up after I leave, Sunday." Dave requested.

Eli first looked at Sarah, "We'd be glad to, Mr. D." he replied, looking at Dave. He and Sarah then said their good-byes and headed to the street. "See you tomorrow, for dinner." Eli said, just before turning the corner.

Dave went inside to find everything had been

cleaned up and put away, "I gotta get me some kids." he joked aloud. With all taken care of, Dave retrieved a joint and went to sit on the front porch, to contemplate one hell of a day.

He had just taken his second hit, when a shadow came across his driveway. A moment later Jody appeared, walking his dog. Dave waved to him to come join him.

"I just got a text from Wall saying I was formally invited to dinner tomorrow," Jody said, "I was hopin' you'd still be up, so I could tell you myself that I would be honored to be fed by you."

Dave choked on his hit, "I don't know if it's an honor," he said, "But I'll do my best." He offered the joint to Jody, who took it with a smile and a nod. They chatted and smoked the rest of the joint, enjoying each others company.

When they were finished with the smoke, Jody looked at Dave, "I can't wait to find out if you can cook," he said, as he got up to leave, "see you tomorrow." He started down the drive with his dog right beside him, he waved as he turned the corner.

"Yup, one hell of a day!" Dave said, as he went in to go to bed.

26

Emma pulled up to Joe's and parked. She looked over at Quinn, who was grinning ear-to-ear.

"You drive well." Quinn stated, still grinning.

"Thank you," Emma said, "I find you can have fun driving and still obey the traffic laws."

"You have got me convinced." Quinn said with enthusiasm. Quinn and Emma exited her car and started up the walk to the porch when Joe came out.

"This, I did not expect." Joe said, bewildered.

"Joey, I would like you to meet my friend, Emma," Quinn started, "Emma, this is my friend, Joey."

"Pleased to meet you," Joe said, "is that your car?" he asked Emma, as he came down the steps.

"The pleasure is mine, and, yes it is." Emma replied with a smile, as she watched Joe walk past her to her car.

Joe's wife came out onto the porch, "Hi, I'm Becky, and you'll have to forgive my husband's manners." she said the last part loud enough for Joe to hear.

"Emma, nice to meet you." Emma said, walking back to her car, "I understand about cars, I'm the same way. Would you like to drive it?" she offered. Joe looked up to his wife, with hope in his eyes.

Rebecca laughed, "All right, but no speeding. You just paid for that ticket you got a couple of weeks ago." she said, warning him.

Quinn looked Joe directly in the eyes, "Joey...under the speed limit, and be careful taking corners." he said.

Joe became unsettled when Quinn caught his gaze, he hadn't made eye contact with him before, and it was unnerving. "Absolutely, total respect." he said, as he took the keys from Emma.

"Be nice, she's old." Emma said, with a smile.

"Thank you, this means a lot." Joe said as he got in the car.

"You got ten minutes." Rebecca yelled from the porch, as he started the car. "You guys come inside." she said as she held the door open for them. They went inside and Rebecca offered them some coffee.

"Yes please, black." They replied, simultaneously.

Rebecca turned to go to the kitchen, "That's just too precious." she said, with a chuckle.

Quinn looked at Emma, "Let us try to never do that again." he said, with an odd look on his face.

Emma giggled and leaned over to give Quinn a hug. As they sat, Quinn could hear the two younger children playing in the back room, this brought a smile to Quinn's face. He loved the sound of children playing, he always had, even when he was a child. Emma noticed Quinn smile at the sounds and it made her feel warm inside, she wasn't ready for that.

Rebecca returned with a tray that had four mugs of coffee, all black, that she set down on the coffee table. "So, how long have you two known each other?" Rebecca asked as she handed each of them a coffee. Quinn looked at Emma with deference.

"About a month." Emma said.

"Really?" Rebecca asked, with feigned surprise.

"I've been seeing her on various buses for three years." Quinn stated.

"And you never thought to talk to her?" Rebecca asked, "In all that time?"

"Most women consider me genetically unacceptable." Quinn said, without emotion.

"I imagine just the ones that don't know you." Rebecca said, "You're smart, you're considerate, and you don't seem to have any bad habits. Honey, you're a catch!" she stated, as she looked at Emma.

Emma tried desperately to not blush, unsuccessfully. "I believe it's called 'preaching to the choir'." she said, with a giggle. This time it was Quinn who blushed as he tried to hide it behind taking a sip of coffee.

"So, Emma, what kind of work do you do?" Rebecca asked.

"I own a software company." Emma replied, paused, then added "Actually, I am the company."

"Well, we all have to start somewhere." Rebecca said, consolingly.

"Yeah, I guess." Emma said, not letting on that she had been doing quite well at it for over ten years.

"Joey's back." Quinn stated.

"You sure? I didn't hear anything," Rebecca asked, "And I got mom-ears." Before Quinn could answer, they all heard a car door close. Rebecca looked at Quinn and shook her head, "Joe told me never to doubt you, now I know." she said, almost to herself.

The front door opened and Joe came in, smiling ear-to-ear, "I have got to get me one of those!" he announced, sounding like the character in the movie Independence Day. "Where did you get a car like that?" Joe asked Emma.

"My mother's brother, Uncle Pi. He bought it new, he wanted to impress a white girl. It must have worked, because she married him. A year later she got pregnant, on the pill, and my uncle parked it, never to drive it again. He would start it, and change the oil, things like that, but he never got the chance to drive it again. He had a stroke just when his youngest entered highschool. I helped them out when they needed it and they wanted me to have the car in return." Emma explained, "My cousins stopped talking to me that day." she added as an afterthought.

"Wow....that's.....that's....sad." Joe said, not really knowing what to say. He looked at his wife, who just shrugged.

"Either way, they're happy and I love the car." Emma said with a smile.

"I second that!" Quinn said, grinning.

"I drove past Dave's," Joe said in a serious tone, "there was a black van, parked about two houses down."

"Could you see anyone in it?" Quinn asked.

"Nah, the windows were too dark." Joe replied.

"Wait, what's going on?" Rebecca asked, concerned.

"We think someone's watching Dave's house." Joe told his wife.

"Why would anyone want to do that?" Rebecca asked.

"That is the question." Quinn said, "Isn't it?"

Rebecca looked around the room at each of them, stopping at her husband, "They're not getting you involved in something, are they?" she asked, in a truly serious tone.

"I asked Joey to look out for them a couple of weeks ago. I'm sure they have no interest in you." Quinn responded in Joe's place. Rebecca continued to look at her husband.

"I'm not involved in anything, Quinn asked me, I asked Dan, he texted me when they showed up, I called Quinn, that's it." Joe explained to his wife.

"That better be it," Rebecca said, giving Joe a look,

"we've been through too much for you to go and do something stupid."

"I promise you, that's it." Joe said, holding his hands up.

"Ok then," Rebecca said, "so, who are these people?" she asked. This made Joe smile.

"One of them said they were from the 'Natural Resources Department'," Quinn said, "they were looking for David, they seemed aggressive."

"That's it?" Rebecca asked in disbelief.

"They tried to force their way into Dave's house and tried to grab Quinn." Emma said, trying to fill in some detail.

"Like I said, they seemed aggressive." Quinn stated.

"Yeah, well," Rebecca said, then looked at Joe, "either way, I don't want you involved." she told her husband.

"You got it." Joe reassured his wife, then looked at Quinn. "You heard her." he said, with a nod to his wife.

"Understood." Quinn said with a nod.

"We should be going." Emma spoke up.

"Yes, I have things to do." Quinn concurred.

"Emma, nice meeting you, and thanks for letting me take your car for a ride," Joe said, "it meant a lot to me."

"It was nice to meet both of you," Emma said, "Is it ok if I leave my car here for a while?" she asked.

"No problem," Joe said, "public streets and all."

Rebecca gave her husband a look, "We'll keep an eye on it for you." she said to Emma.

"Thank you, and thanks for the coffee." Emma said, as she took Quinn's arm.

Quinn looked in Joe's direction and gave a nod, "See you at work, Joey." he said with a smile. They got up and were escorted to the door.

Once outside Emma said "I like your friends, I feel like they're good people."

"I know they are." Quinn stated.

"I think you should walk around the short way to Dave's, go around to the front way. I'll go around the other way and try to get a license plate number. They should be watching you at the house, so they probably won't even notice me." Emma offered as a plan.

"I'll unlock the side door," Quinn said, "you walk by the house and around the corner, then come up the alley and into Dave's, unseen."

"I think we have a plan," Emma said, looking excited, "let's do it."

Quinn smiled, knowing she didn't realize what she said could mean something else, "I'll see you when we get to Dave's." he said, as he turned to go around the block to Dave's.

"Ok then." Emma replied, and walked in the other direction.

As Quinn passed Joey's house he slowed down, because he had never been this way before and he needed to take it all in. As a result, he took longer than expected to come around the corner on Dave's street. When he did, he couldn't see Emma coming towards him as expected. However, he did notice the van shake slightly, like it might when someone sits up or adjusts their position.

Quinn kept his face turned towards Dave's house as he walked, when he saw Emma emerge from a few yards behind the van. She stopped and appeared to be trying to wipe something off the sole of her shoe, then she resumed walking briskly toward him. They passed each other just as Quinn reached Dave's house. He turned up the walkway to the house, then stopped to watch Emma walk away. He did like the way she moved.

After a moment he turned and went up into the house. He unlocked the side door for Emma, when she got there, then went and started to check on the plants. As he did this, he noticed the neighbor, Dan, leave his house. Dan had reached the sidewalk when Quinn saw the side door of the van open and two men, dressed in black suits, exited and walked up behind Dan. They caught up with him just as he turned onto the walkway to Dave's house.

"Excuse me, Dan," the larger of the two men said, "we'd like to ask you some questions."

The hair on the back of Dan's neck was standing straight up, he could not remember giving them his name. Something felt very wrong. Dan walked a few more steps before he turned around to confront the two men. They had stopped at the start of the walkway.

As the larger man took a step onto Dave's property, Quinn stepped out onto the porch. "Agent Johnson, was I not clear...you are not welcome here." Quinn said as he walked to Dan's side.

"We just have a few questions we'd like to have you answer." Agent Johnson said.

"We don't have anything to say to you." Dan said, defiantly.

"We'll see." Agent Johnson said as he reached for Dan.

Quinn responded by reaching for the agent, when the junior agent shot him, from behind, with a taser.

Agent Johnson pushed Dan to the ground and pointed at him, as if to say 'don't move'. Quinn fell to the ground in an explosion of colors and convulsions, when the younger agent handed the taser to Agent Johnson, who pulled on the trigger once more to make Quinn flop around some more.

"Put him in the data base." Agent Johnson told the junior agent. The younger agent pulled out a d.n.a. swab kit and collected a sample from the inside of Quinn's cheek, then packed it away.

Agent Johnson pulled the probes from Quinn's back and the agents returned to their van and drove away.

Emma had just got to Dave's in time to see the van

drive away, so she walked to the front of the house to find Dan trying to pick Quinn up from the ground. She ran out to help Dan pick up Quinn, who was trying to regain his sense of balance.

"What happened?" Emma asked, as she brushed off Quinn's shirt.

"I think it was an ambush," Quinn said, "it seemed choreographed."

"All that to get a d.n.a. sample, it doesn't make sense." Dan said, as if he was trying to understand the minds of their adversaries.

As Quinn regained his ability to walk, they all went into Dave's house. Emma sat Quinn down on the sofa and started cleaning him up, when she lifted his shirt she saw the marks the taser had left on his back.

"This looks awful," Emma said, "where does Dave keep his first-aid kit?"

"It's in the closet next to the bathroom." Quinn stated.

Emma quickly returned with the supplies she needed and went to work on Quinn's wounds.

"The reason I was coming over was to let you know I heard from Dave." Dan explained as he pulled out a paper with Dave's flight information written on it. He handed the paper to Emma, who passed it to Quinn.

Quinn read the information and pulled out his phone, "I told Amanda I would let her know if we heard from Dave." he explained as he called Amanda.

Quinn read her the flight information first, then he told her what had just transpired in the yard. As he was relating what had happened, Emma pulled out her phone and brought up the pictures she had taken of the black van's license plates. She showed Quinn, who read the state and number off to Amanda.

When he had hung up, Emma asked, "Why does she want to know?"

"She told me she can help, she said that she has resources." Quinn answered, "Besides, she's a good friend, and I am thinking that she likes Dave."

"I can't wait to meet her." Emma said, sounding like she hadn't expected Quinn to know any other women.

"She's nice....and smart!" Quinn said, "I think you two will get along."

"I've noticed that your friends are of high caliber," Emma offered, "I expect Amanda's no different." she said, as she finished cleaning up Quinn.

Quinn got up and finished checking on the plants, watering a few and dusting others, leaving Emma and Dan to pass the time with talk of the strangers they had encountered. When Quinn was done with the plants, Dan went home and Emma and Quinn walked around the block to her car.

As Emma drove Quinn home, she kept asking questions they didn't have answers to. Quinn was silent for most of the ride, except to offer counter-questions that couldn't be answered either.

When they arrived at Quinn's place, Emma left the car running as she got out to give Quinn a hug. Quinn smiled and returned the hug before going inside, where Billy said "I knew it was a woman."

27

Their sample collected, Johnson and his partner headed back north, after dropping off their new informant.

"That went better than I thought it would." Agent Johnson said, "Thanks for the good work."

"And we have a name for the sample." the junior agent said.

"Too bad he didn't know when Smith would be back." Johnson complained, "That would have helped more than that freak's name. Now I have to assign a couple of teams to watch both his house and the air-port, and that costs."

"He did say he thought Smith would be back within a week or so." the junior agent said, trying to defend the kid, "And how many flights come in from Belize, anyway?"

"Well, you're going to find out, when we get back." Agent Johnson said, "But first, we have to bring the sample straight to Ctag, orders from Mr. Matthews.

"Looks like we won't be home 'til tomorrow." the junior agent said, sulking.

The younger agent, George Brown, had been taken under the wing of Agent Johnson shortly after he hired on. He wasn't sure why, but enjoyed the protection it afforded him from his co-workers. His crimes had been committed on his computer and he did a little time in a county jail, not monster college.

"What do you think about that kid?" Agent Johnson asked, "What with you sticking up for him and all."

"Wait, I wasn't..." George stopped himself, knowing that it was useless to argue. "He's harmless enough, but he's not as smart as he thinks he is." he said, answering the question.

"Yeah, I got that impression too." Agent Johnson said, with a smile. He liked his new partner, George, he was good at things that he, himself, wasn't. They made up for each other's weaknesses, it seemed to make the job go easier and that was always good.

George spent most of the drive to Ctag looking at his phone, occasionally writing something down. By the time they reached their destination, outside of Colorado Springs, George had a list of flights, and connecting flights, from Belize.

Agent Johnson pulled into the parking lot of Ctag and instructed George to bring the sample straight to the boss. When George returned, they went and got a couple of rooms at a local motel. The next day they returned to Utah, to wait on their next set of orders.

At Ctag, the secretary brought the sample to the lab with orders to expedite. It was placed on top of the next set of samples to be decoded, to be picked up by the next technician who finished their current set.

28

Dave slept in later than usual Saturday morning. When he did wake up, he laid in bed thinking about his adventure, when he realized he had slept through the night without getting up once. This made him get up and head to the bathroom. As he walked down the hall, he could hear quiet noises coming from his yard. He looked out to see Eli washing his car, humming the same tune he had heard from Sarah the day before. He continued on with his morning routine, and when he was done with it, he stepped out onto the porch to find Eli applying a coat of wax to his rental.

"That's really not necessary." Dave said, "I thought I gave you the day off."

"They will have no reason to charge you extra for anything." Eli said with a proud smile, "And I'm on my own time."

Dave grinned and nodded, as he sat down on the steps and lit a joint.

Eli looked over at Dave, "Why you do that, Mr. D.?" he asked.

"Because I'm on vacation, I'm old, I've already made my fortune, had a good life, and now I just want to feel good." Dave replied, "Like you've never tried it." he added as a jibe to his young friend.

"Did once," Eli said, "didn't much care for it,.. at all."

"Well, I find it's better for me than alcohol." Dave explained, "I want to relax, not permanently lower my I.Q."

"Don't like drinking either." Eli said, shaking his head.

Dave laughed, "You're young, wait until your brain stops developing, then you may feel differently." he said.

"How long does my brain need to develop?" Eli asked, not sure if he was being set up for a joke.

"'Til you're about thirty-five, maybe forty, after that you can't do any 'developmental' damage." Dave said matter-of-factly, "No joke."

"Wow! That's, like, twenty years." Eli said, a little stunned.

"There's a lot of things in this world that you have to decide, is this an ally or is this an enemy?" Dave said, "And what works for another may not work for you. Sometimes, something will feel real good, and you devote some time to it and your life seems to spiral down, if you notice at all. Sometimes something will tax your strength, and tire you out, and not feel so good,... but, after a while your life is amounting to something." he explained.

"My Dad says you need to eat, sleep, and work for a living, to stay physically and mentally healthy." Eli said, "And, I think, if you do the third, the first two take care of themselves."

"Your Dad is a smart guy." Dave said.

"Seems like I've heard that before." Eli replied, as he started to buff the car.

Dave finished his smoke and got up to go inside, "Let me know when you're done." he said before going in. Dave was sitting, enjoying a fresh juice and reading the local newspaper, which was delivered on a schedule he hadn't quite figured out. It seemed to arrive every four and a half days, or so. But, it was well written and Dave enjoyed learning what the locals thought was worth writing about.

Eli came to the door, "Knock knock." he said as he opened the screen door.

"Come on in." Dave said, putting down the newspaper, "I know I said I didn't need your help today, but, could you get the two grills set up and ready to light?"

"I can have that done in no time." Eli said with confidence.

"Thanks, man." Dave replied, and went back to finish reading the newspaper.

A short time later, Eli returned to the door, "Knock knock." he said.

"Come on in." Dave called out.

"The grills are ready, I cleaned and oiled the grates, but you should oil them again, once they're hot." Eli said, "Oh, and I cleaned up the coolers for you, they're ready for ice."

"Thanks for thinking ahead," Dave said, "at least ahead of me." he added with a chuckle.

"You taught me well." Eli said with respect.

"You're a quick study." Dave said as he got up and retrieved an envelope from the counter, "I know I already paid you for the week, this is a bonus, for you being so awesome."

"Thanks, Mr. D.," Eli said, "You're cool to hang with, and I learned a lot." he added as he took the envelope. His eyebrows raised as he hefted the envelope in his hand. He put the envelope in his pocket without opening it, he knew Dave had taken care of him.

"See you for dinner, right?" Dave said, as they walked to the door.

"Wouldn't miss it for the world." Eli replied, with a grin. "See you then." he said as he walked out with a wave.

Dave went over his to-do list in his head, first, ice down the beer. He got up and started prepping for his party. He had about three hours until the time people were asked to show up, plenty of time.

He had just finished prepping everything and was about to have a beer, when Jody showed up fifteen minutes early.

"I figured we'd have enough time for this, before everyone's here." Jody said, producing a joint, "You're going to like this, I just got it today." he added as he lit the joint. He took a big hit and passed it to Dave, who took a big hit as well.

"That tastes real good." Dave said, after exhaling.

"It come over from that island off the coast." Jody explained, before hitting the joint again.

"Beer?" Dave asked. Jody nodded and Dave retrieved a beer for him, from the cooler.

They finished the joint in short order, and were joking around, when Wall and his family showed up, followed shortly after by Nessa and Sarah.

"Took you two long enough to smoke that thing." Nessa scowled.

Jody laughed, "You could've joined us at any time." he said, grinning at her.

"P'shaw," Nessa said, "Maybe when I was a lot younger, but you weren't around then." she added, pointing at Jody. "But, it did smell good from over there." she said, pointing with her thumb over her shoulder, at her house.

They all got a good laugh at that, then Dave offered drinks to everybody, taking their orders. "I'm fetching your first drink, after that you're on your own." Dave said, heading to the kitchen for the non-cooler drinks. Soon, everyone had their drinks and Dave raised his beer and said, "Here's to new friends." Everyone cheered and raised their drinks in response.

Dave lit the grills under the watchful eyes of Wall and Jody, "I can do magic, too." he said, looking at the two men.

"We'll see," Jody said, "Won't we." he said to Wall, giving him a nudge with his elbow.

"I'm hoping so." Wall said, with a deep laugh.

Nessa joined the men at the grills, "So... what's on the menu?" she asked.

"I got prime beef steaks, langoustines, and sea bass." Dave stated proudly, "And asparagus and sweet potato slabs, for sides."

"That all sounds good." Nessa said, approvingly.

"Sounds good to me, too." Wall chimed in.

"When does the magic start?" Jody asked, teasingly.

Dave checked the grills and saw that the coals were almost ready, "Soon, my brother, soon." Dave replied, with a grin. He went into the house and returned with the yam slabs and steaks and got them started. He turned to go back in and saw Roxy and Nessa bringing out the seafood and asparagus. "Thanks, but I could've gotten that." he said.

"We didn't want you to leave them steaks." Roxy said with a smile, "I don't want to eat no overdone prime beef."

"Good point." Dave said.

"Those are some pretty rib-eyes." Wall said, "I can't wait to try prime beef."

"I'm sure you've had prime beef before, all the best restaurants serve it." Dave said.

"Like I said, I can't wait to try prime beef." Wall reiterated, to laughter from all.

"How's everyone want their steak done?" Dave asked his guests. He got five mid-rares, and Nessa said "Rare, baby, rare!"

"A woman after my own heart." Dave said, approvingly.

"If I was after your heart, I would want that rare too!" Nessa said to a roar of laughter.

Dave got everything cooked in short order, with all being done within minutes of each other. With the steaks rested and the seafood fresh off the grill, Dave served everyone. They all sat and enjoyed a meal cooked to perfection.

After dinner, while Dave served coffee, Eli and Sarah took their leave. The rest enjoyed their coffee with a smoke, Wall and Nessa each enjoyed a cigar, while Dave and Jody fired up a joint, only to have Roxy join them.

"Special occasion." Roxy said, with a wink to her husband. Wall didn't mind if she got high, she seemed to enjoy sex even more than usual. And they would definitely be having sex when they got home.

When they finished the joint, Dave asked a general question to all, "Has anyone here ever heard of a lost tribe or hidden city around here?" His question brought a round of groans and chuckles.

"White men have been coming here for centuries, asking about El Dorado or whatever, we just point them to the jungle and forget about them." Wall said, to a few nodding heads.

"Consider it this way," Jody started, "the jungle is a very hostile place. It will kill you if you're aren't prepared properly. And if there is a city of gold in there, I don't see them letting you live, let alone leave." he explained. They spent the next half hour talking about the different theories and conspiracies they had heard growing up, and that still came up occasionally.

Evening was approaching when Wall and Roxy said their good-byes and walked home, with Jody following them a few minutes later. Nessa sat enjoying her cigar, with a glass of scotch on the rocks.

"No-one leaves the hidden tribe, unless they were invited in the first place." Nessa said, when they were alone.

"If they don't have contact, how does one get invited?" Dave asked, with a hint of sarcasm.

"Prophecy." Nessa answered, "When something is prophecized, they must follow it." she explained.

"And if they let you go and tell you never to return?" Dave asked, now curious.

"That is them trying to do the minimum, or avoid prophecy." she said, "Is there something you're not telling me?" she asked, sounding a little worried.

"Yeah, I fell." Dave replied.

"You fell?" Nessa queried.

"Off the mountain, when I was hiking up north." Dave started, "I fell into a doorway or something, I was pretty broken up at that point. Anyway, I was trapped in some sort of bed, which Bob said was healing me, and when it was done, they told me to go away and never come back."

"Bob?" Nessa asked, "You met someone named 'Bob'?"

Dave shrugged, "That's what I thought." he said.

"And they just let you go?" Nessa asked, perplexed.

"After a fashion." Dave said, remembering coming to in the jungle.

"So, you know where they are?" Nessa asked, getting curious.

"I'd have to fall off the mountain again, to find them," Dave said, "and even then I would probably miss the entrance." Dave stopped and looked at Nessa, "How is it you know so much about them?" he asked, suddenly suspicious.

"When I was young, I saved an old man from being killed, but I was hurt doing it. I woke up in one of those beds you spoke of, it healed me then he gave me a job. We used to talk about everything." Nessa explained, with a touch of nostalgia in her voice.

"So, one of them had to be living out here." Dave said, thinking out loud.

"They don't... they're not prisoners, they just aren't supposed to interfere." Nessa said defensively, "Anyway, he liked living with us, out here. He liked boats and sailing. It was a long time ago."

"And you never told anyone?" Dave asked.

"Not until now." Nessa said, "And if they said don't come back, you should probably listen, and not go back." she warned.

"I wouldn't know how." Dave replied.

"It's just as well," Nessa said, "they've never been a particularly friendly people." Nessa studied Dave for a moment, "So... what did they tell you?" she asked.

"Just that they've been here a long time, and that they're waiting for the return of Yeshua." Dave answered, "Oh, and that they live a long time."

"Well, that's about what I know, too." Nessa said.

"I'm just glad it wasn't a dream I had when I was knocked out." Dave said, with relief in his voice. Dave thought about telling her about what happened in Mexico, but something held him back from saying anything of his adventures up north.

They talked for a while, about her experiences with 'them' when she was young, but the topic soon switched to Dave and his life in the U.S. After Dave felt he had revealed more of himself than he intended, the evening drew to a close and he sent Nessa home with all of his left-over liquor, which she accepted gladly. He also gave her the last carton of cigarettes that he had, she seemed happy with her haul.

"We don't need the kids finding this stuff in the morning." Dave said, as a reason for his generosity.

"That we don't." Nessa said, knowing that Sarah would have brought it to her anyway. "'Til next time." she said as she walked away.

"Indeed, my lady." Dave responded with a slight bow. He then turned and went in to prepare for his trip home.

29

Dave's plane landed on schedule, about two hours before sunset. The flight home had been uneventful, and Dave had gotten in a good nap along the way. He was looking forward to sleeping in his own bed. Vacations are nice, but you never know what you'll end up sleeping on. A long vacation always reminds you that there is, truly, no place like home.

When the plane had stopped and everyone had de-boarded, Dave went and claimed his luggage. He grabbed his bag and was about to go out and get a cab, when he noticed among three chauffeurs was, in uniform, Amanda holding a sign that read 'Winston Smith'. She was scanning the passengers as if she didn't know who she was there for.

Dave walked up to her, "I'm Winston Smith." he said, acting along with her.

Amanda said, "Very good, sir." and took his bag. She led him out to a waiting limo, opened the rear door for him, without making eye contact with him as he got into the back of the limo. She closed the door and then put his bag in the trunk, before climbing in behind the wheel.

As she pulled into traffic, Dave started to ask what was going on, when Amanda shushed him. She was looking intently in the rear view mirror, to see if they were being followed. When she determined they were alone, she took off her hat.

"What's up?" Dave asked, confused.

"There's people after you." Amanda said, "Didn't you get the message?"

"I guess I thought you guys were messing with me." Dave offered.

"We're not sure of who they are, or what they want, but they're serious." Amanda explained, "They tazed Quinn, I think he's pissed, but, you know, sometimes it's hard to tell with him."

"Tazed? Quinn? You can bet he's pissed. And I wouldn't want to be on the receiving end of that thought process." Dave said, still confused.

"I thought they might be at the airport, so I came to get you, Mr. Smith." Amanda explained.

"So, Winston instead of David, you think that fooled them." Dave said, "And you don't think they know who Winston Smith is?" he asked.

"I doubt it, Quinn said they didn't look like the reading type." she said.

“So… where are we going?” Dave asked.

“I’m pretty sure they’re watching your house, so we’re going to my house, or what used to be my Aunt’s house. I always felt comfortable at my Aunt’s, so I stay there most of the time, but I still have my apartment.” Amanda explained, “I’m pretty sure you’ll like it. It’s kinda out of the way, and it borders the National Forest.”

“Sounds nice.” Dave said, thinking about his own bed.

“Anyway, we’ll see if someone’s coming,” she said, “we’re at the end of the road.”

“What if you need the police, won’t it take them a long time to show up?” Dave asked.

“Dave… I have security, no need to worry.” Amanda replied.

“I don’t worry.” Dave said, almost doubting himself. Dave watched out the window as they drove, seeing the density of housing thin out as they went. “I still can’t figure why anyone would be looking for me.” he pondered aloud.

“You don’t owe the government anything, do you?” Amanda asked, stabbing in the dark.

“You think they were feds?” Dave asked, alarmed.

“I didn’t see them, but Quinn said the men were dressed alike, in dark suits, and that they said they were from the ‘Natural Resources Department’, whatever that means.” Amanda explained.

"I had some strange experiences last week, but there's no way anyone could know about that. Besides, if they've been looking for me for two weeks, then it couldn't have anything to do with that." Dave contemplated aloud.

"Wait, what kind of strange experiences?" Amanda asked as she turned off the highway.

"It's kind of a long story, but basically, I got hurt and received help from an unusual source." Dave said, "I'll tell you about it when we get to your house." he added, not wanting to relate the tale from the back seat. "So... a limo, subtle." he said, jokingly.

"I tried to get Joe to drive, but he said he couldn't get involved." Amanda said, "I think it's his wife."

"Knowing Becky, there's no doubt it's her." Dave said, understanding Joe's situation. He respected Becky's sensibilities, and if she didn't want Joe involved, then he probably didn't want to be involved either. She had a sense for these things, Dave had discovered over time.

Amanda appeared to be watching something in the rear-view mirror. She looked like she was getting worried, but then relaxed. "I saw lights following us," Amanda explained, "but it's Emma and Quinn, she blinked her lights to let me know it's her, not to worry."

"I don't worry." Dave said, sounding even more unconvinced.

They turned onto a road that ended at a large gate,

which opened as they approached. Amanda pulled in a ways and stopped to wait for the other car.

A minute later, Dave saw a faded red Datsun 240Z pull up behind them. He could see Quinn, grinning, in the passenger seat, and a cute Asian girl driving, who waved at him.

Amanda pulled out and continued up the driveway, with Emma and Quinn following close behind. As they approached the house, a garage door opened in the side of the hill the house sat atop. She pulled into the garage and Emma pulled up in the front of the house.

Dave and Amanda walked around to the front porch, where Emma and Quinn were waiting. Quinn introduced Emma to Dave and Amanda as they all entered the house.

"This is a trailer." Quinn stated, upon entering.

"Yes, it is." Amanda said, "It's a triple-wide, special ordered. Most people don't recognize that it's a trailer."

"It's done really well." Dave offered.

"My uncle put it in because the property taxes are a fraction of what a house would be." Amanda explained.

"I love the view from the porch." Emma said, looking out over the valley.

"It is a favorite around here." Amanda agreed.

"It's hard not to like a porch with a view." Quinn said, thoughtfully.

"Well, we can all sit out there and watch the sunset, while Dave tells us all about his vacation." Amanda suggested, omitting why Dave was there in the first place.

"Hey, why not." Dave said, figuring someone would tell him something, sometime.

"Come to the kitchen and grab something to drink," Amanda offered, "and we can have dinner, if you'd like."

"I could use a good hamburger, with American cheese and all the fixin's." Dave responded, sounding hungry.

"Of course, you probably haven't eaten in a while." Amanda said as she walked over to an intercom station. She pressed a button and spoke into it, "Vicky." she said, and let go of the button. A moment later a voice came back, "Yes?" the voice said.

"Vicky, you were right, I am going to need some help this evening." Amanda said into the box.

"I'll be right there, dear." Vicky responded.

A couple of minutes later a late middle-aged woman, of eastern European descent, entered the kitchen.

"Everybody, this is " Amanda started, but got cut off.

"Victoria?" Quinn interrupted.

"Yes, but you can call me Vicky." she said, "And you are?" she asked.

"I am Quinn, Quinn Tucker." he replied.

"And we'll see about him calling you Vicky." Dave said, "I'm Dave, nice to meet you, and this young lady is Emma."

"Hello Dave and Emma, and hello to you Quinn Tucker." Vicky said, "And what are we having for dinner?" she asked.

"Burgers for everyone," Amanda said, looking around at everyone, "and if you want more than one, just let her know now." she added as she turned to look at Vicky. "You and Lenny are welcome to join us." Amanda offered, "It's up to you."

"Thank you, I believe we will." Vicky replied. She took everyone's order and started preparing the meal.

Amanda and her guests grabbed their drinks and a folding chair and retired to the front porch.

The sun was about to set, when Quinn raised his beer, "To Dave's safe return." he toasted.

They all raised their drinks and Dave said, "I second that emotion." and took a drink. Everyone sat and watched the sun slip beyond the horizon.

"So, Dave, tell us all about it." Amanda requested.

"Well as Quinn knows, I expected to drive an ambassador's limo to Belize. It didn't turn out quite that way, instead I had to drive the Ambassador's son's van. It smelled like feet and farts, it pulled to the left, it was awful." Dave started, he told them about the checkpoints, and about Dot and Carlos and the trouble from the cartels. He talked about Eli and his girlfriend, and about Wall and his wife and about Nessa. When he got to the part about waking up inside a mountain, they balked in disbelief. He told them about Bob and the bed, the girl and the device she used. When he told them about Bob speaking in tongues, they, all but Quinn, said that it couldn't be true and that it was a step too far.

Dave pulled out his phone, " I recorded some of our conversation." he said as he set his phone to play back the recording.

They all heard Dave speaking English, but whoever he was talking to, wasn't. Dave was being answered by, what seemed to be, random vowel and consonant sounds mixed in with various clicks and whistles.

The girls sat shaking their heads. "And you understood that?" Emma asked.

"Sounded like perfect English to me, at the time." Dave said, "I didn't believe it myself, until I heard the recording."

"What was he saying there?" Amanda asked.

"Sounded like the Aboriginals in the Kalahari." Quinn interjected.

"I thought so too, when the girl spoke." Dave said, "But as I recall, he was telling me about their history."

"So they've been there all this time and no one has found them?" Emma asked in disbelief.

"Oh, they get found occasionally, but the finders don't get to leave, or some of them, to live." Dave answered, matter-of-factly.

"What about you?" Quinn probed, "How did you get away?"

"Apparently it had something to do with a dream the girl had, they had to let me go." Dave replied, "But they told me not to come back."

"So, you fell into a mountain, got healed by and met an ancient race of people, who had a prophecy about you, and they had to let you go." Amanda posed, "Sounds like your average vacation." she added with a bit of sarcasm.

"Oh, it gets better." Dave said. He then related the story of his return to Mexico, and of finding the tablet. "I kind of wish I had kept that." he said, referring to the device.

"Good luck getting through customs with something like that." Quinn said, "You would probably still be in some shit-hole jail, rotting to death." he added, for effect.

"Thanks for the thought, buddy." Dave said, with a smile, "But I knew I wouldn't get it through customs, kind of a gut feeling."

"Speaking of your gut, looks like you've gotten into better shape since you left." Amanda noted.

"I think it was that healing bed thing I was in." Dave said, "My hips and knees feel better too."

"You look healthy," Quinn said, "Even brighter." he added, almost under his breath.

"Thanks, I guess." Dave responded, "So, is anybody going to tell me why I'm here, and not at home?"

"I thought I explained that." Amanda said, "There

are people after you, and we didn't want you to be abducted in the middle of the night never to be heard from again."

"So you think I wouldn't be safe in my own house?" Dave asked.

"Better safe than sorry." Amanda offered, "Besides, we may have more info tomorrow."

"How's that?" Dave asked, unsure of what was going on.

"Emma got a picture of their real license plate, they put fake plates over the real ones when they're watching your house, and I got people working on that." Amanda explained, "We should have something by time work is done, tomorrow.

"There is something wrong about them." Quinn said, as if stating a fact. This made Dave sit up and take it all more serious. He trusted Quinn, and he trusted the man's instincts.

Just then Lenny stepped out onto the porch, carrying a cooler. Which he set down, retrieved a beer from, then sat upon. "The food will be ready shortly," Lenny said, "ten, maybe fifteen, minutes."

"Sounds good, I'm starved!" Dave said, "So, Lenny, what brings you to the table?" he asked, curious.

Lenny got a nostalgic look on his face, "Me and my wife had a re-sale shop in a little village in Hungary, and one day the Burkmeyers walked in. We didn't raise the prices or pressure them into buying stuff, they said that this was the first place they'd been to that didn't try to rip them off. They came back a couple of times, and Mrs. B and my wife became friends, they just hit it off. They came back, about a year later, and things were bad all over, they offered us work in the U.S. My parents had passed, and her family disowned her, for marrying me, so, we came to work for them. It was more like being adopted, to be honest. They always spoke to us as if we were equals, and took care of us, as much as we did them." he explained.

"They're more like family than anything," Amanda said, smiling at Lenny, "I've known them all my life."

"Wait!" Emma interjected, "Did he say Burkmeyer?" she asked. "Like Burkmeyer the programming genius, like the hardware genius, Burkmeyer?"

"Yes, he said Burkmeyer." Amanda stated.

"I have read his books on programming," Quinn said, "the last one still gives me nightmares."

"Her books," Amanda corrected, "my Aunt Beth wrote the programming books. And she held so many copyrights on programs that pretty much any time anyone uses their phone for just about anything, some money comes our way." she explained, "It's not much per action, like one or two thousanths of a cent."

"Yeah, but that's a lot of volume." Dave said, trying to not do math in his head.

"And it's world wide." Amanda said, wide-eyed, "So... if any of you ever need anything, just let me know." she offered.

"Thank you," Dave said, "I'm sure we all appreciate the thought."

"Yes, I'm good." Quinn said, with Emma nodding beside him. "So, the E stood for Elizabeth?" he asked.

"Yeah, that's right," Amanda said, "and the E. Burkmeyer doing the hardware magic was my uncle, Ernest." she explained.

"I always thought it was the same person." Emma said.

"I did also." Quinn said.

"Believe me, they were as one as two people could be." Amanda said, "They each believed the other made them a whole person." She started to tear up as she talked.

"That's amazing." Emma said.

"It also explains the little style differences in their books." Quinn said, "I am thinking her programming methodology influenced his hardware designs."

"That could allow her software to work more efficiently than others." Emma posed, now realizing why her programs were always a little slower than the E.B. programs.

"I wonder if they were even aware of it." Dave said, "Sublties can influence a person without them ever being aware of it."

"Either way, I end up with more money than I could ever spend, and it just keeps coming." Amanda started,

" It goes to the foundation, which doles it out to numerous charities, I also own a bunch of private companies, which employ thousands of people. Those profits go straight to the foundation, and since we don't accept private donations, we can do whatever we want with our money. I get paid by the foundation, it goes into my account." she went on, "It changes the way you think about things, like what's an appropriate tip, when, while you were eating, you earned more than the waitress makes in a month."

"Yeah, that's one hell of a problem to have." Dave said, with a bit of sarcasm. Dave noticed Quinn would glance his way every couple of minutes, he decided to wait for Quinn to bring up whatever was bouncing around in his brain. He knew Quinn well enough that when he was ready, he would bring it up.

Vicky came to the door, "Food's ready." she proclaimed. Everyone got up and headed to the kitchen to fix themselves a plate. When they returned to the porch, they found a small table had been set up for each of the chairs.

Dave got a burger and a salad headed to the far end of the porch to take a seat. Quinn followed and sat down next to him.

"I would like to hear more about the tablet device." Quinn requested.

"I was wondering what was stirring in that brain of yours." Dave said, with a smile.

The others were getting seated when Dave started explaining how he had only been able to turn the device over to one person, and how the colors told you something about the person you were seeing.

"Tell me more about the colors." Quinn requested, while all the rest were listening intently.

Dave explained how Dorothy had discovered that she could determine if someone was an enemy, a friend, or just indifferent. He also told them that some of the colors hadn't been figured out before he left.

Quinn seemed satisfied with everything Dave had explained, he stopped fidgeting and started eating. He found the device fascinating, but he stopped short of telling them that he saw colors surrounding people.

They all sat and ate, while watching the light fade after the sun had set. When they had finished eating, Emma and Quinn prepared to leave.

"See you at work tomorrow." Amanda said to Quinn, "And Emma, it was wonderful to finally put a face to the voice on the phone... nice meeting you."

"Everything set for tomorrow?" Quinn asked.

"As much as possible." Amanda replied.

"I guess I'll find out as it happens." Dave said, not quite sure what was being talked about.

"Don't worry, everything will be fine." Amanda said, reassuring Dave.

"I keep saying 'I don't worry', don't I." Dave responded, with a weak smile.

“I will see you two tomorrow.” Quinn said, as he and Emma walked to her car.

“Later, buddy.” Dave said, “And Emma, it was nice to meet you.”

“Bye, guys.” Amanda said with a wave.

Emma waved back as she started her car. She let it warm up for a minute, then rolled down the driveway and out of sight.

Amanda turned to Dave, “Let me show you to your room.” she said as she opened the door for him. She led him down a hallway to a nice sized bedroom, where his luggage was waiting for him. “I’m at the end of the hall, if you need anything.” she said, with a coy smile.

30

Amanda and Dave arrived at work early Monday morning. The boss' car was the only car in the lot, when they got there. Jim was waiting for them by the timeclock when they entered. "Welcome back." Jim said to Dave, then he cocked his head toward Amanda, "You still working here?" he asked with a smile.

"Still making you money." Amanda replied, with a wink.

Jim shook Dave's hand, "It's too quiet around here when you're gone." he said.

"What about Rob? That wasn't 'quiet'." Amanda said, reminding her boss.

"Oh yeah, Rob got beat up by someone. I heard he owes money to the wrong people." Jim said.

"Nobody told me anything about Rob getting beat up." Dave said, looking at Amanda.

"I'm sorry, I guess I forgot, what with everything else going on." Amanda said, apologetically, "Besides, I don't spend a lot of time thinking about him, anyway."

"How bad was it?" Dave asked, curious.

"It looked... vengeful," Jim said, "like they wanted him to remember it for a long time."

"Wow, that's messed up." Dave said, shaking his head.

"Yeah, well, he's been acting creepy ever since." Amanda said, "Like, he's always watching Quinn and Joe, listening to what we talk about. And when I helped him, he didn't even say 'thank you'."

"That is creepy, he's up to something." Dave agreed.

They had walked to Jim's office while talking, and some of the employees were starting to arrive. It wasn't long before Quinn showed up. Dave was telling Jim about his vacation, leaving the hidden tribes and grave robbing parts out of the telling, when Quinn came to the office door.

"Did I miss anything?" Quinn asked.

"You rarely do." Dave replied. This made Quinn smile.

"Everything looks normal, so far." Quinn said as he turned to go to his work space.

"Good," Jim said, "maybe I'll make some money this week."

Dave and Amanda looked at each other, knowing Quinn was telling them they weren't being watched.... yet.

"We should get to work, too." Amanda said as she

stood up, with Dave following.

"You guys have a good day, ok." Jim said as they left his office. They each went to their cubicles where Amanda started right away, while Dave took a while to get back into his routine.

At lunch time, Amanda, Quinn, Joe and Dave sat together to strategize. Amanda noticed that Rob wasn't in the lunchroom today. He had been there for the last two weeks, and now he wasn't. This made Amanda suspicious. When she mentioned it out loud Joe said he noticed too, but was just glad to be rid of him.

When they were done eating and headed back to their work spaces, Joe noticed Rob coming in from having his lunch outside of the building. Rob avoided eye contact with Joe, so he wouldn't have to talk to him as he passed by his cubicle.

'That was odd.' Joe thought, 'I'll have to tell the gang at break.' he told himself. Which he did, at the water cooler with Dave and Quinn.

At the end of the day Rob left a few minutes early, before everyone started punching out at the time-clock. Joe was the first to notice, then Amanda soon came up and told Dave and Quinn that Rob wasn't in line, and must have left early for some reason.

"That's ok with me," Quinn said, "I'm tired of him always being near."

"I heard that," Amanda agreed, "And I still think he's creepy."

As they walked out into the parking lot, Quinn noticed three large black vehicles that made him suspicious. Before he could say anything to the others, Rob came from around the corner, grabbed Dave's hand and shook it, saying "It's good to have you back." He then dropped Dave's hand and proceeded to his car, where he got in and started it, but didn't drive away.

"That was weird." Amanda said, "Uh oh." she added when she saw several men exiting the black vehicles and head their way.

Dave looked up and saw the men coming towards them, "At least he didn't kiss me." he said, sounding relieved at how he was betrayed. He looked past the men and saw Lenny, Emma, and an older Chinese man coming up behind them.

Dave stopped, with Amanda by his side, and Quinn took one more step past him. Joe came up from behind and stood next to Dave.

"Hey, Joey." Quinn said, without turning around.

"Hey guys, what's up?" Joe asked, as the men in dark suits formed a semi-circle in front of them.

Quinn recognized Agent Johnson and his partner with the tazer, but the other six men were new to him.

"David Smith, I have been tasked with bringing you in." Agent Johnson said, trying to sound official.

"You got a warrant?" Dave asked, realizing now how serious this was.

"Please, if you would, just come with us." the agent said.

"Or what?" Quinn asked, defiantly.

"This is trouble you don't want." the agent with the tazer said, sounding threatening.

"Well, you can all go fuck yourselves," Dave said, "I ain't going anywhere with you."

The agent with the tazer did a quick draw, to shoot Quinn, but a strike on the agents elbow from behind caused him to shoot one of the other agents. Agent Johnson then swung at Quinn, who grabbed him and in the course of putting him to the ground, tried the new move Emma had shown him. The agents face crashed hard into his knee and he went unconscious, with a broken nose.

Emma and her father took care of three of the agents, while Quinn handled tazer guy and Lenny and Joe kept the others at bay.

With five of the eight agents down, the other three backed off until Dave and his friends had passed, then they collected their wounded and retreated. Dave and his friends watched as the three SUV's pulled away and drove out of sight.

"You were right, Emma." Quinn said, "It was kind of ironical, watching his face and his knee trying to occupy the same space at the same time."

Emma smiled at Quinn, then turned to Dave, "I would like you to meet my father, Jon Cheung," she said, turning to her father, "Father, this is Dave Smith."

"Nice to meet you, and thanks for the help." Dave said, offering his hand.

"When my daughter asked me if I would like to practice what I teach, how could I say no." Jon said, shaking Dave's hand while giving his daughter a hug from the side.

"How can you ever say no to your little girl." Dave said, smiling.

"You must have one." Jon said.

"Yes, I do," Dave replied, "she's all growed up and moved away."

Jon looked at Dave and figured he must be older than he looked, some people were lucky that way, he thought.

Dave turned to Joe, "You are not to get involved." Dave said, "That's what I heard you were told."

"Becky won't fault me for standing with a friend." Joe explained, "Besides, Lenny here, did most of the work." Joe smiled and gave Lenny a pat on the back.

"I'm just here to help." Lenny said, looking Amanda's way.

Dave looked over to Quinn, "Ironical, huh. I like that." Dave said, "Where'd you come up with that one?" he asked. Quinn's face lit up with a grin, Dave knew instantly that Quinn got it from Emma.

"You're coming back to my place." Amanda said to Dave, "You are not safe at home alone."

“I think you may be right.” Dave said, feeling an apprehension he was not used to.

“I gotta get going.” Joe said, as he turned towards his car.

“Thanks, again.” Dave said, with a wave.

Joe got home and found his wife waiting for him. “Look what the kids found on the internet.” Becky said, pointing to the screen where the parking lot fight was being replayed. “You’re not getting involved, are you?” she asked.

“Just helping a friend.” Joe replied as he gave his wife a hug.

Back at the parking lot, Amanda and Dave were about to leave when Emma stopped them. “I want to check something, if you don’t mind.” Emma said, as she took out her phone. She activated an app, which was a frequency analyzer, and walked around Amanda’s car. She stopped at the rear passenger side wheel well. She swept her phone back and forth a few times, then reached into the wheel well and pulled out a small electronic device.

“May I have that?” Quinn requested.

Emma handed the device to Quinn, then turned to Amanda, “I had a feeling they would try something like that.” she explained.

“These guys aren’t stopping, are they?” Amanda said, starting to sound pissed off.

“Doesn’t look like it.” Emma said as Quinn walked up to her.

"I put it on the car pool van," Quinn said, "I'm sure they'll love tracking that."

Jon Cheung walked over and gave his daughter a hug and a kiss on top of her head, "I've got to go." he said, then looking in Amanda's car, "Nice meeting both of you, though I wish it had been under better circumstances." he offered.

"Likewise." Amanda said with a wave. After he left, Amanda turned to Emma, "Your Dad is pretty cool." she noted.

"Yeah, who would've guessed." Emma said, after seeing a side of her father she had never seen. "I'll follow you to your place in a few minutes, I want to sweep my car for bugs. too." she explained.

"I'll take it slow, so you can catch up." Amanda said, "Call me if you see anything suspicious along the way."

"You got it." Emma said as Amanda and Dave pulled away.

Quinn looked around the parking lot, "Robart has left." he said, "I wonder if he saw you get out of your car?" he asked Emma.

"I was out of my car before anyone came out, by at least five minutes." Emma said, "I was over talking with my Dad."

"That's good." Quinn said, relieved, as he scanned the parking lot one more time. Satisfied that there weren't any bad guys around, Quinn sat down in the passenger seat while Emma went around her car, checking it with her phone.

"It's clean." Emma declared as she sat down in the drivers seat, "On to Amanda's." she said as she pulled out of the parking lot.

The drive to Amanda's was uneventful and Quinn saw nothing that would raise any concern. They arrived at Amanda's several seconds after Amanda and Dave reached the front gate. The two cars entered and the gate closed behind them.

They were walking up to the front porch when Dave's phone rang. Dave looked at his phone, "It's the boss, I'll be right in." he said, as he took the call on the porch.

The others went on into Amanda's house. "Can I get you guys anything, a drink or something?" Amanda asked.

"I'll take a beer, thank you." Emma said.

"I'm ok." Quinn answered.

"I'll be right back." Amanda said, as she turned and went into the kitchen. She returned a minute later with three beers and an unopened bottle of water. she set the water down next to Quinn. "Just in case." Amanda said to Quinn. Quinn nodded and smiled in response. He appreciated the fact that Amanda hadn't opened the bottle for him.

"Those guys were bigger than I expected." Emma said, as Amanda handed her a beer. "Thanks." she said as she took the beer.

"That just means their face has more time to pick up speed before it hits their knee." Quinn said, "Ironical, huh." he said, grinning at Emma.

"You two are something else!" Amanda said, shaking her head, "Hard to believe you've only known each other for a month."

The front door opened and Dave came in and sat down behind the unopened beer. "That was Jim," Dave started, "he said the police showed up about five minutes after we left. They talked to him and a few people that were in the parking lot when it happened. They couldn't do anything, with no-one to press charges and no-one to charge. But the whole thing can be seen on the internet. We talked and agreed that I should settle this before I return to work." He explained. Dave paused to think a moment, then looked at Amanda, "Could you box up my personal stuff and bring it to me?" he asked.

"Of course," Amanda said, "but I think I should drive a different car, one they haven't seen."

"Sounds like a good idea to me." Quinn said, "By the way, how many cars do you have?" he asked.

"I have four, not counting the limo," Amanda replied, "I'll take my Aunt's car, it's a sedan, very inconspicuous."

"On second thought, ask Joe if he would drop it off on my porch." Dave said, "I don't want them focusing on you."

"I think it's too late for that." Amanda noted.

"You don't want Robart shaking your hand," Quinn said, "They already know Joey lives by David's."

"Rob is one of the bad guys." Emma chimed in.

"We don't know why he did what he did." Dave said, playing the devil's advocate.

"Maybe we should find out!" Quinn suggested, with emphasis.

"Give it a try," Dave said, "see what you can get out of him, but don't hound him, ok."

"I'm not good at subtle." Quinn stated.

"We'll work on him together, ok." Amanda offered. A light came on, on the intercom, and Amanda walked over and pressed the button.

"The report is here, it just arrived." a voice said through the intercom.

"That sounded like Lenny." Quinn said.

"Bring it up, would you please." Amanda requested.

A minute later came a knock on the back door, and Amanda went to the door to retrieve the report. "I've been waiting for this," Amanda said, "it should tell us who we're dealing with." She sat down and opened the manila envelope and pulled out some papers. She scanned the report quickly, then went back over a few spots a bit slower.

"Well, the SUV's were leased by a 'Martin Services', it's a security company owned by the same guy that owns that 'Ctag DNA corporation." Amanda revealed from the report.

"Ctag.... Did you say Ctag?" Dave asked, "That's the company I sent my DNA to, to find out my genetic history." he said as the color drained from his face.

"I knew it was a bad idea." Quinn said.

"They have your DNA, too." Emma said to Quinn.

"I didn't need to be reminded." Quinn said, with a smile for Emma.

"They must have figured out what my blood can do," Dave said, "or at least suspect."

"I am thinking, they know." Quinn said matter-of-factly.

"Ok, they know," Dave said, "But now we know who they are, and that's gotta be worth something. Right?"

"We need more on them." Amanda said.

"Agreed." Dave said, as he looked over at Emma, who was deep into her laptop. "I think we're about to find out."

"I'm in," Emma said, looking up from her computer, "What do we need?" she asked.

"Names, addresses, location of properties, everything." Amanda requested.

"Everything could take a while." Emma said.

"Start with the goons from the parking lot." Dave suggested.

"Right, we may need some leverage next time we come up against them." Quinn said, moving in behind Emma to get a better view of the screen.

"Ok, H.R. it is." Emma said, tapping on the keyboard,

"let's see, here we go, security department, wow... they have a lot of people doing security. Separate overseas from domestic, focus on local workers... here, we got a dozen and a half men that work mostly for Ctag."

"How much security does a DNA company need anyway?" Dave asked, rhetorically.

"Ok, I'm copying everything I can get from 'Martin services', we can sort it out later." she explained, as she inserted a memory stick into her computer. She tapped a few more keys and files started flowing across the screen.

"The goons from the parking lot all work for Martin Services." Quinn said, as he watched the screen over Emma's shoulder.

"You sure? Those are going by pretty fast." Amanda asked.

Quinn just nodded as he kept watching the screen.

31

Agent Johnson came to, with a start, in the back of his SUV, he looked around and recognized that they were in the strip-mall parking lot where they had met prior to going to get Smith. He exited the vehicle to find Agent Brown had taken charge, even though he couldn't use his right arm. "What happened?" he asked, still dazed.

"It seems they were ready for us." Agent Brown said, "I got a kick in the balls and a dislocated shoulder, but I probably deserved it for tazering the holy shit out of Wilder, over there."

"The last thing I remember is my hand getting crushed and my knee coming at my face." Agent Johnson said, as he prepared to blow his nose.

"STOP!" Agent Brown said, "Don't do that."

"What?" Agent Johnson asked, still readying to blow his nose.

"If you blow your nose, your eyes'll swell shut!"

Agent Brown warned.

"Oh, right." Agent Johnson said, and began wiping off the blood from his face.

"We were surrounded," Agent Brown said, "and we didn't even know it. After you went down, Quinn tried to do the same thing to me. When I saw my knee I tried to stop myself, that's when I felt my shoulder pop. My grip locked on the trigger and my balls landed on my heel, hard. And it took less than a second. What the hell is going on?" he asked, rhetorically.

"This is fucked up." Agent Johnson surmised, "What the hell are we going to tell the boss?"

"I would recommend the truth." Agent Brown said, "Dhu has a way of finding things out, I've noticed."

"Ain't that the truth." Agent Johnson agreed. "So, where are we?" he asked.

"I sent the big guys off with the tracker, to find that blonde's place, and the others I sent back to their motel to get cleaned up. They'll be waiting for your instructions." Agent Brown explained.

"Good enough." Agent Johnson said, "Now, let's have a look at that shoulder." Agent Johnson held Agent Brown's left shoulder against his chest and raised Brown's right arm several inches from his side. He felt Brown wince when he did this. "Hold it there." he instructed, as he put both hands on Agent Brown's right shoulder and pulled him into his chest.

"FUCK!" slipped loudly from Agent Brown, as he

felt his shoulder pop back into it's socket. He moved his arm around slowly, "Thanks." he said with a grimace.

"Anytime." Agent Johnson said, rubbing his hand which was beginning to swell. "Now the hard part, I gotta call the boss." He took out his phone and called Mr. Dhu. He walked around the SUV as he related the events to his boss.

Edgar listened intently to Agent Johnson, Getting madder by the minute. He didn't let Johnson know how he felt, but he was ready to explode. After telling Johnson to return to the office, he hung up and said aloud, "Son of a bitch... what the hell are we dealing with?" He took in some deep breaths, to calm himself. 'Matthews ain't gonna like this' he thought. He was having a moment of regret for selling his business. He did not like having to report to anyone, which was why he started his own business in the first place. But, the first two years drained his resources, not enough capital to keep it going until they got established. That was when his brother introduced him to Martin Matthews. He sold the business, but was well paid to stay and run it. Mr. Matthews created an International Division, and regularly sent people to be hired, which made him more money than he felt he deserved, but less than his girl could find ways to spend it.

Most of the time he was left alone, but every now and then Mr. Matthews stuck his nose in, and this was one of those times. He knew he would have to call his boss and explain the fuck-up. 'This is not going to be pleasant, best to get it over with.' he thought.

He called Mr. Matthews and brought him up to date with the situation. The call lasted much longer than he thought necessary, and he could feel himself getting worked up again. When Mr. Matthews was done, he called his brother in Las Vegas to vent.

The Dhu brothers had been born and raised in Baltimore, to immigrant parents. They grew up fighting on the streets, and honed their skills in the military. John spent ten years in the Marine Corps, Recon Company, And Edgar did eight years in the Army, Special Forces Unit. They both left the service after their parents had been killed during a robbery. They found the lowlifes responsible, and quietly made them disappear. Then they headed west to make a life for themselves. They started the security company together, but John left after the first year, out of money.

32

Amanda arrived at work at the same time as several others, she didn't see Rob's car in the lot so she walked in with the others. 'Safety in numbers, in case I'm being watched.' she thought. She went straight to the boss' office and knocked on the door, which was open, as usual.

Jim looked up from his desk, "Uh oh, here it comes." he said, shaking his head.

"I know, I'm sorry," Amanda said, "but Friday will be my last day." She told him what they had found out, and about Rob's part in what happened.

"Is Dave coming back?" Jim asked, suspecting what the answer would be.

"I can't speak for him, but I don't think so." she told him, "I'll have him call you."

"Thanks," Jim said, "you've been a good employee since the day you started, we're going to miss you."

"Please don't, you'll make me cry." Amanda said, as

she started to tear up. "Please, don't tell anyone, I don't want Rob to find out."

"You have my word." Jim assured her, "We'll talk more later."

Amanda smiled as she turned to head to her cubicle, she went by way of Rob's workspace, "Did those bonus discs help?" she asked the back of his head.

"It wasn't enough." Rob replied, without turning around.

Amanda stood there for a few moments, hoping for a 'thanks anyway', but Rob didn't say anything else. She walked away shaking her head, 'what an asshole' she thought. As she reached her cubicle, she saw Quinn approaching his workspace, she gave him a quick nod, which got a smile out of him as he entered his cubicle.

Amanda took her mid-morning break and went to confer with Joe. They made plans to clean out Dave's desk at lunch. Then she headed to Quinn's corner and told him she was too mad at Rob to talk without punching him in the face, and that he would have Rob all to himself. She couldn't tell how he felt about it, by looking at him. "You ok with that?" she asked.

Quinn smiled and nodded, "OK? Yeah." he replied.

"Remember, subtle." she said, trying to keep a straight face.

"Practice makes perfect." Quinn said, with a grin.

"You make me want to be there," Amanda said, "But I'm still too mad for that."

Mid-day came and Amanda watched Quinn follow Rob into the lunchroom. She grabbed the box she brought from home and met Joe in Dave's cubicle.

"Not much here." Joe said, looking around.

"You're right, I think I can handle it." she said, "You should go and keep a leash on Quinn."

Joe chuckled, "You may be right." he said as he headed off to the lunchroom.

"Catch ya later." Amanda said to the empty doorway. "Now, let's see what we have here." she said aloud, to no-one. She sat down in front of the desk and decided to start from the bottom, up.

The first two drawers were office supplies, things she recognized from the supply closet. The small drawer on top had an unopened bag of circus peanuts, the orange marshmallow things, that had been popular in the middle of the last century. She also found a Polaroid picture of herself. She remembered when Dave took that shot of her, she had been there for about three months when he asked if he could take a picture of her. She agreed, and went into a cutsie pose in front of the window. Looking at the picture, she could see her breast silhouetted from behind, 'I'm holding up pretty well' she thought, 'and at least someone appreciates me'.

Amanda finished collecting Dave's personal items and brought the box to Joe's cubicle. She set the box on his seat so that it couldn't be seen by anyone passing by. That done, she returned to her own space and ate the bagged lunch she had brought from home.

Quinn followed Rob into the lunchroom and got his lunch from the refrigerator right after Rob. Rob went and found an empty table, as usual, and Quinn walked up a moment later and sat down with him.

Joe entered the lunchroom just as Quinn was about to sit down at Rob's table. He went and sat down at an adjacent table, so he could listen in.

"Oh, great." Rob said, not looking happy.

"You were in the van." Quinn said.

"Excuse me?" Rob responded.

"Robart, you were in the van the day I got tazered." Quinn stated, "Start talking." he said, sounding a bit disturbed.

This was the first time Rob had heard anything remotely resembling emotion in Quinn's speech, he found it unnerving, almost scary.

"I didn't have a choice." Rob said, "I had a gambling debt, these guys bought the note. And they're not as easy going as the people I owed at first." he explained, looking lost.

"You must owe a lot." Quinn said, musingly.

Rob glared at Quinn for a moment, "They said I had to pay in full, or else help them and work off what I owe." he said, "Seemed like a no-brainer, I didn't have the money, so...."

"How did they find you?" Quinn asked.

"I asked them that." Rob said, "They said they saw Joe drop you off, then they followed him, first to his house, then to work. Then they checked up on anyone he talked to, lucky me."

"Joey, you remember that day?" Quinn asked, without turning.

"That day I said I felt like I was being watched, yeah I remember." Joe replied.

"Looks like your instincts are serving you well." Quinn said. He looked Rob in the eyes for a moment, "A simple 'thank you' could have gotten you out of all of this." Quinn stated.

Rob felt like his brain was pouring out when he looked into Quinn's eyes, he quickly looked away. "Oh, right, just thank someone and my problems are gone." Rob said sarcastically, "That's how it works."

"It works on more than one level." Quinn said, "Have you ever thanked anybody?" he asked.

"Screw you, dude." Rob said, annoyed. "I don't have to put up with this."

"I guess you have yourself to thank, Robart." Quinn said, "Wouldn't you agree, Joey?"

"Hey, don't bring me into this." Joe said, waving his hands in front of him. "I tried to be nice, and he treats me like I'm not good enough to befriend."

Rob looked over at Joe, "But.." slipped out of his mouth before he could stop it.

"I know, I'm black." Joe said, proudly.

"I didn't mean..." Rob said, embarrassed.

"It's cool, I know where I stand with you and I adjust appropriately." Joe said with a smile.

"I'm done." Rob said abruptly, as he got up and left the room.

"You know what's funny," Joe said, as they watched Rob leave, "I used to catch hell from the other kids, because I chose to speak well. They said I wasn't black enough." he related.

"Kind of ironical." Quinn said, straight faced.

At the end of the day, Amanda covertly watched Rob leave work and head to the parking lot. She watched as Rob opened his car door, reach in for something, and then stood on the running board of his car and scanned the parking lot with the device he retrieved. After a minute he got in his car and drove away.

When she was sure it was clear, she went to her car and drove home. At home she related what had transpired at work that day, and what Quinn had found out about Rob.

When she told him about Rob looking over the parking lot, Dave lit up. "It must have been him that put the tracker on your car." he said, making the connection. "You still have your place in town, right?" he asked, formulating a plan.

"We can drop off your sedan near there, and tomorrow you drive your car and after work, go to your place in town, park, sneak over to your sedan and come home." Dave suggested, "Let them watch an empty apartment."

"That's a good start to a plan," Amanda said, "but I think I can improve on it in a few places."

Just then Dave's phone rang, "It's Quinn." Dave said, as he answered the call. "Hey man, what's up?" he said into the phone. After a minute of listening, he said "Thanks man, I forgot all about it...ok then, bye." He hung up and looked at Amanda.

"That was Quinn," Dave said, "He went to my place, to check on the plants, and he put the box of stuff inside. He also said my house is still being watched."

"He never ceases to amaze me." Amanda said, "He's a good person to have on your side."

"I couldn't agree more." Dave said, thinking about the connection they had developed over the years.

Amanda got up and went to the kitchen and returned with two beers, she handed one to Dave then sat down and opened hers. Dave opened his beer and reached out with it to touch bottles with Amanda.

"Cheers." she said as she touched bottles with Dave.

"Skol." he said, as they both sipped their beer.

"We have to test your powers." Amanda said, changing the subject.

"It's maybe one, not plural, and I'm not sure you can call it a power." Dave replied.

"You know what I mean," Amanda said, "we gotta go somewhere old."

"We got Chaco Canyon and the Pueblo cliff dwellings, both within a half-days drive." Dave said, "I've always thought those places were a lot older than we've been told.

"We should bring Quinn and Emma," Amanda suggested, "just in case, you know."

"I don't think Quinn would let me go without him." Dave said, "But, yeah, I agree." he added thoughtfully.

"Have you heard anything from Ctag?" Amanda asked.

"I collected my mail today," Dave started, "there was a letter from them asking me to come in for an interview. I think they sent it before all the shit started."

"Maybe they didn't like being ignored." Amanda said, "They didn't know you were away."

"That could be," Dave said, "but whatever the reason, they started this and I don't think they're going to stop."

The next morning Amanda drove her car to work, and parked where she regularly parked. She didn't want Rob to have to think.

At lunch, Quinn came to her cubicle to discuss the phone call he received, this morning, from Dave. He also related his encounter with the people who were watching Dave's house.

After he spoke with Dave, yesterday afternoon, he went onto the front porch and waved to the men watching the house. He then walked down to the SUV and knocked on the passenger side window. When the window was lowered, Quinn recognized both men and identified them by name and home address. They raised the window and drove off.

The phone call today was about leaving town for the weekend. Quinn said he had called Emma, and that they were both in.

At the end of the workday, Amanda had her phone in her hand, as most people do, while she walked to her car. Only this time she had turned on the app that Emma had downloaded to her phone. It was the frequency analyzer app, and she was seeing a spike right where Emma said there would be, and it was getting stronger as she approached her car.

She got in and drove to her apartment in town, where Lenny and Vicky were waiting. She parked, went into the building and up to her apartment, and exchanged keys with Lenny. She left Lenny and Vicky at the apartment, to make it appear that she was there, and went out through the rear entrance. She found her sedan near-by and drove away from her old place before heading to the highway and home.

Friday morning Amanda drove the sedan to work and parked far from her normal spot. She looked around and didn't see Rob's car anywhere, this gave her a good feeling about the day.

She worked through the morning, then at lunch she went to Jim's office and gave him a hug before leaving.

Quinn and Joe trapped Rob in his cubicle with questions and meaningless conversation, so he wouldn't see her leave. She didn't have to box anything up because she had been bringing her stuff home a little at a time for the last two weeks. All she had to grab was the nameplate from the outside of her cubicle. She grabbed Dave's nameplate, also, on her way out, it seemed unusually heavy for a cubicle nameplate. She dropped it into her purse, then headed home from here for the last time.

About an hour after lunch Quinn was knocking on the boss' door.

"Come on in." Jim said.

Quinn entered the office and closed the door behind him.

"Oh no, not you too." Jim said, looking worried.

"Not me too, what?" Quinn asked.

"Leaving my employment." Jim explained.

"No, I just came to tell you I'm leaving early today." Quinn said, "And I would like two days of vacation, for Monday and Tuesday."

"You've never taken vacation, this must be important." Jim said, relieved.

"Just a feeling I have." Quinn said.

"Take all the time you want, just come back, please." Jim said.

"That is my intent, James." Quinn said, as he got up to leave.

"Stay out of trouble." Jim said to Quinn's back.

'That's like putting the whammy on it.' Quinn thought, as he left. He went to the parking lot where Emma was waiting to drive them to Amanda's.

Rob had gotten a call from his handler, earlier that day, telling him that Amanda's car hadn't moved and asked if she was there at work. He responded that she was there and assured them that he would find out what she was driving by the end of the workday. He left work fifteen minutes early, and sat in his car until the parking lot was empty. He didn't understand how he could have missed her, these people were not going to be happy. This was the third time he had tried to find out where Amanda was staying, and the third time he had failed.

33

Emma, with Quinn, pulled up to Amanda's house to find a full size, military style, Hummer parked outside of the garage. "Very cool!" Emma said, as she exited her vehicle. She walked around the truck, looking over, under, and occasionally crawling upon.

Amanda and Dave came out onto the front porch. "Would you like to drive it?" Amanda asked Emma.

"Oh yeah," Emma said, "it's been a dream of mine." she explained.

"Dave and I have already been ok'd to drive it, but all three of us are on the insurance." Amanda said, "Come on, I'll give you the rundown,..you drive."

Dave and Quinn watched as the ladies climbed into the Hummer. "Emma looks even smaller in that thing." Dave said, watching them.

Quinn snorted a laugh, "I never thought of her as small, until now." he said, smiling.

"Still, I wouldn't want to piss her off." Dave said,

"I'm pretty sure she could kick my ass."

"Mine, too." Quinn said, nodding.

"Yeah, and it takes a tazer to stop you." Dave said, poking at Quinn. They both had a good laugh as they watched Emma drive out of sight behind the house. A few minutes later the truck reappeared and Emma seemed much more confident behind the wheel. She pulled the truck back into its original parking spot.

"Once you get used to where the wheels are under you, it's pretty easy to drive." Emma said, climbing down from the cab.

Amanda came around the truck, she looked at Dave, "She's pretty good!" she said, with a smile.

"Excellent." Dave said as he turned and slapped Quinn on the back lightly and proceeded into the house. The others followed him in, and they made plans for their weekend adventure over dinner, along with a few beers.

After dinner, Quinn went to his bag and retrieved a metal mint box. He handed the box to Dave, "I had Joey roll them," Quinn said, as Dave opened the box, "I kept tearing the papers."

Dave opened the box to find it packed with joints, "Thank you, to all involved." Dave said, smiling, "I could use an attitude adjustment." He pulled out one of the joints and looked over at Amanda, to get an ok before he lit up.

"Who do you think bought it?" Amanda said,

striking a lighter for Dave.

Dave leaned in to get a light, and after a few puffs Quinn's hand went up to take the next hit. After his turn he passed the joint to Emma, who was on her third beer, she passed it, without hitting it, to Amanda.

"I'm fine with one or the other, but rarely both," Emma said, "both puts me to sleep."

"I'm the same way," Quinn said, "but it's pretty rare that I drink." he explained, as he was passed the joint from Amanda.

"I don't think I've ever seen you take a drink." Dave said to Quinn.

"I had a beer at the first poker game I attended." Quinn reminded Dave.

"Oh yeah, I remember now, you didn't say more than a half-dozen words all night." Dave said, smiling.

"Alcohol makes me quiet," Quinn said, "unlike the alternative."

"I'd rather have you talking." Emma said, "I learn things when you talk."

"Don't we all." Amanda said, nodding in agreement.

"In that case, would you like to hear a poem I wrote?" Quinn asked, "It's my first."

"How could we say no?" Dave replied, looking at the ladies, who were nodding in agreement.

"I am thinking it would be better if you read it," Quinn said, as he stood up, "but here goes;

Some walk

Some fly
Some talk
All die " he recited.

Dave was taking a sip of beer when Quinn gave his reading, and he tried his best to keep from spraying beer across the room, with limited success.

Emma looked at him wide eyed, "Were you drinking when you wrote that?" she asked, blinking once.

Amanda laughed at Emma's remark, "Really, a bit terse, wouldn't you say?" she asked, playfully.

"At least it rhymes." Dave said, still wiping up.

Quinn tried his best to hide his smile and act defensive, "How comprehensive can you get with eight words?" he asked.

"And still rhyme." Dave threw in.

"It does cover quite a bit." Emma said, thoughtfully.

"And it rhymes." Dave said. This made Quinn break out in a huge grin.

Amanda smacked Dave on the back of his head, "I was expecting something more..."

"Flowery?" Quinn asked.

"Not exactly," Amanda replied, "but certainly something more...verbose."

"I had to start somewhere." Quinn said, straight faced.

Emma leaned over and gave Quinn a hug. Dave noticed that Quinn didn't flinch when Emma touched him, a vast improvement in Quinn's tolerance.

"Well, if we're to get going before sun-up we should think about getting some sleep." Dave suggested.

"You're right," Amanda said, "everyone know where their room is?" she asked.

"First door on the right." Quinn responded.

"First door on the left." Emma chimed in.

"Second door on the right is the bathroom," Amanda said, "across from Dave. I'm at the end of the hall if you need anything."

"Please, no mistakes," Dave said, "I don't need to be peed on in the middle of the night." he joked.

"Or worse." Quinn added.

Dave stopped in his tracks, "Why would you even say that?" he asked Quinn.

"Going for a laugh, I guess." Quinn answered, hearing Amanda and Emma giggle.

"Good night, everyone." Amanda said, then turned to Emma, "You can use the master-bath, in my room." she offered.

"Thanks, I'll be right in." Emma said as she opened the door to her room.

"Good night, ladies." Dave and Quinn chimed, as they went to their respective rooms.

About ten minutes after it sounded like everybody had settled, Amanda decided to go see Dave. She realized how much she cared for him when he was on vacation, and she had been trying to get his interest since he had been back. She knew he liked her, especially after finding the picture, but couldn't figure out why he never hit on her. She was going to find out tonight. She quietly opened her door and stepped into the hallway, only to look up and see Emma doing the same.

Emma smiled a gave a little wave as she crossed the hall and tapped on Quinn's door.

Amanda walked by and went to the kitchen to get a bottle of water, as if this had been her intent all along. When she got back to the hallway, it was empty. She stopped at Dave's door, and after a short moment of doubt, she tapped lightly.

The door opened almost instantly, "I thought I heard someone out there." Dave said quietly.

"May I come in?" Amanda asked.

"You are always welcome." Dave said looking at her. He could tell she was wearing nothing but her robe. She entered his room, and when he had closed the door, she stepped over to him and gave him a hug. Not a hug like you give to family, but one pressing her pelvis into his. Her robe was open enough that she could feel her naked flesh rubbing him through the thin fabric of his sleepwear. She could feel him starting to get an erection.

Dave initially returned Amanda's hug, but when he started to get excited he pulled back. "What are you doing?" he asked, confused.

"Proposing, I do believe." she replied, pulling him close again.

"Look, I'm flattered." Dave started.

"I know you like me," Amanda interrupted, "I can tell." she said as she wiggled against him.

"There's something you don't know about me." Dave said.

"What, that you're old?" Amanda replied, "Like, old enough to be my father."

"Who told you that?" Dave asked, stunned.

"Chrissy told me." she said.

"You know Chrissy?" he asked.

"Poker game, about three years ago." Amanda said, "We just hit it off, and we keep in touch. When I expressed an interest in you, she told me that you two had dated until she found out how old you were. She said she saw a photo of a woman on the table next to your bed and she asked if it was an old girlfriend." she explained.

"I remember that," he said, "When I said it was my daughter, she said my daughter looked older than her. That was the end of our dating." Dave recounted.

"Well, I don't care about age," Amanda started, "look, I'm over thirty, and I can't have kids. I have the same thing my Aunt had, it's a genetic thing that won't let my eggs 'ripen' and become viable. So, I figure you already have a kid, so that won't be a problem, plus I really like you. I can't think of anyone I would rather spend my time with." she finished, putting her head against his chest.

“Wow!” Dave said, head spinning. He had always had a thing for Amanda, but didn't think she would want an old man for an old man. “I never thought I would ever get married again.” he said, smiling.

“So...” She asked, pulling her head back to look him in the eyes.

“So...I accept,” Dave replied, “but we still have to wait until we’re married to have sex.” he explained.

“No problem.” Amanda said, pushing Dave onto the bed.

34

Agent Johnson sat at his desk, Friday morning, reading the reports from his team and wondering how things could have gone so wrong. He had spent six hours in surgery, getting his hand repaired after his last encounter with Quinn Tucker. Now his hand was in a traction device that looked like some sort of medival torture machine. His eyes were still black, after a week, and in the week since he had reset his nose, he was finally starting to breathe through it.

And now, reading the E-mails from his squad, one failure after another. They haven't found Smith, haven't located where the blonde lives, which were probably connected, and now it appears that they've been hacked. It was the only way to explain how Tucker could have the names and addresses of his men.

He called the I.T. department and told them of the incursion, and instructed them to see if they could get anything on the hacker. He figured that there must be some kind of electronic trail to follow, or maybe a signature, or something.

After speaking to I.T., Agent Johnson called his boss and gave him the information he had gleaned from all the reports he had received. Mr. Dhu was not happy, this thing was getting expensive and not producing any results, and now he had to call Mr. Matthews with more bad news.

After the call, which went better than he expected, Edgar went to Agent Johnson's office to see the reports for himself. It was the first time he had seen Agent Johnson, face to face, since his release from the hospital.

"Holy shit!" Edgar said, upon seeing Johnson's face and hand. "How in the world did you let someone do that to you?" he asked.

"You can see it on the internet," Johnson replied, "I've been studying it for a week, and I still don't know."

"Pull it up." Edgar requested, "I want to see these people."

Agent Johnson pulled up the video of the attempt at bringing in Smith. Edgar studied the fight for a couple of minutes, replaying it in slow-motion over and over. Edgar noticed Agent Johnson seemed uncomfortable, "Looks like they had your number from the start," Edgar said, "How's that, I wonder?"

Agent Johnson stared at the floor, "I think it was the hacker, he must have seen my E-mails." he admitted.

"Oh yeah, the hacker." Edgar said, "It doesn't look good for a security company to get hacked."

"It doesn't look good to have a security guard leaving a nose print on his knee, either." Agent Johnson said, "I don't like not looking good."

Edgar smiled, "We have got to get on top of this," he said, "find out who those other people are, the ones that helped him."

"Already working on that," Agent Johnson said, "Though, it's not going so well, yet."

"Bring in that snitch," Edgar suggested, "he might be able to help."

"That would certainly be a change." Agent Johnson said, "You'll see when you read the reports."

"Forward them to me," Edgar said, "I'll read them as soon as I'm finished talking to I.T."

"Would you be wanting to talk to Bott when he gets here?" Agent Johnson asked, not sure how involved in this case his boss wanted to get.

"I'll let you know after I read the reports." Edgar said, as he left Johnson's office to go visit the I.T. department.

After fifteen minutes of thoroughly excoriating the I.T. department, to their repeated claims that they could find no evidence that they had been hacked, Edgar went to his office to calm down.

The chance of him relaxing dwindled away when he started reading the reports. The first report was about the fiasco in the parking lot. It had been submitted by Agent Brown, it was well written and very detailed. He was thinking Brown had some potential.

The second one detailed how two of his men spent an hour following a car-pool van. The third report told of following the blonde to her apartment, seeing lights being turned on and off, seeing her shadow in the windows, and of her never leaving, despite the fact that she was at work the next day.

The final report revealed that they had lost track of Smith and the blonde, and everything seemed to be going back to its normal routine. Until the men watching the house were identified. That last part really bothered him, 'How did they get their names and addresses' he asked himself. There were only two possible answers, either they were hacked or someone talked.

He couldn't believe any of his men would rat out their co-workers, they were all well paid and seemed happy to be there. Most were happy to have legitimate jobs, after being released from prison. He knew, in his heart, that his men were loyal to him. That left being hacked, and since whoever got in and out without leaving a trace, it meant that he had skills.

He wondered if he had accidently run afoul of some kind of organization. That would explain how they seemed to be one step ahead of his team the whole way. All he could do now was wait, and hope for a break.

Saturday, Rob drove to Martin Services, in Utah,

arriving around noon. It wasn't long before Agent Johnson determined that Bott wasn't going to be much help. They had a first name for the blonde, Amanda, but no names for the other three in the parking lot.

Agent Johnson called Mr. Dhu and informed him that talking to Bott would only piss him off. Edgar acquiesced to his agent, 'No break here' he thought.

Sunday morning Edgar woke to find he had an E-mail from his brother in Las Vegas.

35

Emma was disoriented when she woke up, she looked around the room and saw her bag on the chair. She knew she was in her room at Amanda's, but the last thing she remembered was cuddling up against Quinn with his arm around her. They had been watching the news, with him explaining what was really going on. Obviously, she had fallen asleep, but how did she end up in her room? Her parents couldn't move her, when she was a baby, without waking her. Yet, here she was.

She shook off the odd feeling and went to Amanda's room, who's door was ajar. She tapped lightly before going in. Amanda had told her to just come on in, but she felt it wouldn't be polite to enter without a warning.

Amanda was dressed and sitting on her bed, with some maps, papers and envelopes, when Emma entered. "Morning, dear." Amanda said, "How'd you sleep?" she asked.

"Like a rock." Emma replied as she headed to the bathroom.

"And how was Quinn?" Amanda teased.

"We just watched the news," Emma said, "boy, he does not like progressives."

Amanda chuckled, "So I've heard," she said, "ask him about Catholics some time."

"I just might, it's a long ride." Emma said, teasing a threat, as she closed the bathroom door. Amanda was in the kitchen when Emma emerged from her morning routine. She went to her room and put her kit together, then went outside to wait.

It was still dark, with just a hint of dawn on the horizon behind the mountains, when Emma approached the truck. She found Quinn's bag sitting next to the truck when she got there and set her bag next to his. She stepped back a couple of paces and saw Quinn in front of the truck, standing motionless facing the mountains. She stood and watched him for a couple of minutes.

Dave came out of his room with his bag and found Amanda's two bags sitting next to his door. He picked them up and went out onto the porch, and after a couple of steps, he could see Emma staring into the dark in front of the truck. Every now and then she would tilt her head to the side, it reminded Dave of when a dog cocks it's head trying to understand human behavior. As his eyes adjusted to the dark, he could see Quinn standing in front of the truck. 'That explains what she's looking at' Dave thought.

Amanda came out carrying a cooler and the maps and saw Dave watching Emma watching Quinn. "What have I got myself into?" she quietly asked herself, shaking her head.

Quinn turned around, "Sounds like everyone's ready." he stated.

Dave and Quinn packed the bags into the back and they all climbed in, Dave driving and Amanda next to him. Emma sat in the middle of the rear seat, to be closer to Quinn.

They had gone about ten miles when Amanda noticed that Quinn had fallen asleep, "Must not have slept well." she said quietly to Dave, nodding in Quinn's direction. Quinn slept for the first three hours of the trip. He woke up when Dave pulled onto the interstate highway.

"I fell asleep." Quinn said, rubbing his eyes, "I'm sorry, I didn't drool on you, did I?" he asked Emma.

"You're fine," Emma said, "all the drool landed on your shirt." she teased. Quinn instantly looked down at his shirt, only to see a small wet spot. He was relieved that he hadn't been flowing, he could remember mornings waking up with his pillow soaked.

"I feel better." Quinn stated.

"I feel with my hands." Emma whispered into Quinn's ear.

"As funny as that is," Quinn said looking in her

direction, “that’s not funny.” The thought of someone, even Emma, running their hands all over his body terrified him. Too much contact, especially on his genitals, would break down the defenses he had developed over the years. He worked hard keeping the assault on his senses at bay.

Emma let out a nervous giggle, “Sorry.” she said, not sure of where their relationship was going.

“We’ll talk when we’re alone.” Quinn said quietly to her.

“You two ok back there?” Dave asked over his shoulder.

“Yup!” Quinn and Emma responded simultaneously, they looked at each other and Emma started to giggle, with Quinn following with a quiet laugh. For the next five minutes they couldn’t look in the others direction without laughing.

Finally under control, Quinn wondered aloud, “What the hell was that?” He had never been close enough, emotionally, to anybody else to have experienced anything like that before. He made momentary eye contact with Emma, that wasn’t unpleasant, turned and shook his head rapidly for a second.

“A giggle fit, that’s what my Dad called it.” Emma offered, “You mean that’s never happened to you before?” she asked, surprised.

“A giggle fit, huh. And no, never before.” Quinn said, “I didn’t realize laughing could get out of control, but it wasn't bad, like if I slip."

Amanda looked at Dave, "You kids behave yourselves back there." she joked, over her shoulder.

"Are we there yet?" Emma asked in a childlike voice. Quinn started to giggle again, and Emma followed quickly.

"Looks like we may be parents after all." Amanda teased with Dave, who did not look amused.

The giggling stopped after a minute or so, "Almost in New Mexico." Quinn noted.

"Yeah, about a half hour away." Dave clarified, "You ok back there?" he asked.

"I will be, David, I will be." Quinn answered, looking straight ahead, "How 'bout some radio?" he asked.

"I didn't want to disturb your sleep." Amanda said, as she turned on the stereo and found some classic rock.

"Disturb his sleep?" Dave said, "He grew up in an orphanage, he could sleep through just about anything, believe me, I know."

"So, you've been driving in silence for me?" Quinn said, "Unnecessary, but thanks, I guess."

"I'm just glad you didn't snore," Dave said, with a smile, "I would've cranked the stereo to eleven!"

"I don't snore." Quinn stated, "I know, I stayed up one night and listened." This got a giggle from Emma, which Quinn stopped with a gentle nudge and a smile.

"What do we expect to find at Chaco Canyon?" Emma asked.

"Hopefully, something old that Dave can open." Amanda said.

"And by old, we mean pre-flood." Dave said, "So, don't get your hopes up."

"Low hopes, right." Quinn said, nodding, "It will be good to see one of the places I've read about."

"I've seen it on T.V." Emma said, "But you never get the feeling you get seeing something live. Like the Grand Canyon, pictures and T.V. don't do it justice."

"I've never seen the Grand Canyon." Quinn stated.

"You've never...." Dave said, astounded, "We have got to go, on the way back." he said, looking at Amanda, who nodded in agreement.

"How is it you've never been to the Grand Canyon?" Emma asked, "You've been here your whole life."

"I don't travel much." Quinn said.

"Oh, I'm sorry." Emma said, realizing she had forgot about his condition.

"Don't be," Quinn said to her, "you treat me like you do everyone else. I like that about you." he explained. Emma leaned into Quinn and gave him a hug.

"So, it's set," Amanda said, "Grand Canyon on the way back."

"Are you going to be ok for all this?" Emma quietly asked Quinn.

"We're going to find out, aren't we?" Quinn asked rhetorically. Twice now, Quinn had slept in a bed other than his own. The first time he slept ok, not so much the second time. He knew that it would be a good thing to grow in this way, but it was a bit unsettling.

They rode in silence for a while, until Emma saw a billboard that said; Jesus saves.

"What does Jesus save?" Emma asked, innocently.

"Yeshua." Quinn corrected.

"Huh?" Emma said, confused.

"His name is Yeshua," Quinn explained, "and He'll save your soul, if you ask."

"Then why does everybody call him Jesus?" she asked, now curious.

"Good question," Amanda said from the front, "I'm guessing Quinn is going to tell us."

"She asked," Quinn said, "and it's some of what I believe."

"I know," Amanda said, "I was just teasing." Amanda had been raised as a Catholic, but had stopped attending Mass a few years earlier.

"I'm not completely sure about why, but the Catholics started calling him that around the twelfth century." Quinn explained, "I think that if you pray in someone's name, you should use their name. It seems pretty simple to me."

"It's weird that they would change His name." Emma said.

"Yeah, weird." Quinn agreed, not wanting to talk about the Catholics any more. He didn't want to upset Amanda by talking down her religion. "You should read the New Testament." he suggested.

"My Dad raised me as a Zen Buddhist," Emma offered, "but he wasn't very strict about it."

"I am thinking that may be the point of Zen." Quinn said, joking.

"I am thinking you may be right." Emma said, emulating Quinn. This made Quinn smile, and he gave her a little squeeze, as she sat leaning against him.

In the past, people had mocked the way he spoke, it bothered him on some level, but he would never let them see that he didn't like it. He wasn't about to give them the satisfaction, so he stopped listening to them, for good. He didn't get the feeling she was mocking him, it came from a good place and he got a good feeling hearing her.

"So, why are you a Christian?" Emma asked.

"It makes the most sense to me," Quinn explained, "He was killed be cause He said; I am the Way, the Truth and the Life, no-one comes unto the Father, but by Me. All it takes is faith, no hoops to jump through, nothing to earn, nothing to prove, just believe. It can't get any simpler than that. Plus, more than five-hundred people saw him walking around and talking, after the crucifiction. I have read a lot, and nothing has caused me to doubt Him. He also fullfilled more than one hundred prophecies, from the Old Testament."

"Wow, I never heard anything about that," Emma said, "that's a lot."

"Did you read about Buddha saying to watch for another in five-hundred years?" Quinn asked.

"Yeah, I remember, in one of my Dad's books." she said.

"That was around twenty-five hundred years ago, right?" Quinn posed.

"Yeah....you mean..?" Emma said, starting to make the connection.

"Yup, Buddha saw His coming." Quinn answered.

"I didn't know that." Dave said from the front, "I find that to be fascinating."

"Yeah, he's got me thinking about the validity of the Catholic Church," Amanda said, "it's not a good feeling."

"I did not intend to make you feel bad," Quinn said, "just wanted to make you think."

"Yeah, thanks a lot for that." Amanda quipped, "But, the more I read the Bible, the more I see that you're right about the Catholics. They don't follow what He told us to do."

"So, I did get you to think!" Quinn said.

"It all sounds very involved." Emma said, "Why are there so many different sects?"

"Just keep it simple, read it for yourself and don't listen to people that tell you what he meant. Figure it out for yourself, the way it is intended." Quinn explained.

"All that, and now Dave tells us of some hidden tribe that believes in Him, and are waiting for His return."

Emma posed, “Maybe I should read the Bible.”

“Not maybe.” Quinn said, softly.

“I get the feeling you would have had me read it at some point.” Emma said, with a smile.

“I’ll get you one,” Quinn offered, “one that uses His real name.”

“Sounds like the beginning of a study group.” Dave said to Quinn.

“Hey, me too.” Amanda said, “I’d like to find out what’s real and what’s been made up by men, no offense.” she added, looking at Dave.

“None taken,” Dave replied, “I’m old, but not old enough to have been involved in creating traditions for the Catholics.”

“Maybe I should have said ‘made up by man’.” Amanda mused.

“Too literal, David, too literal.” Quinn said, joking.

“Yeah, my humor can be dry.” Dave said.

“Anyway,” Amanda spoke up, “if you start a Bible study group, I want in.”

“I think that I would like to try it, too.” Emma said to Quinn.

“What about your father?” Quinn asked her.

“He will understand,” Emma said, “he said that if a ‘way’ cannot handle challenge, then it is not to be followed.”

“That makes sense.” Amanda said.

“And if he doesn’t understand?” Quinn asked, not

wanting to cause discord in her family.

"Then he can get Mother and himself a place of their own." Emma said, defiantly.

"Wow... didn't see that coming." Quinn said, stunned.

"My parents moved to the Valley, from San Francisco, three years ago. They asked to stay with me while they shopped around for a house." Emma explained.

"They must be picky." Quinn mused.

"That might have been funny, in the first year." Emma replied.

"Is it something money can fix?" Amanda offered, hoping to help.

"No, my Dad's pretty well off." Emma answered, "They're too comfortable, and it's my fault." She took in a deep breath and let out a sad sigh.

"Something will present itself." Quinn said, trying not to smile.

"That's very Zen of you." Emma said, "I don't even want to think of what 'it' might be."

"What does Zen say about surrounding yourself with positive people?" Dave asked.

"That it is desirable." Emma replied.

"There are two creatures fighting in our brains, one is good, and one is evil. The one that wins is the one we feed." Quinn stated.

"That makes sense." Amanda said, "You figure that out by yourself?"

“Read it somewhere.” Quinn replied, looking out the window.

“Still, it makes sense.” Emma said, “You must read a lot.”

“Books, and the computer.” Quinn explained, “When I’m not working, I’m reading.”

“I liked ‘The Hobbit’ and ‘The Lord of the Rings’ trilogy. Have you ever read them?” Emma asked.

“When I was seven, I read them.” Quinn said, “Why didn’t the wizard have the eagles take Frodo and the ring to the volcano right away? No one would have died unnecessarily.”

“Wouldn’t have made much of a story,” Emma said, “now would it.”

“I liked Dr. Seuss, when I started reading, I learned about interactions between people and what is to be expected of you.” Quinn explained, “After that, it was all just variations on a theme. I’ve kept to non-fiction, except for the newspapers lately, since about the time I turned eight.”

“What about movies?” Emma asked.

“I don’t watch T.V.” Quinn said, “Never liked it.”

“So, when I turned it on last night, why didn’t you say something?” Emma asked.

“I like you more than I dislike T.V.” Quinn replied, with a smile.

“Wow” Emma said, “You don’t have to make yourself uncomfortable on my account, ok.”

"That's my call." Quinn stated, "I know what's important to me."

"Wow!" Emma repeated, as she leaned against him.

Quinn liked her show of affection, it was all very new to him, and it felt good. He could feel himself starting to get an erection, this made him stare out of the window and try to think of something else.

Emma noticed him getting hard and immediately sat up straight. She tried her best not to look at it, she knew from last night that he didn't want her to touch it. He had told her it would send him into convulsions, and she believed him, having never met a man that didn't want it touched.

After a few minutes of looking out the window, Quinn relaxed and everything went back to normal. He remembered that twice, at the orphanage, two different girls tried to give him a hand-job. Both times, once when he was nine and once when he was fifteen, ended with him flopping around on the ground, erection disappearing immediately without a happy ending. He didn't want to go through that ever again. He appreciated that she understood his situation. Quinn turned and looked Emma in the eyes, "Thank you." he said with a smile.

Emma, already aroused from seeing him get hard, had an orgasm when he locked eyes with her. She could feel herself blush, so she quickly looked away and just nodded.

Quinn watched as the green glow that surrounded Emma suddenly turned blue. He hadn't seen this happen before, but figured she felt more comfortable with him. She leaned against him and he put his arm around her, feeling pretty comfortable himself.

"Here's the turn off for the park." Amanda announced, as Dave slowed for the turn onto the road to Chaco Canyon.

After about fifteen minutes, Emma was getting fidgety, "I thought you meant we were there." she complained, as Dave made a turn.

"Pavement ends." Amanda read aloud from a sign.

"What?" Emma asked as the road turned bumpy.

After another ten minutes of having the vehicle pounded by the road, Quinn said, "I am thinking we have the right vehicle for this road." This brought agreement from all.

"I gotta say," Dave said, "you really have to want to see these ruins, to put up with a road like this."

Several minutes later they could see the visitors center, and soon the road was paved, once again. Dave found a parking spot and Amanda got out and went into the visitors center to pay their entrance fee. She bought everyone a memento and got some maps of the park. She climbed back into the truck and gave everybody their gift and a map.

"Where do we go first?" Amanda asked.

"Let's drive, and we can stop at each ruin." Dave

suggested, “Don’t want to miss anything.” Dave pulled out of the parking area and onto the loop, they reached the first pull out and parked. “Hungo Pavi, everyone.” Dave announced, bus driver-like.

“We have the place to ourselves.” Quinn noted, “Must not be one of the main attractions.”

“Hey,” Emma spoke up, looking at her map, “we missed a ruin. A trail at the visitors center.”

“We can check it out on the way back.” Amanda suggested, “We got plenty of time.”

Hungo Pavi was a smaller ruin, set in a side canyon. They explored the ruins for about twenty minutes, with no-one else stopping to see this sight.

“There used to be a road going through here.” Quinn noted, “Before this site was built here.”

“I don’t see it,” Dave said, “but if you say so, I’m not going to argue.” Dave and the ladies had spent most of their time looking over the ruins, while Quinn spent his time staring out at the mountains surrounding them. “Everybody ready to move on?” Dave asked. They walked back to the truck, and soon were on their way to the main attraction, Pueblo Bonito.

Dave slowed to a crawl as he entered the parking area, which was empty on this end.

“Park here.” Quinn said, pointing at an empty part of the parking lot.

“Ok buddy,” Dave said, “you got it.” As he pulled into the first spot that he could. They were much closer to the Chetro Ketl ruin than the Pueblo Bonito, so there were plenty of spaces available.

They climbed out of the truck and the ladies were consulting the map, while Dave and Quinn checked their bags and locked up the truck. The men met up with the girls at the trail head, Quinn headed up the trail to Chetro Ketl, walking slowly, looking side to side. Dave and Amanda passed him as Dave said, "We'll be waiting for you at the ruins."

"I'm staying with Quinn," Emma said, "I want to see what he sees."

"Good luck with that." Dave quipped, smiling towards Quinn. Quinn nodded and returned the smile.

Emma took Quinn's arm, and they watched Dave and Amanda head towards Chetro Ketl. They walked along together, slowly, and Emma did her best to see what he was seeing.

"I'm seeing trails running through here," Quinn said, "some old, and some really old."

"It all looks like desert to me." Emma offered.

"A trail heads west, towards Pueblo Bonito, and a spur heads to the mountain face." Quinn told her, "That way." he said as he pointed at the cliff face.

"There's no trail for us, that way." Emma noted, looking at the map, "The map shows a trail along the cliff face, between the two ruins, we'll get there." They continued up the trail to meet up with Dave and Amanda at Chetro Ketl.

As Emma and Quinn approached, Dave said, "I think this is all very impressive, but it's not as old as I had hoped."

"I am thinking that they got the dates from the wood in the floors," Quinn said, "Carbon-14 dating."

"I suppose so." Dave said, looking disappointed.

"I see sections of a very old road," Quinn said, "I think they built this place on part of that road."

"It would be an advantage to have a level area to start building on." Dave said, with a nod. Dave and Quinn followed the women through the ruins, when they got to the eastern side of the complex Quinn stopped, as the others kept walking.

Emma walked back to Quinn, who was staring at the opposite cliff face, "What do you see?" Emma asked.

"Not sure," Quinn responded, "I think the road continues, mostly buried."

"Well, there's no trail to over there." Emma said, tugging on his arm, "C'mon, let's catch up." Quinn turned and let Emma lead him until they caught up with their friends. They finished the trail through the ruins, then started down the trail to Pueblo Bonito. They all slowed to Quinn's pace, and stayed within a few yards of him.

"This used to be a road," Quinn said, "and I'm seeing bugs."

"Ew!" Amanda said with a start, then started looking at the ground around her feet.

"Carved on the rock." Quinn explained, trying not to smile.

Dave laughed out loud, "Now, that's funny!" he said to Amanda, who smiled at herself.

"Hey, this isn't a bug." Emma said from a few yards down the trail. A moment later, they were all staring at a petroglyph of a man.

"He's got really big hands." Amanda noted.

"You know what that means." Emma replied, with a giggle. She turned and walked down the trail a few yards. "Oh, I see a bug," She said, looking up at the cliff face, "kinda like a caterpillar."

Amanda joined Emma in looking for more bugs. "I'm seeing bits of figures, but it's like they've been erased." Amanda said, scanning the wall. Dave joined the girls to look for more petroglyphs, while Quinn remained inspecting the area around the man with the big hands. They all quieted down when a small group approached.

The approaching family stopped short of them, as the eldest of them pointed out things on the wall. Dave could hear the silver haired man explaining things, in his native tongue, to his family. The group consisted of the Elder, a younger couple and, what looked like, their four kids, all not yet teens. As they passed, the three all smiled and nodded, with Emma waving at the children. The Elder kept an eye on Dave as he passed by, then said something to the other man as they walked on.

Dave shook his head, "That was weird." he said to the ladies, as they watched the group nearing Quinn.

"Really weird." Amanda agreed, as she went to see what the old man was pointing out to his family.

Dave watched as the youngsters walked right up next to Quinn and looked to see what he was staring at. They giggled and traded looks, when they realized Quinn wasn't like them. The Elder said something to them, and they moved on.

Quinn didn't understand the words, but he recognized the tone of an admonishment. The parents apologized as they passed. "I am not offended by the honesty of children." Quinn said, without turning.

The man smiled and moved on as the silver haired man walked up and stood at Quinn's side. The family walked several yards up the trail, then stopped and turned to watch the interaction between the two men.

Without moving his head, Quinn glanced down at the man standing at his left, to check the glow of this person. He could tell a lot about a person by reading their aura. He looked at the man's body and saw an aura that was green, surrounded by purple, and smoother than anything he had ever seen on a person. The man leaned over to his left, to catch Quinn's eye.

Quinn avoided eye contact because, from most people, it was a flood of fear and confusion. He did not like it, and so, rarely looked anyone in the eyes. He didn't want to know that much about anybody.

The old man leaned another inch, and caught Quinn's eye. He straightened up, keeping eye contact with Quinn, who turned and faced the old man.

Quinn did not get blasted with the usual deluge when they locked eyes, instead he felt control and calmness. He sensed that the old man was like him as a youth, but had learned much more than he, himself, had.

The old man smiled and nodded at Quinn, then turned and joined his family. He started speaking to them in the old tongue, saying that if that guy had been born in their tribe, he would have been trained as a shaman. Like they did for him as a youth.

Quinn didn't understand what was being said, but recognized that it was about him, and that it wasn't malicious. He looked to see Dave watching, he shrugged and Dave smiled. They both looked over at the family to see the old man gesturing, occasionally pointing at the cliff face. Again, Quinn knew that he was talking about them.

The old man was telling his family that it was rare to meet a man with power, that didn't understand his power. But, to meet two men, each with power, and neither understanding, this was an omen. Something was coming in the near future. The native family soon moved on and left the four friends to continue exploring.

"Hey guys." Amanda called out, from a little way

down the trail. She was looking up at the cliff face, and when Emma reached her she pointed up at the wall.

Emma looked up to see a stain on the rock above, it looked like an arrow, the kind that shows where to go. the two women looked to where the arrow was pointing, to see Quinn standing at the spot. They looked at each other, then back at Quinn, then back at each other. They turned and headed back up the trail towards Quinn. When they reached Dave, they each took an arm and they walked on to where Quinn was standing.

Quinn glanced up and down the trail, to insure they were alone, then stepped off the trail and placed his hand gently on the petroglyph of the man. Nothing happened. Quinn stepped back onto the trail, again looking up and down the trail. As the others reached him, he pointed at the petroglyph, "That's it," he said, "Put your hand on him,...the big hands, it's a clue."

They all looked in both directions, insuring they were alone. Dave moved off the trail, towards the petroglyph, feeling the excitement building as he approached. He placed his hand on the 'glyph and felt a tiny stab on his palm. He pulled his hand away and stepped back a step.

"Did you feel a little prick?" Quinn asked, pointing at the petroglyph, which now had a drop of blood near the crotch.

Dave looked down and watched as the blood was drawn into the rock and disappeared. A few seconds passed before the rock to his right started to move, making a low pitched grinding noise, revealing a partially blocked passageway.

Again, looking up and down the trail, seeing that they were still alone, Quinn pulled out a small flashlight, "This is what we're here for!" he said, handing the flashlight to Emma as she passed him and entered the opening.

"There's plenty of room." Emma called back to them, "Just watch your heads."

Quinn followed Emma into the cliff face, with Amanda following him and Dave bringing up the rear. As soon as Dave reached the others, past the rubble, the door closed with a thud that echoed down the hallway.

"That didn't sound good." Dave noted, "The door in Mexico was pretty much silent, by comparison."

Emma lit up the rocks in the passageway, "It looks like a cave-in." she said.

"I am thinking it was probably an earthquake." Quinn said, sounding a bit nervous. He had never experienced such a lack of input, and was afraid he would become too sensitive to be of use to his friends.

Dave pulled out a flashlight of his own and started looking at the wall by the entrance. "I don't see anything here to press, to open the door." he stated, as he started looking behind the fallen rocks, "Must be behind this mess."

"You mean we can't get out?" Amanda said, not

happy with the situation.

"Not this way." Dave answered, "Looks like we're walking." He shone his light down the hallway, revealing little. Dave walked over to Amanda and handed her his flashlight. "Didn't think we'd find anything, did you?" Dave teased. Amanda looked over at Emma, who looked down at the ground. Dave chuckled and kissed Amanda on the forehead, "Next time, right." he said quietly.

Emma turned and started down the passage, with Quinn at her side. "You're keeping up pretty well." Emma said to Quinn.

"Very empty, nothing to note." Quinn replied.

They walked for five minutes before coming upon a door, on the left side of the hall. There was a raised area beside the closed door, which Emma pressed, then Quinn, then Amanda. The ladies both pointed their lights at the raised spot, while all three stared at Dave.

"Oh, now you believe." Dave said, "I guess I'm up." He walked up to the door and placed his hand on the raised spot and pressed. Nothing happened. He pressed a couple more times, with no results. "Must be locked." he said, turning to the others. They continued on for a few minutes until they came to a tee.

After a minute of them looking back and forth, Quinn said "The air is moving to the left."

"Pueblo Bonito is to the left." Dave offered.

They all looked at each other, and with a nod Quinn

and Emma said "To the left." And they started down the passage in their chosen direction.

After a short walk they came upon another door, Emma and Quinn both tried to open it, without success. When Dave pressed the spot the door opened, sliding silently to the side. Dave stepped halfway through the door, to check for a raised spot on the inside. He didn't want to be trapped in an even smaller space. Upon seeing the spot, he entered the room, with Emma and Quinn following behind him. Amanda was about to follow Quinn when she caught a glint of light out of the corner of her eye.

"I'll be right there." Amanda said, as she headed further down the hall.

Inside the room, the ceiling started to glow softly, slowly increasing in intensity until they no longer needed their flashlights. They looked around to see shelf after shelf of scrolls.

"This is amazing," Emma quipped, "there must be hundreds of them."

"More like thousands." Dave said, leaning in to get a better look at the scrolls. "I don't recognize this writing."

"Looks like a cross between hieroglyphics and quantum math." Quinn offered, also looking close.

Amanda moved slowly as she proceeded down the passageway to where she thought she saw a light. After several yards she started to see a soft glow coming from a partially open door. She walked up to the door and reached out to open it further, when she felt a punch to her gut. She let out a short sound, then lost her wind. It felt like she had been hit hard by a burning torch. Her hands went to her gut as she fell back and watched the door slam shut, before she hit the ground.

Dave straightened up suddenly, then they all heard a loud clap. "Amanda" escaped from Dave's lips as he ran out of the room and down the hall. He arrived, seconds later, to find Amanda on her back, trying to hold her head up, eyes wide and blinking, reaching out to him with a bloodied hand. "No no no..." Dave cried softly as he took her hand, "Here, put pressure on it." he said as he pressed her hand on her belly. He scooped her up and ran past Quinn and Emma.

"Oh shit!" Emma cried, seeing the blood as they passed. Emma and Quinn ran behind Dave as he ran past the hallway they came in.

"Where are we going?" Quinn asked, as he watched Dave, almost in a panic, hit the pad of every door he passed. Occasionally one would open, Dave would look in then continue up the hall. After a couple of minutes of doing this, they came to what at first looked like another side passage. Dave turned into the opening, to find that it was just a room.

Dave looked around the room and began to recognize where he was. He, in his panic, had almost turned and continued up the hall. Quinn and Emma turned the corner a moment later. "Move that." Dave said, indicating for Quinn to grab the tablet that was on the table.

Quinn picked up the device, and felt a tingle come from it. He watched as Dave carefully placed Amanda on the table, which looked more like a slab of rock. Dave snatched the tablet from Quinn's hands.

"Sorry." he said as he pressed the side of the device with his finger. He tried several different spots along the edge of the tablet, until it woke up and started to glow. He pointed the device at Amanda and pressed one more time.

At the foot of the bed an arch formed and pulled what looked like a metallic fabric over Amanda. It covered her entirely, from head to toe, but within moments it retracted from her head. Dave collapsed to the floor, with a sigh of relief.

"I am thinking I need to know what happened." Quinn said, obviously nervous. He looked at Dave, the blood on his hand dripped onto the floor, where it seemed to get absorbed.

"I don't know," Dave responded, "maybe a booby-trap or something. I found her on her back and bleeding, and not able to talk."

"I am thinking you knew this thing was here." Quinn said, looking around the room.

"I was hoping," Dave said, "thank the Lord we found it!" Dave looked over at Emma, who looked confused and worried. He caught her eye, then glanced over at

Quinn. She nodded and went to be near Quinn, who put his arm over her shoulders and gently pulled her close.

"What now?" Emma asked.

"Now we wait." Dave replied. A moment later the blanket retreated to just above her wound. "That appears promising." he said, as he got up off of the floor.

"How long were you in the bed, after your fall?" Quinn asked, appearing much calmer.

"More than two days." Dave answered, looking over Amanda.

"They'll be looking for us by then." Emma said, "We'll tell them that we were abducted by aliens."

"That's after we find a way out of here." Quinn said, reminding them of their original dilemma. The three friends fell silent in contemplation and prayer. After about twenty minutes Amanda started to wake.

"Where am I?" Amanda asked, then tried to move, "I can't feel my legs." she said, scared.

"Relax," Dave said, "you're being held down, you were stabbed and now you're being healed. You'll be fine."

She looked at Dave and saw the blood on his shirt, "Oh my..." Amanda uttered, "Are you ok?" she asked.

"I'm fine," Dave replied, "it's your blood."

Amanda blinked a few times, "There was an open door," She said, "I thought I saw something move, then I got hit with more pain than I thought existed. I remember seeing Dave, then nothing." she explained.

"So, you didn't see what stabbed you?" Emma asked.

"Nope, just pain and the door slamming shut." Amanda offered, "Then waking up here, wherever 'here' is."

"I am so sorry," Dave said, "I don't know why I let you talk me into this, we don't know what we're doing."

"We all wanted to do this," Amanda said, "it's no-one's fault."

"I'm going to check out the passage." Quinn said, as he offered his arm to Emma. She took his arm and they walked out of the room, leaving Dave alone with Amanda.

"I was so scared." Dave said as he leaned in to give Amanda a hug. "What if there hadn't been one of these things here, or we didn't find it in time?"

"Let's not think about that now." Amanda replied, holding Dave as close as she could. They talked quietly for a while when she asked, "Where'd those two go, they should be back by now."

"I'm sure they're ok." Dave said, "After what happened to you, I'm sure Quinn will be careful." Just then, the blanket retracted into the foot of the bed.

Amanda swung her feet over the side of the bed and slowly stood up, expecting to feel some pain. When there wasn't any pain she looked at Dave and smiled broadly. She looked down at her blouse, there wasn't any blood but there was a hole in it, where she had been stabbed. It looked like it had been cut with a three edged knife, with each blade about three-quarters of an inch high. She lifted her blouse to examine her belly where she had been stabbed, revealing a small three-pointed scar. She ran her hand over the spot a few times, "I guess I'm good to go." she proclaimed with a smile.

Dave placed the tablet on the bed, where he had found it, and they stepped out into the passageway. They could see Quinn and Emma coming towards them from up the hall.

"I think we found it." Emma said, "It didn't open for either of us, but it is a pad at a dead end of a hallway."

"Sounds promising," Dave said, "let's get going." They walked about a quarter of a mile when they came to a tee. Dave stood for a half-a-minute looking in each direction, "Right turn, right?" Dave asked.

"Correct," Quinn answered, "that's where the air was coming from."

"That's what I felt," Dave said, "so, I tried to think like you, like everything's a clue."

"I don't believe in coincidence." Quinn stated.

They walked another five minutes when Dave passed a side hall, Emma and Quinn stopped at the passage.

Dave stopped and looked back, "I missed a turn, huh?" he said as he walked back to his friends.

Emma led the way down the hallway, and after a

minute of walking she stopped and stood against the wall, shining her light on a raised spot on the opposite wall, about two feet from the end of the hall. Quinn and Amanda fell in beside Emma, against the wall, now with two lights illuminating the raised spot.

"Let's hope this works." Dave said as he placed his hand on the pad. Almost instantly the end of the passage opened with a flood of light and hot air. They stepped out into the light and waited for their eyes to adjust, after several seconds the door closed silently behind them.

Quinn pointed to the west, "I am thinking that is Chetro Ketl, over there." They all looked to where Quinn was pointing and could see ruins on the other side of the wash. They made their way, carefully, across the open desert to the ruins, without being seen.

"I know there's a lot more to see, but I'm done." Dave said.

"We can come back and be tourists another time." Amanda offered, "What do you guys think?"

"I'm with Quinn." Emma said, giving him proxy.

"I'm just along for the ride." Quinn said, with a smile.

"Ok then, we're outta here." Amanda proclaimed, "I'm feeling pretty good, I'll drive, if you don't mind."

"Thank you." Dave said, as he handed her the keys. They climbed into the truck and were soon back on the loop.

"There's a road south coming up." Emma said, looking at the park map, "It looks like it should be paved for a while."

"It couldn't be any worse than what we came in on." Amanda said as she slowed for the turn. After a couple of minutes the pavement ran out and they were presented with a sign that said the road may be unpassable and it was at your own risk.

"I thought the real road would last longer." Emma said, comparing all the maps they had. The road south turned out to be not much better than the road going in, it was, however, twice as long.

There wasn't a lot of conversation as Amanda tried her best to find the smoothest route along the road. After being rattled for what seemed like forever, they came to a tee at a paved road.

"We went by here," Quinn stated, "on the way in."

"Turn right," Emma said, "That'll get us out the way we came in."

Amanda did as she was directed and soon they were headed west on the interstate.

"Are we still going to see the Grand Canyon?" Quinn asked.

"You bet we are." Amanda said, "We have a place to go first, but we'll get there."

Dave turned his head towards Amanda, "Should we tell them?" he mouthed.

"Let it be a surprise." Amanda replied softly.

It wasn't long before Quinn fell asleep, with Emma curled up under his arm. She couldn't sleep, with everything they went through running through her brain, but felt better being nestled under his arm.

36

It was just before sunset when Amanda pulled off of the interstate and Quinn woke up.

"How long was I out?" Quinn asked, trying to get orientated.

"How about all of Arizona." Dave said, now in a better mood.

"And part of New Mexico." Amanda added.

"You slept through two stops," Emma said, "and I got out both times." she teased.

Quinn, now awake, noticed the road signs, "Are we on the way to" he started, getting cut off.

"Vegas, baby!" Amanda said, "And I'm going to need your help when we get there."

"I am thinking I don't know how much help I will be, there." Quinn said, sounding a bit nervous, "I don't like crowds."

"I'm sure you'll be fine." Amanda said, trying to be reassuring, "I got us some rooms, so you don't have to worry about that, and the envelopes I gave you are to get you started. If you need more, just ask."

Emma reached over the back of the seat and retrieved her bag, she reached in and got the envelope Amanda had given her at the start of the day. "There's a thousand dollars in here!" Emma said, stunned.

"That's to have fun with," Amanda instructed, "if you want anything, just put it on your room. It's covered."

"What do you mean by anything?" Quinn asked, innocently.

"You know, food, clothes,...a car, anything!" Amanda replied, with a smile.

"Any kind of car?" Quinn asked, now joking.

"Any kind of car you can drive, buddy." Dave answered, calling Quinn's bluff.

Quinn had kept his eyes on his feet since they had hit the strip. The lights dimmed a little as Amanda pulled into the valet parking area, where they were met by four people and two luggage carts. Amanda stopped where directed and the valet stepped up and opened Amanda's door. The valet, trying not to smile, accepted the keys from Amanda.

"I know, it's a lot of fun to drive." Amanda said to the valet, "Ever driven one of these?" she asked quietly.

The young man shook his head, "Not the military style." he answered, as he accepted a tip.

Dave got out and walked to the back of the truck and stopped when the trunk popped open. The concierge opened Quinn's door and he and Emma exited the vehicle, while the two bellhops unloaded the luggage under Dave's direction.

Quinn stepped away from the vehicle and began stretching, while Emma spoke to the concierge in an animated fashion. The young lady took out her phone and began tapping vigorously on the screen, then looked up at Emma and nodded. The concierge turned to Amanda and held out two room key cards.

"Amanda?" She asked, waiting for a nod, "I'm Bobbie, we spoke on the phone." she said, handing the cards to Amanda.

"Hi Bobbie, nice to finally meet you." Amanda said, as she handed Bobbie an envelope.

Bobbie accepted the envelope and pocketed it without looking inside. "Everything has been arranged, per your request." she said, "Please, follow me." Bobbie turned and led the foursome into the hotel. Just as they reached the entrance, a young man ran up to Bobbie and handed her a package. Bobbie stopped and relayed the package to Emma.

Emma opened the bag and produced a pair of sunglasses, which she had requested when they first arrived. The glasses were only twenty percent dark, but they had opaque side pieces. Emma turned and looked at Quinn, "These are for you," she said, "Here, put them on."

"What are these?" Quinn asked, without looking up.

"Blinders." Emma stated as she put the glasses on Quinn.

Quinn slowly lifted his head, "These help." he said, with a smile, "Thank you."

"I was thinking, this place is designed to be an assault on the senses," Emma replied, "I can't imagine what it must be like for you, but I was hoping these would help."

"As long as I have you watching my periphery." Quinn said, looking side to side.

They continued through the lobby, stopping at the front desk for a minute, then on up to their rooms. Amanda handed a key card to Emma, "You get the presidential suite." she said, "we're next door. You got half an hour to get cleaned up and meet us out here, ok?"

"If you say so." Quinn said as he followed Emma into their suite. Their bags were already there, Quinn's in the master bedroom and Emma's in the other. The suite was two bedroom, two and a half bath, with a kitchenette and a sitting room with a fully stocked bar.

"This place is nice." Emma said after they explored the suite.

"Can we switch rooms?" Quinn asked.

"Why would you want to do that?" Emma asked, happy with her room.

"Too big." Quinn said, after seeing her room and feeling more comfortable in the smaller space.

"If you insist." Emma said, grabbing her bag and heading to the master bedroom. Quinn followed and retrieved his bag, then headed back to his room.

Twenty minutes later, showered and dressed, Emma came into the sitting room to find Quinn waiting patiently.

"Cute." Quinn said, upon seeing Emma wearing sweats.

"Great." Emma replied, "I didn't know that we would be around people, it's this or what I was wearing, and at least these are clean."

"I just meant that you look cute." Quinn said, sensing her discomfort, "I don't think anybody will complain."

Emma smiled, "Sorry, I worry too much about what people think, when they see me." she explained.

"I find, mostly, that people don't think." Quinn said, straight faced. He stood up and walked to the door, "Shall we?" he asked, offering his arm. Quinn had on a fresh pair of jeans and a dress shirt, his usual attire, with his new sunglasses in his shirt pocket.

They stepped into the hallway and within a minute Dave came out, dressed in a suit. "She'll be out in a minute." he said.

"I'm starting to feel underdressed." Emma said softly to Quinn.

Amanda emerged from her suite wearing a dress, "Everybody's ready, I see." she said, "Let's get going."

Dave and Amanda led the way down the hall to the elevators.

"Now I'm really feeling underdressed." Emma whispered to Quinn, as Dave and Amanda got on the elevator.

"No need to worry," Quinn said, "you look great!" He stepped aside to let Emma get on the elevator first, then he followed and the door slid shut.

"We can get you something else to wear, if you'd like." Amanda offered, "I couldn't help but overhear, sorry."

"That would be nice, thank you." Emma said.

"You could have ordered it brought to your room." Amanda said, "I said if you need something, just get it." Amanda pressed the button for the shopping level and the elevator started down.

Dave and Quinn waited by the elevators while Emma and Amanda went into the store. It didn't take long before the ladies came out with Emma sporting a new outfit.

"Wow." Dave said, upon seeing Emma in her new clothes.

"You look beautiful." Quinn said, with a big smile.

"Alright ladies, let's get moving." Amanda said as the elevator arrived. They soon reached the ground floor and Dave and Amanda led the way through the lobby and out to a waiting limo. They climbed in and the two couples sat facing each other as the limo started down the strip.

Emma caught Amanda's eye, "Is what's happening what I think is happening?" Emma asked, wide-eyed. Amanda smiled and gave a little nod. Emma grinned and turned to tell Quinn.

"They're getting married." Quinn stated, taking the wind out of her sails.

"You knew?" Emma said, "And didn't tell me."

"I figured it out when Amanda came out of her room." Quinn explained, "I thought you figured it out, too."

"Vegas, the suit and dress, the suites," Emma said, thinking out loud, "yeah, I should've figured it out. I must have been distracted." She leaned into Quinn's side and gave him a hug.

Soon, they were pulling into the parking lot of The Wedding Chapel. The limo door opened and as Quinn emerged he looked up at the driver, "Lenny?" he asked rhetorically, "I'm sorry I didn't recognize you when we got in." he said. Lenny just smiled and nodded.

"A private limo to a wedding in Las Vegas," Emma said, "I guess I can cross that off my bucket list."

"Bucket list?" Quinn asked.

"Yeah, bucket list. I'll explain later," Emma replied, "I have got to get some fiction into you." All five entered the Chapel to find Joe and Becky, along with Vicky, waiting for them.

Amanda went and greeted them, "I'm so glad you

guys could make it." she said, with a warm smile. Lenny went over and sat down next to his wife.

"All expenses paid trip to Vegas," Joe replied, "I'm in."

"Either way," Becky spoke up, "I wasn't going to miss this."

"The private jet was a nice touch," Joe added, "unexpected, but very cool."

Thirty minutes later Quinn emerged from the Chapel, propped the doors open and went to the door of the limo, standing valet like. Dave and Amanda came next, Amanda with a bouquet and Dave with a bottle of Dom Perignon, followed by the rest of the party.

Quinn opened the door of the limo, "Mr. and Mrs. Smith." he said, as he straightened up, holding the door. He stood with one hand, palm up, pointing inside the limo. Amanda got in first, then Dave, who stopped and dropped a silver dollar into Quinn's palm.

The couple took their seat and Amanda looked at Dave, "What was that?" she asked, curious.

"The day you started, Quinn said I was going to marry again. I said no-way." Dave explained, "Heck, neither of us had seen you yet, and he didn't say who I would marry, so I bet him a dollar it would never happen."

Amanda giggled, "I like a man that pays up." she said, leaning into him.

Joe got in next, and sat next to Amanda, leaving

Quinn to sit between Becky and Emma. Vicky sat up front with Lenny.

During the ride to the hotel, Becky leaned over to see Emma, “So, when are you two getting hitched?” she asked, as a joke.

Quinn looked at Emma, who looked him in the eyes. Quinn watched as her aura turned blue, this time with waves of brighter blue.

Emma turned away after a few seconds, “Not necessary.” she said softly, as she nestled into Quinn’s side.

When they pulled up to the hotel, Amanda gave a few instructions to Joe then told everyone to have a good time, and that her and Dave were going for a ride and would see them in the morning.

As they watched the limo pull away, Joe leaned over to Quinn, “He probably had a hard-on and didn’t want to get out.” he said, giving Quinn a nudge with his elbow.

Meanwhile, Becky pulled Emma aside, “What the hell was that?” she asked quietly.

“What was what?” Emma replied, acting innocent.

“I got a rush from you,” Becky explained, “a rush that made me blush!”

Emma turned bright red, embarrassed that someone could know.

“I got a way of feeling what other people feel.” Becky told her, “But I never felt anything like that.”

“So, you’re, like, an empath?” Emma asked, trying

to change the subject.

"We call it 'the gift'," Becky revealed, "It come down through the women in my family, though not all the women have it. My Aunt and my Gramma had it, but not my Ma, and I got two sisters that don't, either."

"Wow, that's amazing." Emma said.

"So...what was that?" Becky pressed.

"I don't know, but sometimes when we make eye contact, I have an orgasm." Emma said, shyly.

"That was one hell of an orgasm!" Becky said, shaking her head.

"This time it didn't stop until I turned away." Emma said, blushing again, "Lucky thing I had on a pad."

Becky snorted, "Girl, you are something else." she said, "I caught Quinn's eye once, for about half a second, it was like getting punched in the brain."

"Right," Emma said, "it was kinda like that for me, too, the first time. But with, like, being bare. It was unsettling, for sure."

"Like he got X-ray vision and could see you naked?" Becky asked.

"No, not naked, worse." Emma tried to explain, "Like being read like a book, with nothing redacted."

"Well, don't worry." Becky said, "Your secret is safe with me."

"Thank you." Emma replied, giving Becky a hug.

The limo gone, the two men turned to see the women hugging.

"Bonding over sex talk, no doubt." Joe said, giving Quinn another nudge.

"Then I'd say you were in trouble." Quinn said, returning the nudge. Quinn had never told anyone, until Emma, that he was a virgin, and most people just assumed he wasn't.

"Oh great," Joe said, "you got some secret sex knowledge that I can never match, right."

"No comment." Quinn replied, with a grin.

"Oh, that's just evil, bro." Joe said, with a shake of his head.

"A little research never hurt," Quinn offered, "but, no pictures, drawings only. Otherwise it's pornography."

Joe laughed out loud, "You never let up, do you?" he said.

"I don't know how." Quinn stated, as he put on his sunglasses and headed towards their ladies.

As the men approached, Emma turned towards them, "I'm starving!" she proclaimed.

"Me too." Quinn said, offering his arm to Emma.

They entered the lobby and Joe went to the front desk, as instructed, and within a minute he returned holding three electronic cards. "Two for gambling and one for the room." Joe said, holding up the cards.

"Suite." Quinn stated.

"This whole deal is sweet!" Joe replied.

"I mean you have a suite, not just a room." Quinn explained.

Becky's eyebrow went up, then she took two of the cards from Joe. "I'll be in our suite." she said, turning to the elevators.

"What about dinner?" Joe asked.

"I'll order something and have it brought up." Becky said, with a coy smile.

"I'll see you guys later," Joe said, "I want to check out our suite, too." He caught up with his wife and they disappeared into an elevator.

"That leaves us." Quinn said, smiling.

"Perfect!" Emma replied.

After dinner they headed into the casino, they were walking down an almost deserted aisle of slot machines when Quinn stopped. He raised his sunglasses and looked at a stool in front of a slot machine. "Play this one." he said to Emma, pointing at the machine behind the stool he had noticed. "I want to try blackjack."

Emma tilted her head, looking at Quinn, "If you say so," she said, "But why this one?" she asked quietly as she sat down.

"I think someone was sitting here that left feeling very down," he whispered, "like they spent a lot and didn't win."

"You think it's ready to pay out." Emma said as she inserted a hundred-dollar bill.

"I'll be at the blackjack tables, when you finish up here." Quinn said, and headed to the card tables.

After fifteen minutes, and another hundred dollars,

the machine Emma was playing exploded in a burst of bells, lights and whistles. She had just won forty-five thousand dollars!

She felt someone move in beside her, she looked over to see their concierge smiling at her. “Bobbie,” Emma stammered, “I just won.”

“Yes, yes you did, indeed.” Bobbie said, as she inserted a card into the machine. She pressed a few buttons on the slot machine, then pulled the card out and handed it to Emma. “Don’t lose this.” Bobbie said, looking serious.

Emma took the card, “I gotta tell Quinn.” she said as she took off to find him. Bobbie looked up at one of the cameras, then followed Emma.

In the security room, the man in charge had backed up the video to where Quinn had stopped and pointed. He studied the picture in front of him, “What the fuck.” he said, “Is he some kind of psychic?” he asked rhetorically. His staff made some nervous noises and shifted around a bit. His crew knew he didn’t like things he couldn’t explain, and that it put him a bad mood.

“We’ll keep an eye on him, Mr. Dhu.” one of the staff said.

“I want to talk to him.” John Dhu told his underling, “Bring him here.”

The second in charge scanned the screens, “There he is, at the blackjack table.” he said, as he turned and left the room. He picked up two more security guards on the way to retrieve Quinn.

Emma had located Quinn just in time to see a large man about to grab Quinn's shoulder. "Don't!" she called out, as the man touched Quinn, who grabbed the man's fingers and spun around in his seat, stopping just before smashing the man's face into the floor.

Bobbie pushed past Emma and stopped the other two guards, she looked at Quinn, who didn't return the look, and said, "Let him up, please."

Quinn scooped the man up to his feet, "Sorry, it was reflex." he said to the guard.

The guard, rattled by Quinn's gaze and rubbing his hand, said, "My boss would like to see you."

Bobbie stepped in between Quinn and the guard, "You should've come to me." she told the guard.

"They want to see me for losing?" Quinn asked, "Because I've lost a lot here."

Bobbie turned to Quinn, "I'm not sure why, but the head of security wants to talk to you." she said, "I'll be with you the whole time."

"Me too." Emma said, taking Quinn's arm.

John had watched the entire interaction between the man and his guard. 'I have got to tell my brother about this one.' he thought.

The guard led the threesome to the security office, where Quinn, pointing at a machine, was up on the main screen. "I didn't see that part." Bobbie said, bewildered.

“I’m John Dhu.” the chief said, putting out his hand.

“Quinn Tucker, and this is Emma. She’s with me.” Quinn replied, ignoring the man’s hand.

John pulled his hand back, “Ok,” he said, “can you explain this?” He pointed at the screen behind him.

Emma noticed the man get irritated at Quinn’s rejection and stepped up, putting out her hand, “He doesn’t like touching others.” she explained. John shook her hand and visibly relaxed. “He said he had a hunch.” Emma told him, “And I have learned to listen to him.” She leaned her head to his shoulder.

“A hunch, huh.” John said, as he backed up the video to the point where Quinn raised his glasses. “And what do you see here?” he asked, almost smug.

“Nothing.” Quinn stated.

“Nothing, huh.” John said, annoyed, “You stopped and focused on nothing, that’s what you want me to believe. You stop, focus on nothing, and in less than twenty minutes she gets a major payout. Nah..., you saw something.”

“You want me to say I saw an angel pointing at that machine, or something?” Quinn asked, sarcastically.

“I just want to know how you did it.” John replied.

“Like she said, I had a hunch.” Quinn said, “And I was looking at her butt.”

John let the video advance slowly, and saw that when Emma turned, Quinn lowered his glasses. He looked at Quinn and Emma with a suspicious eye, “I guess so," he said, "but I'll be watching you."

"Right." Emma said, feeling intimidated.

"You two can go." Bobbie said to them, "I'll see you later." Bobbie stayed behind, to explain how to treat a whale and their party, while Quinn and Emma headed back to the casino.

"That was scary." Emma said, holding Quinn's arm.

"Let's do it again." Quinn suggested, "I didn't like that man."

"But, he said he would be watching us." Emma said, still worried.

"But he's not as smart as us." he said, "He can watch all he wants." Quinn removed his sunglasses as they walked along the wall, until he turned down a relatively empty aisle.

Quinn led the way, this time, and gave an almost imperceptible twitch of his elbow as he passed a machine. He walked past the indicated machine, seeing another likely winner.

Emma stopped at the machine Quinn had chosen and called to him. He turned around and Emma waved him back, to get him to sit down at, what appeared to be, her choice of machines. Quinn returned to her and whispered 'four' as he sat down. Emma continued down the aisle to the fourth machine and sat down. Ten minutes later, Quinn had won twenty-five thousand dollars, and a few minutes after that, Emma won another fifty-thousand.

John and Bobbie watched on the screen as the couple walked around the casino and turned down an aisle of slots. They watched as Emma appeared to pick out a machine for Quinn, then find a machine of her own to play. “I better get down there. “Bobbie said, sounding annoyed.

“I apologize again, for not opening your E-mail right away.” John said sincerely.

Bobbie was at the end of the aisle when Quinn’s machine paid out. She put his winnings on a card for him, “Are you trying to piss him off?” she asked.

“We’ve done nothing against the rules.” Quinn stated.

“That may be true, but he’s paid to be suspicious.” Bobbie said, as Emma’s machine started going wild. “You have got to be kidding.” she said, as she watched Emma press a few buttons and then pull her card out of the machine.

Emma held her card up and smiled broadly, “Fifty.” she said excitedly

“He’s not going to let go of this,” Bobbie warned, “I only got so much pull.”

“Beginners luck.” Quinn said, then looked at Emma, “I think I should try poker, I didn’t do so good at black-jack.” He offered his arm to Emma, who took it, and they walked away as Bobbie’s phone signaled that she had received a text.

They found the poker tables and Quinn entered a

twenty-thousand dollar buy-in, single table tournament. There weren't enough people entered to start, so he sat down at a sit-and-go table to warm up before the big money tournament.

Quinn had tripled his money when he was told that the tournament was about to begin. He moved to the tournament table and Emma stayed on the rail, watching him win, for a while, until she told him that she was going to bed.

Emma smiled as she passed the two doors nearest to the Presidential suite, they both had 'Do Not Disturb' signs hanging on the doorknobs. She went into her suite, and while making herself a drink she noticed a small container on the bar. She opened it and found that it contained several joints. She went to her room to change and saw her sweats, folded, sitting on her bed, she had forgotten all about them. Soon, she was sitting on the balcony, in her sweats, sipping her drink and puffing on a really tasty joint, before going to bed.

37

Sunday morning, Edgar woke up when it started to get light, just before sun-up. He enjoyed his Sundays, it was his only day off and he made a point of disconnecting from anything that had to do with work. He put on a pot of coffee and leisurely went about his morning routine. When the coffee was ready, he poured himself a mug and sat down to check out the news on his computer. That was when he saw that he had an E-mail from his brother, John. He opened it and read;

> Hey Eddy,
>
> There's a guy here that made me think of you. After your call about that guy in Phoenix, I thought you might like to see this guy I found in my casino. Check out the attached video.
>
> John

Edgar opened the video file and watched a guy, from a sitting position, put a guy twice his size to the floor. He made it look effortless, and he was fast. He replayed the video a few times before he recognized Quinn from the video of the fight in the parking lot.

"Son of a bitch." Edgar said out loud, as he reached for his phone. He stopped before making the call to his brother when he saw the time on his phone. He knew his brother would be asleep, and he didn't want to disturb him, he knew his brother worked noon to midnight, so he would call later. He spent the next hour comparing the two videos. There was a girl in the Vegas video, right at the end, that he was pretty sure was the dark-haired girl that was in the Phoenix video.

It was about nine o'clock when his girlfriend called, wanting to go to brunch. He dressed and went to pick her up. After brunch they went to her place, to fool around and spend some time together before she had to go to work. It was after three o'clock when Edgar finally got home and had a chance to call his brother.

John was at work when his phone rang, he looked to see that it was his brother. He went to his office to take the call. "Hey Eddy," John said, "what did you think of that video I sent? You ever see anything like that?"

"It's the same guy," Edgar said, "you know, the one I called you about."

"No shit!" John said, "What're the odds?"

"I need to know everything you can tell me about

him, and the dark-haired girl with him." Edgar requested.

"Ok," John said, pulling up the file, "they're part of the Smith party, a whale that we've never seen before. Smith transferred a million into the hotel account, and they took the top three suites in the hotel. The Smith party consists of three couples, the Smith's, the Tucker's and the Coleman's. The suites are paid for through to Wednesday, and they've won more than they've lost."

"That's it?" Edgar asked, hoping for more.

"You mean besides the fact that this Tucker character is really pissing me off." John said.

"He seems to do that to a lot of people," Edgar replied, "like he's got a talent for it."

"At first look, he appeared autistic," John explained, "but that changed the first time someone touched him. I've never seen anything like it."

"You should talk to my agent that went up against him." Edgar said, "The man's got two black eyes and a hand in traction."

"All from this freak?" John asked.

"You can see it on the internet." Edgar said, giving him the address to see the video of the parking lot fight. "So, you say they're going to be there until Wednesday."

"That's what I read here." John said, "Why?"

"I'm coming to see you, bro," Edgar said, "I'll leave first thing in the morning."

"See you then." John said, before hanging up.

38

Sunday morning, Emma woke after sunrise and when she came out of her room, she found Quinn looking in the refrigerator. He turned around, holding a bottle of water, and smiled broadly.

"I done well." Quinn said, beaming.

"Oh yeah, how well?" she asked, walking to the bar to show Quinn the small container. She grabbed the room service menu, "You hungry?" she asked.

Quinn perused the contents of the container, "A little over four hundred G's, after taxes." he said, as he picked out a joint and headed to the balcony.

"You cashed out?" she asked.

"Had to," he replied, "John and one of his goons, and a guy from the I.R.S. accompanied me to the window."

"John, that scary guy from security?" Emma asked.

"Yeah, he didn't seem happy." Quinn said, "But right after they left, I ran into Joey and Rebecca. I picked out a couple of machines for them."

"John's going to explode when he sees that!" Emma said, "You're not going to be welcome here."

"That's ok." Quinn said, "I don't plan on coming back."

Emma looked at him, 'He looks tired' she thought. "I'm thinking bagels for breakfast." she suggested, "Whaddya think?"

Quinn smiled and nodded, "Sounds good." he replied. Emma got up and went inside to call in their order.

A short time later, Emma answered a knock on the door. The cart was brought in and Emma tipped the man as she walked him to the door. "Thank you." she said, closing the door.

The man, once in the hallway, looked at the bill in his hand. It was a hundred-dollar bill, "Thank you!" he said, pocketing the tip.

Emma rolled the cart to the balcony door, and Quinn came in and rolled back the cart lid. "That's a lot of bagels." Quinn said, looking at a dozen and a half of assorted bagels with all the fixins.

"You're right." Emma said as she got her phone and texted their neighbors. A minute later she received a reply. "They'll be here in a few minutes." she said, smiling.

As Dave and Amanda came out of their suite, Amanda looked down the hall to see Joe and Becky approaching. "Hey guys," Amanda called, "They got bagels, come on."

Joe and Becky looked at each other, Joe shrugged and Becky said, "Sounds good to me."

Emma watching through the peephole, opened the door right before they could knock. "Come on in, everyone." Emma said, opening the door wide. The two couples entered the suite and began looking around.

"This is even bigger than I thought." Amanda said.

"I could get used to this." Becky said.

"I could get three of my apartments in here." Quinn said, "Hello everyone." He turned the cart around and opened it.

"That's a lot of bagels." Dave said, slackjawed.

Emma giggled, "Dig in, everybody." She offered.

They were enjoying their breakfast while Dave told Joe and Becky of his adventures down south, and of what happened at Chaco Canyon. While Dave was telling them of yesterday's exploits, Joe and Becky also got three different points of view thrown in, for effect.

Becky had stopped eating, and was staring at Dave, while Joe appeared deep in thought. "So, these D.N.A. people see something in your genes, probably what gives you access, and they want you for some reason." Joe summed up.

"Yeah, that pretty much covers it." Dave replied, "Anyway, I got to apologize to these guys for getting them involved in something so dangerous. We got lucky this time, and I think we should quit while we're ahead, and by ahead, I mean alive."

The room got quiet, and Quinn became motionless and stared at the floor in front of his feet. Amanda and Emma traded looks, "I don't want to stop." Amanda said, looking at Dave.

"I almost lost you." Dave said, "I vote no." Dave and Amanda both turned to Emma.

"It was scary...,but definitely not boring!" Emma said, "I'm with Quinn, but I would vote yes."

"Girl power!" Amanda said, bumping knuckles with Emma. Dave, Amanda and Emma all turned to Quinn.

"Well, buddy?" Dave asked, "What do you think?"

Quinn looked Becky's way, "I give my vote to Rebecca," he said, "if she doesn't mind."

"I don't mind, Becky said, "I think I understand. You don't mind, do you, Dave?" she asked.

"I wouldn't mind an outside opinion," Dave replied, "just think of all of us as Joe."

Becky smiled, "It is dangerous, but so is getting chased by an evil millionaire. If he's going to chase you, make it cost him. This stuff is on another level, if I didn't have the kids I would probably ask to join you. Quinn votes yes!" Becky declared, making Quinn smile.

"Put like that, I want to change my vote to 'not no'." Dave said, still a little worried, "That leaves the question; where to next."

Amanda looked at Becky, "You home school, don't you?" she asked.

"Yes, we do." Becky answered, "Why? What are you thinking?"

"I'm thinking that some world travel would improve any kind of education." Amanda said, "You guys could be our base of operations, out of danger."

"I'd feel better having someone to call, that knows where we are." Dave put in.

Joe looked at Becky, "I always wanted to see the Sphinx and the pyramids." Joe said.

"Machu Picchu," Becky said, "or any of a number of places in South America."

"Angor Wat." Emma said, "That place is fascinating."

"Mount Shasta, in Cali." Amanda said, "Lots of U.F.O. sightings."

Dave shook his head, "I think we should head back to Mexico," he said, "maybe even Belize, but somewhere we won't get killed." They all turned to Quinn.

"I need to get a passport." Quinn stated.

"You're not the only one." Joe said as he looked at his wife, "We both do, too"

"Since we're all here," Amanda said, "The rooms are all paid for 'til Wednesday, but we'd like to leave first thing in the morning."

"We still have to see the Grand Canyon." Emma said.

Joe looked at Becky, "What do you think?" he asked her.

"You can ride back with us," Amanda offered, "or

you can stay and take the jet back to Phoenix."

"You don't mind if we stay?" Becky asked, "Cuz we've seen the Grand Canyon."

"As long as you put everything on the room." Amanda said, with a smile.

"It'll give us a chance to marinate on your offer." Becky said, "In comfort."

"It may bias you." Quinn said.

"I'm hoping it does." Joe said smiling.

Having decimated the bagels, the party broke up and the two visiting couples took their leave. Quinn picked out another joint and smoked it with Emma, before he went to bed. Emma went down to the casino and started giving the casino back their money.

Quinn woke around four o'clock, he cleaned up and went down to the casino to find Emma. He saw Joe and Becky out at the pool and waved when they saw him. He went into the casino and walked along the wall, looking down the aisles for Emma. He found her when he walked past the poker room. Emma, with Dave and Amanda, were sitting at a sit-and-go Texas hold'em table.

Quinn walked along the rail, until he was behind Emma, "How are you doing?" he asked her. All three turned and saw Quinn watching them play, they told the dealer they were sitting out and went to the rail.

"Down around ten thou' on the slots," Emma replied, "thought I might do better at this."

"We saw her over here," Amanda said, "so we thought we could find out what kind of poker player she is."

"Turns out, she's pretty good." Dave said.

"I'm hungry." Emma said, "Let's find a place for dinner."

"I'll get Joey and Rebecca." Quinn said, "I'll meet you in the lobby."

"Got'cha." Emma said, as she went back to the table to cash out of the game. Dave and Amanda followed suit, and soon they were in the lobby with Quinn.

"They'll be back down in a few minutes." Quinn told them.

"I'm going to check out the gift shop," Emma said, "until they get here."

"Sounds good," Dave said, "you coming?" he asked Amanda.

"Yeah," Amanda said, "But I'll be right there, I got something to do." She took out her phone and sent a text to Bobbie, then went into the shop.

Joe and Becky entered the lobby and saw Quinn standing by the door to the gift shop, and soon they were being seated, without reservations, in the hotel's top restaurant.

"Those hundred dollar tips sure help!" Dave said to Amanda.

"This table cost two hundred," Amanda replied, "and that was just the maître'd'."

“That’s crazy.” Joe said.

“This better be worth all that.” Becky said.

“I’ll have made it back by time our food gets here,” Amanda explained, “so don’t worry about what anything costs, ok.”

Joe and Becky sat and stared at Amanda.

“I inherited some money when my Aunt died.” Amanda said, to Joe and Becky, who were still staring. “Ok, a lot of money.” she conceded.

“That explains a lot.” Joe said, “The private jet, the limo, the suites. We thought you were blowing your wad making memories. You sure are making some for us.

“Yeah, well,” Amanda said, “it’s new to me, too. So don’t be shy, go ahead and splurge.”

They spent the next two hours eating, drinking and talking about what they may find.

Early Monday morning, Dave, Amanda, Quinn and Emma were on their way to the Grand Canyon. While Joe and Becky decided to stay and be pampered until Wednesday.

39

At the top center of his computer screen, Bill watched as a small red square appeared and started pulsing. Bill clicked on the square and received the list of instructions. He followed the instructions, but on the way back from dropping off the file he stopped to talk to Curtis.

"You get a 'BB'?" Curtis asked.

Bill moved in closer, "No, it was red." he said quietly.

"Red?" Curtis whispered, "I never heard of a red one." he said, acting surprised.

"Yeah," Bill replied, "it was a guy named Quinn Tucker, and I had to bring it to the boss, not H.R. like a 'BB'.

"Best not to think about it." Curtis offered.

"You're probably right, but..." Bill said, as he turned to return to his workstation.

"Later." Curtis replied, as he returned to his work. As lunch time approached, he found himself at a good point to take a break. He walked past Bill's space and saw he was in the middle of working through a sample. He went on to eat by himself.

When he returned from lunch, he looked for Bill, who wasn't there. 'Must be at lunch' he thought, then he started to notice that there weren't any of Bill's personal items. He stepped back and saw that Bill's name plate was no longer there.

He turned and went to his space and returned to work, without stopping to ask anyone about what happened to Bill. He had a pretty good idea what happened, and that came with the realization that everyone here was being monitored. It was all he could do to keep his head down and keep working, as if everything was normal.

When Curtis finally got home, he disconnected his computer from the internet, then he had a brief panic attack. "What kind of people am I working for?" he asked aloud, as he poured himself a drink. He was glad he knew how to follow instructions, and still had a job. At the same time he felt apprehension about working at such a place. He never liked the idea that he was being watched, but he knew that most places had cameras, just in case something happens, they have a record. But to have your private conversations listened to, that was on another level. He sat thinking for a while, when he pulled out his phone and called up the spectrum analyzer app. and started sweeping his apartment.

He finished looking for a signal, without finding one. Relieved, he went and checked on his hidden file, it was where he had left it. he opened it and wrote down the name 'Quinn Tucker'. He returned the file to it's hiding place, making sure it was safe. That done, he switched his computer back on and went through it, to see if there was any spyware on it.

Satisfied his computer wasn't compromised, he reconnected to the internet and contacted a few friends to tell them what a great company he worked for, and how much he loved his new job.

After Bill had left the office the secretary, excited, brought the file to her boss. As she entered the office she said, "Three years with nothing, and now twice in as many months."

Martin looked up from his computer, eyes wide, "Another one?" he asked, "This has got to mean something." he said as he took the file from Janet. He quickly scanned the file, then looked up at his secretary, 'She looks eager' he thought.

When they had finished having sex, Janet returned to her desk and Martin returned to studying the file. He started to recognize a similarity to the Smith file, so he retrieved the first file and compared it to the new file. After a few minutes he confirmed what he first suspected.

Martin reached for the intercom, "Janet, could you connect me with Mr. Dhu?" he requested. Edgar was driving to Las Vegas, when his phone rang, it was Mr. Matthews. He told his car to accept the call.

A minute later, Martin's phone rang, he answered it and learned that Edgar had located Smith and was on his way to catch up with them. Then Martin relayed the information he had received, and what he had discovered. On the other end of the call, Edgar listened intently. When Mr. Matthews had finished relaying everything he could, Edgar replied "My source says that they both claim to be orphans. I don't think they know." He said his good-byes and ended the call. He continued on to Las Vegas, anticipating finally meeting these guys in person.

40

After spending the night at the Grand Canyon, they headed home by driving to Winslow then turning south. When they reached Payson, Quinn's phone signaled that he had a message. He tried to retrieve the message before they got through town but only got part of the message before he lost the signal.

"That was Joey," Quinn said, "he said someone was there looking for us."

Amanda sat up, "Who was looking for us?" she asked.

"Don't know, I lost the signal when we left town." Quinn replied. He put his phone away and looked toward Emma, "How would anyone know we were there?" he wondered.

"This is getting weird." Emma said, sounding confused.

"I guess we'll find out when we get home." Amanda offered.

They arrived at the ranch about an hour later, and Quinn went to his messages before he got out of the truck. He sat and listened for a minute or so, then he hung up.

"Joey said that John guy showed up outside their room with another guy, who looked even bigger and dumber, and they said they were looking for Dave and I." Quinn stated, "Joey thought that they looked, and acted, like brothers."

"I wonder if he's from the d.n.a. people." Dave pondered, as he climbed out of the truck.

"Oh great, more people after us." Amanda said as she retrieved her luggage. Dave came around the truck to get the luggage from Amanda.

"I got this, babe" Dave said with a smile, taking the luggage from his wife. He carried her bags to the porch, then went back for his own. Quinn had emptied the back of the truck by time Dave returned.

"Thanks, man." Dave said as he grabbed his bag.

Quinn carried his and Emma's bags over to where she had parked her car and set them down. She came up next to him and leaned into him a little bit, then proceeded to unlock the car. Quinn was no longer surprised that he enjoyed the attention from her, it was starting to feel natural. This made him smile as he loaded the bags into the back of her car.

As Quinn and Emma walked to the house his phone started to ring.

"Hello Joey," Quinn said, answering his phone, "how's Vegas doing?"

"We left this morning, the wife was getting a bad feeling." Joe said, "Are you guys back?" he asked.

"Yes, we are." Quinn replied, "For about ten minutes now."

"Cool, we're about ten minutes away," Joe said, "see you soon."

"Joey's coming!" Quinn called out to the others, as they approached the porch. "He said about ten minutes."

Amada came back out onto the porch, "They must've flown back this morning," she said. "I hope they're alright."

"He sounded fine." Quinn told her, "But me, I have to pee."

"Go right in, you guys." Amanda said, "I'll wait for Joe."

Quinn and Emma went inside to take care of business. Dave was coming down the hall when they turned the corner, Quinn nodded and went into the restroom, while Emma went past them into Amanda's room. Quinn finished first and waited outside the door for Emma, when she came out they went to the porch together, where they found Dave and Amanda unwinding from the drive. They had just sat down when Joe pulled up to the gate. Amanda got up and reached through the door to press the button to let him in.

Joe parked next to the Hummer and got out and opened the door for Becky, she got out and they proceeded on to the porch.

"Didn't expect to see you guys until tomorrow." Amanda said with a smile. The three behind her all waved at the arriving couple.

"Well, we already made our decision and those guys that were looking for you, they gave me a real bad feeling. We agreed that we had enough of Las Vegas for quite some time, and here we are." Becky explained, "Oh, and we told those guys that you were out seeing shows, I'll bet they're still looking for you!"

Amanda led them into the house and told them to get comfy, then asked if anyone wanted anything. She headed to the kitchen to fill their orders. She came back with four beers and two bottles of water. Emma and Joe each took a water, while the others opened their beers.

"So, tell us about the guy that was looking for us." Dave requested.

"He looked like a bigger, dumber version of that security dude." Joe said.

"John Dhu." Becky added.

"Yeah, and he seemed disappointed that you weren't there." Joe said.

"Disappointed, hah, he was pissed! Didn't show much, but he was mad." Becky explained.

"Anyway, she didn't want to stay any longer, so I

made a call to the pilot, and we came back this morning." Joe finished.

"So, what did you decide?" Amanda asked, looking at Becky.

"We," Joe started, "decided that we would like to join you on your journeys. We talked to the kids, they're all in, with one stipulation."

"And that would be?" Amanda asked, wondering what the kids could possibly hold out for.

"They want their aunt, my sister, to come with." Joe stated, "She doesn't know yet, but she's between jobs and she's really great with the kids, so I'm thinking she'll be happy to come with."

Amanda smiled, "If she's anything like you she'd be more than welcome." She said, "And besides, that will give the girls a four-to-three advantage in voting."

"Then I should be making a phone call." Joe said and stepped off the side.

"So, where are we heading?" Becky asked, looking at Amanda.

"We haven't even determined if we should be doing this." Dave said firmly.

"I think we should get some experts to help us." Emma interjected.

"Ex – has been, spurt – drip under pressure." Quinn stated.

Emma leaned over and looked at Quinn, "What?" she asked, trying not to laugh. She had never heard 'expert' defined quite like that and found it amusing.

"I think what Quinn is saying is that anyone who truly knows about this stuff isn't going to want us poking around." Dave started, "And all those theorists out there don't know any more than we do."

"I guess you got a point." Emma conceded, "But, still."

"I think we got all we need, as far as personnel is concerned." Amanda said, "What I think we need is technology."

"Technology may make us easier to find." Quinn offered.

Joe walked back over and joined the conversation, "Sissy says she's in!" he announced, "So where are we going?" he asked, looking around at everybody.

"Haven't figured it out yet." Dave said, "But, I think we should go back to Belize, you know, get our feet under us first. Plus, it should be safer."

Just then a knock came at the front door. "What the fu....?" Amanda said. She walked to the door, with Dave at her side. "Who's there?" She asked loudly.

There was no answer. Dave stepped to the door and opened it, there were two men in dark suits, wearing fedoras, standing there. "Can I help you?" he asked.

"Screw that," Amanda interrupted, "How did you get in here?" she asked forcibly.

"Amanda Nordmon," one of the men started, "it has come to our attention that you were somewhere that is forbidden to civilians."

"Amanda Smith, thank you very much." She said, liking the way it sounded.

"We are here to inform you that you should not talk about such things." The second man started, "It would be detrimental for everyone involved if this were to reach the media."

"Wait," Emma said, "you mean there's no flashy thingy?"

"There's not going to be a problem here, is there?" the first man said, looking irritated.

"No, no problem at all." Dave said, reassuringly, looking at the men.

The two men looked over the small crowd, then at each other, and turned and walked to their car. They got in and headed towards the gate, which opened by itself, and left the ranch. The gate closed itself and the car was gone.

Amanda reached over to the security panel and turned a knob and threw a switch, "They're gone!" she said.

"Good riddance." Joe said.

"You don't get it," Amanda said, "they're gone, not on the road leading to the highway, not out front, disappeared, vanished, no-where, gone!" Everyone got real quiet. "This changes things." She muttered.

"I don't think they were human." Quinn stated. Everyone looked at him, "They didn't look right, their skin looked like tiny feathers." he added.

"They didn't feel right, either." Becky said, taking Quinn's side.

"Looks like it ended before we even got started." Amanda said, sadly.

CPSIA information can be obtained
at www.ICGtesting.com
Printed in the USA
LVHW051231270723
753394LV00001B/33